The

CW00493558

Pluto Crime

Edited by Ronald Segal

'. . . Is there anything inherently illogical with the concept of socialist – or, at least, politically and socially aware – crime fiction? Pluto Press, publishers of serious left wing books, have inaugurated a crime list to prove that the two can mix . . . the first batch of pinko whodunits augurs well for the genre.' *The Times*

'. . . the most innovative publishing experiment of the crime-story year!' *The Guardian*

Julian Rathbone

The Euro-Killers

Pluto Press

London and Sydney

This edition published in 1986 by Pluto Press Limited,
The Works, 105a Torriano Avenue, London NW5 2RX
and Pluto Press Australia Limited, PO Box 199, Leichhardt,
New South Wales 2040, Australia. Also Pluto Press,
51 Washington Street, Dover, New Hampshire 03820 USA.

First published by Michael Joseph Limited, London WC1.

7   6   5   4   3   2   1

90   89   88   87   86

Printed in Great Britain by Cox & Wyman, Reading, Berks

British Library Cataloguing in Publication Data
Rathbone, Julian
    The Euro-killers.
    I. Title
    823'.914[F]   PR6068.A8

ISBN 0 7453 0160 6

Contents

Author's Note

Brabt, Province and City, is imagined. Clearly its imagined existence lies not a hundred miles from the modern province of Brabant which is part of Belgium, but I had more in mind a more direct descendant of the medieval duchy. In Brabt a dialect confusing Flemish, Dutch, and German is spoken, and there are about 150 gelds to the pound sterling.

I

Public Servant

Jan Argand was punctilious in his personal habits, in the routine aspects of his job, in the personal relationships which were left to him. His son was married and they met rarely, often only at the mental home to which his wife had long since retired and which Argand visited every third Sunday. Her place in his life had been taken by an elderly widow who lived in the apartment above him: she had a key, came down and 'did' for him in the late morning when she had finished her own housework, and prepared an evening meal for him. Usually this was a matter of cold meats, rye bread, a salad, but if the weather was cold and she was feeling inclined towards him she would leave a casserole in his oven. He saw her only once a week, when he settled up with her. Breakfast he took on the way to work, always in the Café Louis Bonaparte, always after buying *The Brabanter* at the kiosk on the pavement outside.

The Louis Bonaparte, named after Napoleon's brother, a kingling who had ruled in the Province for four brief years, was as solid and unchanging as Argand himself, or at least he supposed it was. The walls were panelled in dark wood, the place was lit – neither brightly nor dully – by white globes hung in threes, the tables were dressed in plain spotless white linen and the chairs were solid, foursquare, upholstered in red leather fixed with brass studs. The coffee was poured from pewter jugs embossed with an LB monogram surmounted with a crown into large white cups similarly decorated; the croissants came wrapped in hot napkins and the butter was always exactly the right temperature, cool but spreadable.

On this morning in late March, however, things were not as they had always been though Jan Argand did not immediately notice the differences. Three minutes went by during which he read the news items on the front page of his paper – new Community regulations regarding the growth and marketing of cut flowers, steps to be taken to maintain the value of the dollar, agreement reached between European leaders on yet more measures to counter terrorism – before he reached for the pewter sugar pot. And it was not there – not there at all. In its place a shallow bowl contained four wrapped lumps of sugar. Shaking his head with disbelief and then irritation Argand looked over his table more carefully and found to his dismay that the usual butter dish, with its creamy slices of butter crumbling at the edges, had been similarly replaced with foil-wrapped cubes. The glass jam-dish with its chrome lid and spoon had also gone – in its place were three tiny foil tubs imported from Scotland.

Argand's eyebrows were bushy, grey and high-arched, and now they rose a further centimetre, giving his grey face a momentarily comic look, not unlike a painted wooden doll. He thought of calling the waiter, asking for the manager, then he pulled his brows together, sighed, and with obvious distaste used stubby capable fingers to remove the offensive wrappers. The coffee at least was unchanged. Scarcely formulated guesses at the excuses he would have been given had he complained went through his mind – reasons of economy, Excellency, of hygiene, the new regulations you understand, by buying these things pre-packed we have been able to sack two of the kitchen staff and thus postpone an inevitable increase of our charges.

'Excellency', for so decreed the City Fathers of Brabt when they first inaugurated the post of Commissioner of Police in the early nineteenth century. Now there were three Commissioners, all of them Excellencies, and each in their own way excellent – or at least so Argand supposed, though he recognised that his colleagues' excellence was not always his.

Commissioner Argand turned to the inside pages of *The Brabanter* and tried to forget how tangibly and irritatingly the twentieth century had spoiled his breakfast.

Of the several items he took in and mentally noted, two particularly caught his attention and three may catch ours – in different ways they all had a bearing on the events of the next two weeks. He read of the continuing campaign of civil disobedience, organised by the League for Life, against the proposed expansion of the EUREAC works on the coast near Spartshaven; of how Sports Union Brabt had been drawn against Kirkshield Wanderers in the semi-final of the Euro-Cup, first leg to be played in Brabt on Sunday week in thirteen days' time; of how Wolfgang Herm, Vice-President and until lately Managing Director of EUREAC was not available to comment on an item printed in a scandal sheet the previous evening alleging that his daughter was actively campaigning for full civil rights for the City prostitutes.

The resistance to EUREAC's expansion interested him as a professional, though not professionally: public order in an area where local sympathy lay with the dissidents was always a problem, a problem which he considered more or less dispassionately in this case since Spartshaven lay eighteen kilometres beyond the City boundaries and in the jurisdiction of the Rural Guard. The second item concerned him personally for Kirkshield Wanderers, or rather their supporters, were notorious throughout Europe — Barcelona and St Étienne were still estimating the claims they would make against the Scottish club for damage done in the previous rounds. Argand now believed that his day would begin by calling together his colleagues and officers in other branches of the City's administration to plan a counter-campaign against foreign football hooligans.

The third item interested him not at all, provoked only distaste. He had had no dealings with Wolfgang Herm's daughter though his colleagues, the Commissioners for Crime and State Security, knew her only too well. When she was sixteen her father in person had dragged her down to the police headquarters in Wilhelmstras and denounced her for distributing pot free to her friends; three years later she had been unsuccessfully but justifiably prosecuted for harbouring two members of Red Spectre, the local version of the Red Brigades. These two escapades, of one so young, removed her from the class of ordinary criminals judged by Argand to be weak and lazy, and put her into that of those who have an ineradicable inclination towards moral evil — freaks, drug-takers, vandals, perverts. The fact that she was now putting herself on the side of those who profited from vice confirmed this judgement.

The report alluded to Victoria Herm's past, and printed an old picture of her with Wolfgang. The industrialist looked absurdly young, as he always did — he had a smile and a mop of boyish fair hair that Argand associated with some film star whose name he could not recollect. The man in question had for some years been a decisive influence on the appearance of well-to-do men in their late forties. The ambience of chic wealth in which he and the Herms moved irritated Jan, for he could not bear waste and he knew it boasted waste.

He folded *The Brabanter*, dabbed his mouth with the napkin that had wrapped his croissant and put money, the exact amount, beside his cup. The table looked messy and that annoyed him too. He had opened a second butter cube and had not finished it; there was jam left in the tub he had sampled. It was an absurd world where it was cheaper for a restaurant to throw away food and wrappers than pay a man to look after its stores properly.

At the door he slipped on his light-weight grey coat and greyish-brown hat – the waiter knew better than to offer to help him – and stepped out smartly into the brisk, gusty sunshine of Wilhelmstras. Behind him an almost imperceptible but nevertheless real feeling of relief blossomed like an aroma above the spotless white tables of the Louis Bonaparte.

Jan Argand believed in hierarchy and thought that the outward forms of rank should be observed. Half an hour later then he was irritated again when his desk phone rang and he learned that Secretary Prinz, the permanent official to whom he was immediately responsible, was on his way down to see him. Argand would have preferred to have gone up to the Secretary's office, would have preferred to have been sent for. He knew that behind this reversal of the outward forms of rank there was more than jolly if spurious democracy – Secretary Prinz was on his way to ask a favour, and a favour meant, at best, an irregularity.

When the Secretary arrived Jan was standing in the large dormer window looking down at the chestnut leaves already bursting out of sticky buds and tossing in the wind below him: he did not intend to interview his superior from behind his desk. He turned, their hands touched briefly, and courtesies about the weekend were exchanged.

Secretary Prinz moved in the Herms' world. He was a large man, perhaps five years older than Argand, but with a florid look about him that suggested that the pleasures of the table, which he had never neglected, were on the point of supplanting more energetic pursuits. His lower lip drooped heavily – not entirely the result of pipe-smoking – and his large hands were already mottled. After the war he had made a name as an amateur show-jumper, had represented the Province at the Helsinki Olympics, and he still rode. He was no fool, had achieved academic distinction when studying the law but would probably not have reached his position as one of the three most senior permanent civil servants in the Province had he not been distantly connected with the Archduke – an achievement that Argand respected.

There was little else he liked about his superior. He distrusted the man's ostentation and glibness; disliked his bonhomous manners and the pipe he now busied himself with, keeping the Commissioner waiting until smoke was billowing satisfyingly around him.

'Well, I won't waste your time,' he said at last, 'I'll come straight to the point. Wolfgang Herm of EUREAC has disappeared, has not been seen since last Friday evening, and I am absolutely certain that you are the man to look into it.'

Argand's irritation sharpened, and he turned away to conceal it.

'Dear old Jan,' Prinz went on, 'I didn't expect you to be pleased. But hear me out. This has cropped up at a very sensitive time. I'm sure you know the Spartshaven Project gets under way in exactly a fortnight, and in the public eye the Spartshaven Project is Herm's project. Then there are family problems too. For EUREAC this couldn't have come at a worse moment. There is a strong feeling on the board that for the next few months they must at best appear in a very good light indeed, at the worst keep a lower profile than usual . . .'

'I don't have to tell you, Secretary, that the disappearance of anyone, no matter who, is not my business, not my business at all, comes quite outside the responsibilities laid down. . .'

'Oh quite, Argand. Quite. I take your point and respect you for making it, but at this stage in the game it's difficult to pinpoint exactly who should be looking into it. You see, no crime has been committed as far as we know, there is as yet no question of state security being compromised. The firm and the family are simply a little perturbed, as is to be expected at this time which, as I said, is a sensitive one for all concerned. They approached me as they are entitled to, and have asked me to appoint someone, someone of irreproachable integrity, yet as discreet as may be, to look around.' Prinz sucked his pipe and watched the Commissioner with benevolent if somewhat rheumy eyes.

Argand left the window, returned to his desk and the large solid leather chair behind it. Prinz sensed withdrawal in this move, stood over the broad desk, looked down at Jan and puffed rich smoke into the air above him.

'Exactly what is it you want me to do?'

'Find the man, that's all.'

A private detective should do this, Argand thought, but EUREAC don't want a private investigator nosing about in its cupboards and beneath the stairs. He could understand too Secretary Prinz's reluctance to call in the Commissioner for Crime: in the first place, if the press heard of it they would want to know what was in the air, while the Commissioner for Public Order could be having talks with EUREAC of a purely routine nature; in the second place the Crime Commissioner was a bluff and direct man who sought publicity.

In the Louis Bonaparte complaint had been pointless

because the answers were predictable. The same was true now. Anyway, Secretary Prinz was his superior, and Argand always did as he was told.

'I was in the middle of setting up a meeting to formulate plans for the Euro-Cup match on Sunday week . . .'

'When have you fixed that meeting for?'

'Tomorrow at three.'

'Well, you must attend it. And any other functions where your absence would occasion remark. But you have very competent deputies to see to details and routine matters. I'm sure this won't take more than a few days, a few days at the most. I take it you will look into it for us?'

Argand shrugged.

'Good man. They're expecting you at EUREAC. Ask for Christian Kratt, he's the Company Secretary. Mrs Herm is expecting you too, at her home. Keep in touch with me, won't you? Let me know how things are going?'

Secretary Prinz knocked his pipe out in Argand's alabaster ashtray which, being a non-smoker, he never used himself, and went to the door. Argand did not move to open it for him.

'Well, Jan. All we do is in the public service you know. Even if sometimes we have to act a little less openly than we like.'

With this Prinz went. A layer of blue smoke hung in the still air behind him.

2

Company Servants

Argand was driven to the EUREAC offices in a police department car. He paused for a moment before getting out, looked up at the tall elegant building – a squashed hexagon in rose-tinted concrete with glass that was tinted to look like bronze from the outside. Not all EUREAC's problems have been connected with the Spartshaven Project, he reflected, and recalled how Baron de Merle, the President of the Company, had been shot in the knees on these pink marble steps just over a year before. Red Spectre had claimed responsibility. The incident, the first of the sort Brabt had experienced, had been shocking: now a discreet reminder remained to jog the memories of passing Brabanters that their streets were no longer safe – a ramp matching the marble smoothed out the steps so that the principal shareholder could negotiate the entrance in his electrically powered wheel-chair. Less discreetly, two armed guards flanked the heavy glass doors. The tinted visors of their helmets followed Argand into the foyer and continued to watch his back, while a third guard inside scrutinised his documents and phoned up the identity of the caller through to some further security check in the floors above.

'Commissioner Argand?'

Jan turned from a large mural depicting the River

Flot Plant near Spartshaven – tall white stacks, cooling towers, storage tanks against a blue sky swept with white clouds; in the foreground, marshes and dunes with two white birds, a little like seagulls but more elegant, black-capped with forked tails, swooping playfully over the water.

'Yes,' he replied, and ignored the hand offered. He had resented the challenge at the door. Now he was faced with a man in his middle thirties and therefore younger than the vanished industrialist, but otherwise a very similar sort of person. This man had the same boyish quiff, the same toothy smile, the same sort of expensive light-weight tweed suit.

'My name is Hector Macher and I'm Wolfgang Herm's personal assistant. Commissioner, it is awfully good of you to come and help us like this, a person of your position. Secretary Prinz could not speak highly enough of you, and I'm sure all of us here are tremendously relieved to have you amongst us . . .'

Noiseless lift doors closed behind them. Jan wrinkled his nose – the confined space was scented. Automatically, as it always did whenever he smelt a sweet, commercial scent, his mother's phrase 'stinks like a brothel' came into his head.

'Mr Kratt, Christian Kratt, our Company Secretary, is waiting to see you, but first we thought you'd like to see Wolfgang's office, help to put you in the picture and so on, get the feel of things.'

The doors breathed open and they stepped straight into a large room furnished like a sitting-room with easy chairs, a sofa, cabinets, occasional tables, the whole in a bleak and very modern style, variously textured, the colours muted greys and ochres. Only a large desk in a window, with two telephones on it, suggested that it was a room for work rather than dull but luxurious leisure.

'That is Mr Herm's private lift?'

'Almost. Baron de Merle, Mr Kratt and I are the only other people who use it. Apart from the maintenance staff, of course.'

Argand nodded slowly, then walked further into the room. The flooring seemed to snuggle against his feet in a way he did not like. The windows, huge sheets of bronze-tinted glass, looked down thirty floors and this disturbed him more than anything else so far – he had not realised that the lift had travelled so fast.

'This is where Mr Herm works?'

'Of course. Well, that is when he is here.'

'What do you mean "when he is here"?'

'He spends more time at the River Flot Plant than he does here. He has an office there too. Really he uses this quite infrequently, perhaps not more than four or five hours a week. Before meetings. To see people.'

'Do you go to the Plant with him?'

'No, no. I stay here and keep an eye on things for him. That's really my job.' Macher now strode across the room to a door which he opened. 'And this is where I do it.' Jan looked past him into a smaller office, a far more business-like affair with filing cabinets, a copier, various other gadgets; the effect was still one of wealth, but at least purpose was suggested as well.

'I shall want a full account of Mr Herm's movements, over the last three weeks to begin with, perhaps over a longer period. Appointments made for the future. I shall want you to help me to build up a complete and accurate picture, as far as you are able, of his main preoccupations at the moment. I mean those relevant to EUREAC, of course.'

Hector Macher smiled, pushed the quiff back off his forehead. 'Why Commissioner, that's easily answered. In two words. The Spartshaven Project.' He bent at the knees as if he were about to genuflect but in fact he scooped up off a rose-veined marble coffee-table something that looked like a cross between a very expensively produced company report and a brochure advertising a luxury holiday, a cruise to the Bahamas perhaps. The glossy laminated cover carried a photograph of the view of the EUREAC plant resembling the mural in the foyer. Across it, in embossed letters of gold, Argand read: 'EUREAC MOVES INTO THE TWENTY-FIRST CENTURY' and then in smaller letters, but still in gold, 'at Spartshaven'. As colophon there was a gold cut-out silhouette of one of the birds that had featured in the painting. In gold it looked more like a long-billed swallow than a gull.

Macher's voice rose; almost he began to bubble. 'Really this is Wolfgang's. Really it is. The idea was his in the first place, just over five years ago. The largest single stage expansion of any chemical or plastic firm in Europe. Combined with the comprehensive development of the environment adjacent to it. It was his inspiration, but in practice too he has been in on every aspect: financing it, planning it, dealing with all the government departments concerned at Provincial level and at Community level in Brussels. And of course he has tried to have all the technical side at his fingertips too. Lately he's given most of his time to the environmental aspects and he has taught us all so much in that area, helped us to see the importance of it . . . and now, a fortnight exactly before the earth-movers break the ground, a fortnight before the whole thing becomes a physical reality, he disappears. Really, it doesn't make sense, Commissioner, there's no sense to it . . .'

'But I'm sure the Commissioner will make *sense* of it for us.'

Argand turned. A second door behind them had opened, and a tall thin man with short grey hair came towards them through the soundless carpet.

'Commissioner Argand. I'm Christian Kratt.'

'Our Company Secretary,' murmured Macher.

'I'm very *pleased* to meet you. Very pleased you can be here. Won't you sit down? Hector, see to some coffee for us, there's a good boy.'

Here at least was someone whose appearance owed nothing at all to Robert Redford. Kratt's suit was dark, no doubt as expensive as Macher's, but ill-fitting at the shoulders and hips, the pockets baggy, the flaps half tucked in. His face had a lean unhealthy look, and his hair, short though it was, was stringy. Argand fancied that Kratt gave off a very slight sour odour. Yet he was impressive too. His pale blue eyes behind thickish spectacles were unblinking, expressionless, his voice a calm monotone which added force to the occasional words he emphasised, his movements decisive and economical. He settled himself at the opposite end of the sofa from Argand so that his long legs reached down one side of a triangle and his feet almost touched the policeman's. He put his fingers together beneath his chin.

'Hector was right to say that Wolfgang's overriding interest is the Spartshaven Project, but he exaggerated to make it so much Wolfgang's own project. The media too like to see things in crude personal terms, like to make a *story* out of what is a very technical, very complicated process, what is essentially a *corporate* process. But yes, it is strange for Wolfgang to disappear now. That is, if we are assuming that he has disappeared voluntarily.'

'That's not very likely, is it?'

'No. Really very unlikely, quite untypical. It is just that we would all like to *hope* that that is what has happened: that Wolfgang has taken it into his head to have a long and private weekend somewhere, and will turn up tomorrow or the day after, alive and well. But it is not *likely*.'

'What do you see as the likely possibilities, Mr Kratt?'

Kratt glanced at him, eyes alert behind the spectacles, like a carrion-eater – bird or mammal – suddenly aware of another, if smaller, guest at the feast.

'Kidnap or illness. I understand that the fact that there has been no ransom demand yet is *not* significant. Often, I believe, kidnappers wait a few days to allow the anxiety to become intolerable – ' He paused; Argand murmured assent. 'Illness seems less likely. Of course all hospitals in the Province and even as far away as Brussels and Antwerp have been checked. I suppose amnesia need not be ruled out, nor the sort of accident which might leave a person, if not dead, then hidden or incapable of movement. But these possibilities seem intrinsically less likely than kidnap. I *hope* it is kidnap. We have the means and the will to meet almost *any* demand.'

Macher returned with coffee. As the personal assistant busied himself with modern porcelain and silver, Argand realised that he was watching the movements of an athlete – neat, smooth, co-ordinated, a squash-player perhaps, but judging by his tan, a skiier and surfer as well. When they were settled and Argand had tasted the coffee, which was rich and strong, he began to speak.

'There are of course possibilities other than kidnap or accident.'

Cold silence followed. Neither man was prepared to risk possible self-exposure by offering his ideas as to what these might be.

'Broadly speaking,' Argand went on, 'I am talking about scandal. I will be blunt. There are two sorts of scandal – financial and sexual. I should like to know why it has not occurred to either of you that Mr Herm might voluntarily disappear to avoid facing exposure for some irregularity in either of these spheres.'

The silence returned, though Macher leant forward out of the deep chair he was in and pushed his heavy lock of hair back off his forehead, then fixed expressionless eyes on Kratt as if waiting for guidance.

At last Kratt set down his cup.

'I appreciate, Commissioner, that you have to suggest these things, that you are not prompted by impertinence. Well, let *me* be blunt. EUREAC is not some tuppenny-halfpenny bank. It is not the sort of business where an employee or even director can cook the books or get his fingers caught in the till. There is a limit to the amount of money an intelligent man needs or wants. EUREAC's ability to pay its senior members goes *beyond* that limit.'

Argand waited.

'As to the other thing, well Hector was more intimate with Wolfgang than I.' He turned to the personal assistant. 'I *think* you are a friend of the family?'

'Yes, yes indeed.' Again the boyish push at his hair, and a slight blush under the tan. 'And really Commissioner, there's nothing there to explain this, nothing there, I'm sure.'

'It was from his home that he disappeared.'

'Oh quite. Walked out at six o'clock on Friday evening for a breath of fresh air, he said, and well . . . that was it.'

'You weren't there at the time?'

'No. Lena, Mrs Herm, phoned me an hour or so later, to see if I knew where he was. Later, at about ten, when he still hadn't come back I went over, and in fact spent the rest of the week-end there. I do that quite often, they keep a room for me. It's convenient when we have to travel the next day, or if Wolfgang is entertaining business guests and requires my services.'

'You are not married.'

'No. That is, no longer.'

'Is it a happy marriage? The Herms, I mean.'

There was a fractional pause.

'Yes . . . oh yes, I'd say so. A very stable marriage.' Again the hesitation which Argand read as an indication that Macher was calculating how much to say, how

23

much to hide, how likely it was that he would be caught in a lie or an incomplete truth. 'Of course, they have been together for a long time. More than twenty years, and in that time there have been ups and downs, strains and so on. Wolfgang is hopelessly tied up with EUREAC and I think this has told on Lena at times. But nothing more. Nothing more, I assure you.'

Both company men now sat still and waiting.

'There's one other possibility I'd like to have your opinion on. And that is that Mr Herm has been murdered.'

Kratt answered briskly. 'A maniac might have done it. Or a *near* maniac like the Red Spectre people. But they make their attacks in broad daylight, do they not? To get publicity. That at least was the case when poor Baron de Merle was shot in the knees. But I cannot think Wolfgang is the victim of a premeditated, planned murder, for that is what you are implying is it not? I cannot see that there could possibly be *any* motive for such a crime.'

Macher nodded his head in vigorous assent with Kratt, vigorous rejection of Argand's suggestion.

Argand got to his feet, walked over to the huge tinted window and looked down at the complex of traffic flows beneath him. The company men also stood, puzzled by his sudden move, waited in the middle of the room to see what was coming next. Argand turned and faced them.

'Mr Herm may have been kidnapped. We shall know very soon if he has. He may be ill or in physical distress following an accident or even a mugging attack. If this is the case he will be found. If he does not reappear in the next twenty-four hours, if he is not heard of in that time then one of the other possibilities I have mentioned – that he has taken himself off to escape some nemesis, or enjoy some gain, or that he has been murdered – becomes increasingly likely. Now I am here, at your request, to find Mr Herm. I believe Secretary Prinz asked me to come because he believes me to be discreet as well as thorough, and I do assure you of my discretion. I will not cover up crime but beyond that I think you will find me discreet. I must work now on these possibilities, there is no other line open to me. In other words I must pry into Mr Herm's business affairs and into his personal life if I am to find any clue as to what has happened to him. I should like to be assured that I have your support.'

Macher looked at Kratt, Kratt finally looked at Argand. His stoop became more pronounced, his head seemed to shrink away between his bony shoulders. 'Yes, yes, Commissioner. Clearly we must give you all the help we can. The extent to which we are free to do so is of course limited, especially where company affairs are concerned. I have no idea what you particularly have in mind at the moment, but I can envisage that you might ask to see things I could not, on my own authority, show you. I should have to consult my board first. But with these reservations we will do whatever you want.'

He moved towards the policeman, briefly took his hand. Again Argand was conscious of a sour tang in the air.

'I will leave you now with Hector who I know will look after you far better than I. He was far more familiar with Wolfgang's *habits*. Now please excuse me Commissioner, and please believe how grateful we are that you felt that you could come.'

The Company Secretary moved away through the carpet. Before he reached the door he twice lifted a gold cigarette case half clear from his side pocket, only to let it drop back. Finally he clenched both thin hands tightly behind him. The door slid open before he reached it.

For an hour Macher took Argand through Herm's appointment diaries explaining each entry for the previous month; agreed, subject to Lena Herm's permission, to make available papers connected with all financial transactions during the same period, both personal and those connected with EUREAC; explained how Herm would have been occupied during the next three weeks. Much of all this seemed to be related to the Spartshaven Project – at least Macher said so, but again and again the missing man's movements had taken him to his office at the Plant and there was only Macher's word that these visits were related to the Project. Finally there had been three meetings with what was termed in the diary the "cabinet", two of them on successive days during the previous week.

'What is this "cabinet"?' Jan asked.

'It's a sort of inner board, approved by the full board which has over thirty people on it and meets infrequently. The cabinet makes decisions of importance where they are beyond the scope of individual managers or heads of department, but it cannot of course formulate new policy.'

'Who sits on it?'

'Wolfgang and Christian, of course. Baron de Merle, Joseph Dax . . .'

'The ex-minister?'

'Yes. And Paul Brandt who is in charge at the Plant.'

'What is a quorum for this cabinet?'

'Four. I should have mentioned that as second shareholder in the whole firm Lena Herm also has the right to sit, but she does not exercise it very often.'

'And these meetings are minuted. Company law would, I think, indicate that they should be.'

'Yes, technically they are minuted.' He laughed. 'Perhaps I should say technologically minuted. They are recorded, the tapes stored and print-outs prepared when required.'

'I should like to see the print-outs of the last two

meetings, those last week.'

'Of course. But you will appreciate that I can't authorise that myself . . .'

'Then ask Mr Kratt if I can have them.'

'Now?'

'Why not?'

Macher shrugged, pushed at his hair, blushed beneath his tan again. After a moment he had Kratt on the office intercom.

'The Commissioner would like to see the minutes of the last two cabinet meetings.'

There was a pause.

'Of course. But I don't think I should authorise that without first consulting the *others* who were present. Would you ask the Commissioner if he would mind waiting for them until, let's say, tomorrow morning.'

At last Argand felt that he had got together as much as Macher would give him, though he sensed that in two or three areas he had been headed off, areas he had to admit might have no relevance at all to Herm's disappearance. At half-past twelve he was ready to go.

'Mrs Herm is expecting me today. Would you ring her for me and ask her when I can come?'

Again Macher hesitated and then to Argand's surprise spoke to a secretary and asked her to ring Mrs Herm. The answer came back in only a minute or so — Mrs Herm had a lunch appointment but would be free to see the Commissioner at three o'clock.

On his way out, on the marble steps into the street, the same two guards who had been on duty when he arrived saluted him again. Their smart dark green uniforms, helmets with perspex visors, and black combat boots; their riot sticks and their webbing belts supporting revolvers and bullet pouches all infuriated him — he hated private armies. But in this case he hated the name too. He recalled how Wolfgang Herm had won praise

27

from the ecological movement when he instituted a squad of technicians trained to track down and control EUREAÇ's pollution – and how, when ecology went out of fashion, they were converted into what they now were, a private security and police force, but still called the EUREAC Health Guards.

3

Two Dossiers

Argand lunched in his office and went through a folder of information prepared for him by the research department on the recent history of EUREAC and the life of Wolfgang Herm. Near the top of the pile was a copy of the brochure EUREAC MOVES INTO THE TWENTY-FIRST CENTURY.

The frontispiece was a studio photograph of Herm signed by a name with an international reputation. Showing him in profile and facing what appeared to be a source of soft, almost mystic light, the picture managed to suggest vision and determination, as well as the boyish bonhomie the face usually expressed. Opposite was an introduction presented in the form of a typed letter with a facsimile of Herm's signature at the bottom. It spoke of the sense of privilege, of the feelings of adventure and endeavour that filled Wolfgang as he contemplated the Project, of the satisfaction it gave him to share these emotions through the medium of the brochure.

The arrangement inside was logical. It started with photographs of the Plant as it then was, standing on a broad headland between the estuary of the River Flot which links the City of Brabt with the sea, and the silted-up marsh to the south. Beyond the narrow gap through which the sea flows in to the marsh, a spit of shingle continues south for a mile before broadening out into an area of dunes and salt pasture where sheep, highly rated for their characteristic flavour, are grazed. On the neck of land between the shingle spit, the sea to the west and the salt pasture and marsh to the east lies Spartshaven. The brochure spent little space on Spartshaven beyond saying that it was a run-down area ripe for development. There was no photograph.

The second section dealt with proposed expansion of the plant, in other words with the Project itself. It began with a description of the new processes and products that were to be introduced, which would double the output of the Plant, already one of the largest chemical complexes in Europe. It went to some length to say how the effluents from these new processes were noxious and had a long life, how in the past such effluents had been pumped into rivers and the sea to the serious detriment of the environment. But that was not the EUREAC way. They proposed initially to dam the tidal inlet to the marsh, drain it, and then on the north side, the side nearest the plant, build into the marsh huge concrete-lined tanks capable of holding millions of gallons of effluent. In these tanks effluent would be treated by slow but natural processes using the water from the brook which still drained into the marsh from the land side. When the effluent had thus been rendered quite harmless, and only then, it would be allowed to flow out into the sea. Although these tanks would be huge they would occupy only one third of the total area of the marsh. Once they had been built the tidal mouth of the marsh would be reopened

This led to the third and final section of the brochure. This described how EUREAC's care for the environment went far beyond simply processing the toxic substances out of the effluent. Since the marsh, even the two thirds left apparently unaltered, would be seriously affected by the whole business, especially during the year or eighteen months when the sea would be cut off from it, EUREAC proposed to alter its character, to develop it from a dull area of mudflats which was no use to anyone and had little if any aesthetic appeal, into a splendid new pleasure complex with a marina and areas of water set aside for small boat sailing, water-skiing, and so on. The centre of this complex would be Spartshaven, which was ideally situated with the sea on one side and the marsh where the marina would be on the other, and was already provided with water, electricity and a good road back to Brabt. This section concluded with a gatefold spread – one side showing an aerial photograph of the site as it then was and the other, an artist's impression of how it would look when the whole development was complete.

The brochure itself closed with another piece purporting to be by Wolfgang Herm. This described how a beautiful but increasingly rare bird, the little tern, nests and breeds on the spit of shingle near the tidal entrance to the marsh; how EUREAC planned to begin operations with the closing of the entrance in October when the nesting season was over, and how by March the returning terns would find their nesting area completely restored. He was so confident that this would work out that the silhouette of a tern which appeared on the front of the brochure and which had been designed by his very good friend Emil Schneider, the painter, had been adopted as the badge of the Project and the symbol of EUREAC's intention to keep good faith with the environment.

Newspaper cuttings told the story of public enquiries into the Project, resistance from environmentalists organised into a group calling itself the League for Life, and finally from the inhabitants of Spartshaven who appeared to be living in shanties with leases of twenty years to run. These had finally been offered sums large enough to buy proper houses or flats in the suburbs of Brabt; yet even so, some thirty families had refused to move and a bill had had to go before the Moot, as the Provincial parliament is called, to give EUREAC the right to make compulsory purchases and evict. The evictions had not yet taken place – EUREAC had said that it would not exercise its right over the properties until the very last moment, the actual day for closing the tidal gap.

One of the last cuttings spoke of how the financing of the Project had run into difficulties a year ago, through the currency crisis and a drop in liquidity. As a result, the first operation, the closing of the tidal gap, had had to be postponed from October to the following April and the remaining residents had thus gained an extra five months. There was no mention of how this postponement might affect the nesting habits of terns, though Argand remembered that the part of the press that felt it could ignore the hard facts of economic reality had made a fuss about the birds. But all that was now forgotten.

So much for EUREAC and the Project. Most of what he had read he had known before from the papers and television, only details had been forgotten. He thought he knew far less about Wolfgang Herm, and turned to the second folder hoping to find out more.

Inevitably he was disappointed – he discovered again that he knew more than he thought he did. The picture built up through newspaper and magazine cuttings was familiar and superficial. Wolfgang was nearly fifty years old, and came from a poorish family of village schoolteachers. In 1943, at the age of eighteen he had been arrested by the Gestapo on suspicion of being connected with the Resistance, and after the war he had received the Resistance Medal from the re-established Moot. This did not mean much – in an attempt to persuade themselves that their resistance to the Nazi invasion had been heroic and unanimous the Moot had given this medal to almost anyone who asked for it, even blatant collaborators.

In the next ten years Wolfgang pursued a brilliant career as a chemist, though finally he did not take his doctorate, preferring to enter EUREAC which was then known as Brabt Chemical Industries. His rise in the firm had been meteoric, as the media say, and well deserved. Initially his contribution had been as a technologist: he improved old processes and developed new ones at a time when new discoveries in both plastics and man-made fibres were creating a boom in the industry. Capital under the Marshall Plan was available. At the age of thirty he became the youngest director on the board and married Lena de Merle, ten years younger than himself and the niece of the Baron who was then President of the firm, though her cousin had since succeeded to both titles.

At about this time Wolfgang had phased himself out of the technical side of the business, though he remained very closely in touch with it through the team of younger and possibly even more brilliant scientists that he had built up. For the next fifteen years he had been the chief force behind the firm's steady expansion into the rest of Europe and had shown remarkable gifts for financing and organisation which the media, encouraged by his perennially youthful appearance and the increasing glamour of his life-style, exaggerated and sensationalised. As Christian Kratt had implied, no one man can possibly exert more than a superficial influence over a corporation of such size and complexity, yet to the media and public Wolfgang had come for a time to be known as "Mr EUREAC".

He had developed a taste for the chic in art and the

fashionable in leisure: he and Lena were photographed skiing with an ex-Olympic champion, sailing with British royalty, and of course he piloted his own plane. Then his daughter took to distributing pot and in a moment of uncharacteristic over-reaction he took her himself to Wilhelmstras and handed her over to the Commissioner for Crime, who liked publicity and leaked the story to the press. The coverage was enormous, and since then Wolfgang had tried to keep out of the papers. However, he had provided copy for too long – the only difference now, was that where before the tone had been adulatory it now became critical, even accusatory. But as Brabt's one member of the jet set, he could not expect to be left alone.

Victoria, his daughter, now supplied most of the material – first unwittingly, by talking freely to people who later turned out to be journalists, and then with real *éclat* when she was arrested for harbouring terrorists.

Argand remembered the case well and had no need to turn up the relevant cuttings. For a time two youths had shared the single room Victoria rented on the edge of Brabt's tiny red light district. Later they were identified and charged with complicity in several attacks on industrialists and politicians, including the 'kneeing' of Victoria's mother's cousin the Baron de Merle. One of these youths, Hans Punt, was now serving a life sentence in Brabt's top security jail; the other had fallen from the roof of the Wilhelmstras building while attempting to escape. The prosecution had been unable, many of course said unwilling, to prove that Victoria had known they were members of Red Spectre. She claimed that they had come to her as machinists made redundant by a new process developed at EUREAC, and she had been happy to give them a free roof until they got work.

In all this collection of material one paper figured more often than any other, a fact which annoyed Argand for he did not even like handling the thing. This was a paper called *Slik Stien* named in dialect after a folk hero of the Province who, much in the style of Till in Germany, had gained a reputation as a prankster, a satirist, a pricker of authoritarian ballons. *Slik Stien*, which came out on three evenings a week, but occasionally pushed out extra editions when it had scooped the rest of the press, had been particularly critical of EUREAC in general and Herm in particular for over five years, but this was not the reason why Argand hated it.

Slik Stien stood for most of the things he abhorred about the times: it defended drug-taking and offered advice to those prosecuted under the anti-drug laws; it defended the right, as it called it, of adults to read pornography and in fact ran a porn colour supplement called *Slik Prik*. Its latest campaign Argand found mad as well as repugnant – it called for the right *not* to work to be established where the only work available was dehumanising. Three times Argand had instituted prosecutions against the paper under laws relating to public order, and in the first two cases it had got off scotfree and in the third had escaped with a derisory fine. It had got its own back by lampooning him in a satirical comic-strip which alluded in its time to everyone who was anyone in Brabt.

By half-past two Argand was sick of all this, sick indeed of the whole business of Herm's disappearance. However, not one cell of his body rebelled against the call of duty: he put on his coat, picked up his hat, left instructions to cover the running of his department including preparations for the Euro-Cup tie, and called for a car to take him to the Herms' house.

4

Company Wife

Brabt, a large town with over two hundred thousand inhabitants and the capital of the wealthy Province that shares its name, stands on the River Flot in the middle of a large and fertile plain. The only high ground for miles around is a low range of small hills not more than one hundred metres high occupying an area little more than three kilometres by two; the river takes a dog-leg bend to get round this eminence which forms exactly one quarter of the old part of the town, the other three-quarters being spread round the outer bank of the dog-leg. There is a small castle, and a public park overlooking the river and the rest of the town, but the reverse slopes, which face south, are the preserve of the rich and the notable. There are about a thousand dwellings in all, most of them set in their own grounds, and larger, grander, more modern as they near the crest. The Herms' house, a long low building that looked as if Frank Lloyd Wright might have designed it, was almost at the top and extended right across the ground it stood in. From that height one could see clear across the fen to the North Sea, a strip of glowing silver twenty kilometres to the west, and the stacks and towers of the EUREAC Plant beneath plumes of white vapour at the mouth of the River Flot. EUREAC chimneys smoke white at all times, never black or yellow.

An Indonesian servant took Jan's hat and coat and showed him into a large living-room, muttering that Madame would be told of his arrival. The Commissioner wondered, a little angrily as the servant's manner had been so off-hand, if his immigration papers and work permit were in order.

He looked around and did not like what he saw. The room was large and oddly shaped with unexpected alcoves and angles. It was on at least three different levels – and the ceiling was oppressively low in places. The furniture was low too and upholstered in a range of muted blues, greens and purples in a variety of fabrics and dyed skins. There were only four pictures, all large, all framed in matt chrome, and to Argand's eye identical – rectangles of bright orange each with a vermilion square in the upper half. Against the colour scheme of the room the effect was shattering – but meaningless.

'Commissioner Argand? How good of you to come.' He turned and was for a moment quite at a loss, his eyes held by eyes of an extraordinary lilac hue, his fingers touched by cool alabaster, his nose responding gratefully to slight but magical fragrances. On several occasions Argand had met the rather frumpish minor royalty who still presided over the Province and he had always been disappointed. What he now for a moment felt was what he would have liked to have felt on those occasions.

But Lena Herm was human and the moment did not last. She was a beauty – turned forty but in perfect condition, fit and lithe, only perhaps just a shade too thin to be completely attractive. Her hair was a shade of pale gold which managed to suggest the presence of silver in perfect keeping with her age. It was dressed simply, but very much dressed for all that. Her clothes were simple too, even dull – an English jumper and a light tweed skirt, but there was a richness about their textures, a

37

rightness in the way they moved and hung that declared the perfection of the style.

'Hector has been singing your praises to me. I'm sure we owe much to Secretary Prinz for finding you for us. Won't you sit down? Would you like something? Tea, coffee, something to drink? No? Well then, where shall we begin?'

From the depths of a chair that felt as if it was upholstered in chamois Argand heard himself ask her to tell him exactly what Herm had done during the hour he had been in the house before his disappearance.

'I don't know exactly what he did. You see I hardly saw him. We met, accidentally, you know? just as he arrived.' As she spoke her hands, small, white, long-fingered with nails immaculately lacquered, floated and fluttered before her – an unflamboyant recollection of Balinese dancing. A chain or bracelet on one wrist chimed fragile notes. Her voice was cool, her speech measured as if a touch unsure of her listener's ability to comprehend her. 'I was coming in from playing tennis at a neighbour's. I asked him if he wanted anything, sometimes he has tea, but he said he had had some at the office. That is the office at the Plant – I believe he had been there all day, not in town. Then I said I would go and change and he said he would too, he felt he wanted to shower. We met here again at about ten to six. I asked him if he wanted a drink, for we were going to eat early, we usually do when we have no guests. He said no but that he would take a short walk. I asked should I come too, he said no, he didn't want to trouble me, he knew I had spent the afternoon out of doors. He added that he wouldn't be more than a quarter of an hour. And that was it: the last I saw of him.'

As she spoke the last three words, she gave a slight toss of her head and finished with a sharp little bark which might have been a laugh but which registered chagrin.

'Which way did he go?'

'Through the door there into the garden. It did not occur to me that he was going any further than that.'

'Could you show me?'

'Of course.'

She led the way through the French window on to a lawn which rolled immaculately down landscaped slopes towards some shrubs which had been artfully arranged to suggest greater depth to the area than there actually was.

'There is a way out down there?'

'Yes, I'll show you.'

He followed her across the lawn. She did not hesitate, nor did she look back to see if he was behind her. Argand had the impression that people usually did as Lena Herm expected them to; the idea formed that surprise and a sense of offence were still her chief reactions to her husband's disappearance. At the bottom a small path wound between a handsome laurel and a clump of pampas grass to a high wall protected with barbed wire. Set in it was a door which appeared to be wood, but when Lena Herm opened it, which she did by pressing a button that released a lock, Jan realised it was steel. She remained in the doorway keeping it open while he walked into a narrow lane that wound down the hill between neighbouring properties, a service road linked to the main road further down. All the walls seemed to be as thoroughly defensive as the Herms' and this gave it an unattractive bleak air, not a place to go for a stroll in the evening.

'Once out through this door, how could Mr Herm get back in?'

'Only by speaking in the microphone here.' She pointed to a small square grill set in the wall. 'Then once his voice had been identified in the house, whoever was there would press a button to release the locks. As you

39

see there is no handle or lock of any sort on the outside.'

'Could he not have gone round to the front of the house and so on to the main road?'

'No. To get to the front he would have had to go through the house, and it's unlikely that he would have done so without being seen. There are only three ways in. One through the room we have just left, one through the dining-room where Mustafa was preparing the table for dinner, and one through the kitchen area where the other servants were working.'

'So your husband must have gone out through this door, though no one actually saw him do so?'

'Yes.'

'And since no one can get in, he must have gone out of his own free will. I mean if he was kidnapped the kidnap must have taken place after he had gone through the door.'

'Yes.'

'To get back into the house he would either have had to use this microphone, or walk down this lane and then back up the main road to the front door.'

'Yes.'

'Mrs Herm, did he often do that? I mean was it any sort of evening routine with him to make that circuit when he felt he needed a breath of fresh air?'

At last she hesitated, perhaps seeing which way things were tending. Her voice was cool when she replied.

'I have already said, Commissioner, that it did not occur to me at the time that he could have gone anywhere but into the garden.'

She moved her head impatiently and he passed back into the shrubbery. She allowed the door to swing solidly shut behind her and he followed her back to the living-room.

They sat down as they had done before and it was Lena Herm who spoke first.

'Hector has already told me on the telephone that you seem inclined to assume that my husband disappeared because he wanted to.'

'Yes. Or was murdered. But I don't believe that either of these is necessarily what happened. Just that if he was kidnapped or had an accident or has fallen ill we shall hear soon enough. So I have the other two possibilities in mind as the only two worth pursuing at the moment.'

'It is quite impossible that he should have chosen to disappear, and I should prefer it if you would drop that line of enquiry.'

Again Jan felt angry, albeit momentarily. Then he remembered who this woman was and his voice continued evenly.

'Mrs Herm. We have already established that he went through that steel door of his own free will. At least his first step into limbo was voluntary.'

She shrugged.

'Yes I see that. What I mean you to understand is that I know my husband very well. There is no possibility that any chicanery on his part is at the bottom of this, or liaison, and time spent trying to uncover something of the sort will be time wasted.'

Argand nodded. 'Well, Mrs Herm, let us not waste any more time. Would you mind showing me any other rooms in the house your husband uses? A study perhaps? Does he have his own bathroom?'

These turned out to be part of what was virtually a self-contained apartment lacking only a kitchen. There were three rooms on the first floor and with an ambience quite different from that of the rest of the house. Here the predominant colours were whites and greys; the furniture, though good and no doubt expensive was upright, wooden, stained dark. There were pictures on the walls, real pictures – fresh water-colours of the North Sea coasts, framed sketches of birds, mostly sea birds, many of them terns, and a fine portrait of a girl of about eighteen or nineteen. She was blond, like Lena, but plumper and freckled.

'My daughter.'

Not, Argand noted, *our* daughter.

'It's a good likeness,' he said.

Lena Herm looked at him sharply. 'Of course. Her face will be familiar to you in Wilhelmstras.'

'Only from photographs. I don't think I have ever seen her.'

'My husband was very pleased with this picture. It was a gift from Victoria, a sort of peace offering after that absurd business with . . . pot.' She said the word as if it was "shit". 'I'm afraid the reconciliation was short-lived, though it had other consequences. Through it my husband met the painter, Emil Schneider. Most of what you see here is by him.'

'And the mural in the EUREAC Building?'

'Yes. They are very close friends. Perhaps you should interview Emil Schneider about this disappearance.'

This was said drily. Argand wondered why.

When they had seen all the rooms Argand faced her again.

'I know you will think I am returning to a line you would prefer me not to take, but I must ask you if anything is missing from these rooms?'

'You mean, did he take anything personal when he went? You can see for yourself that his washing things and so on are still in the bathroom. For the rest, well I am not too sure. You may ask Mustafa if you like. He looks after my husband's clothes.'

'But the rest is as it usually is?'

She looked round the room they were in — a sitting-room with most of the bird pictures in it. For a fraction of a second her gaze hesitated, and an almost stillborn sound died in her throat.

'Well?'

'No. Nothing. But I must confess, Commissioner, I do not spend much time in these rooms. They are my husband's retreat and I respect it, as he respects mine.'

An hour or so later Argand left. He had questioned briefly and fruitlessly the staff, which included the butler/valet Mustafa, and a Brabanter couple who cooked, kept house and gardened. He had also obtained Lena Herm's permission to send up two of his subordinates the following morning — they would perform routine checks such as identifying and recording Wolfgang's fingerprints and so on. One of them was also an expert on financial matters; Argand was mildly surprised when she said that she would authorise a thorough examination of Wolfgang's personal documents over the previous three months.

As he was about to leave a green Land Rover pulled up behind his official car. It carried on its door the flaming torch of the EUREAC Health Guards.

'This is Christian Kratt's idea, since my husband went for his breath of fresh air. They stay here until nine o'clock in the morning. I must say I am glad to have them though I feel sorry for the one who stays outside. They take it in turns.'

'You know you could have asked Secretary Prinz for regular police protection.'

'Really?'

Back in Wilhelmstras Argand was shown the evening edition of *Slik Stien*. At the foot of the front page was a thick black headline: 'Our Chief Industrialist Disappears . . .' and it went on in smaller print '. . . . and no one knows where he has gone or why. A spokesman for EUREAC has confirmed that Wolfgang Herm has not been into work today, but that's not unusual. However, he's not been at home either, nor at the EUREAC Plant, so where is he? Watch this space for exciting revelations in the next few days.'

Do they really know anything? Argand asked himself. Probably not, apart from the fact that he has disappeared. But it was interesting that they knew as much when everyone seemed concerned to keep it quiet.

Later still, at home now, sitting in his leather armchair which had been his father's before him, Jan Argand thought over the whole day. He had finished the salad and cold meats Mrs Esslin, the widow upstairs, had left out for him and was enjoying his one self-indulgence of the day, a thimbleful of plum-flavoured dry gin. There was much he had found repugnant, not least the break from routine. But now, relaxing a little, he allowed himself a half-smile of self-mockery – he was intrigued. There was a puzzle, questions to be answered, odd areas where he had been blocked, others where people had been oddly cooperative. There was to be no financial or sexual scandal but they didn't mind if he pried into Herm's finances. And then they had stalled on the Inner Board minutes . . . would they go on refusing to show them? Why had EUREAC and Lena Herm called him in if they were going to be less than open? Well, clearly they really did not know where Herm was, clearly they wanted to know. But he also had the feeling that this disappearance was not entirely unexpected. Or perhaps it was more the case that they had been expecting something to happen but were not yet sure that this disappearance was it.

One thing Argand was sure of, and that was that Herm's disappearance had been in the first instance voluntary, whatever had happened to him since, and premeditated. EUREAC and Mrs Herm were of this opinion too, but did not want him to discover it for himself. What did they want then? They wanted him to find Herm but believe that Herm had gone involuntarily –

there were contradictions here.

Lena Herm had drawn his attention to the presence of Herm's wash things in his bathroom. But the toothbrush had been brand-new and the plastic case it had been bought in was still in the wicker basket by the sink. And from Herm's sitting-room the last in a series of framed tern sketches had also gone – the gap in the sequence was what she, Lena Herm, had noticed for the first time, and she had been unwilling to draw his attention to it.

Argand's feelings about Lena Herm remained distressingly ambivalent. He respected her – respect is too weak a word – as a member of a family that had been rich and powerful in Brabt for a hundred years, and he did not feel let down, as he did with people like Prinz or even the Archduke, by her manner, her presence. But he literally sweated with morbid embarrassment at the thought that she might lie to him. This acute discomfort, a sort of transferred shame, masked his refusal to admit to himself that she was clearly one of those who believe that the law is an institution whose chief function is to protect and assist the rich and powerful.

5

Turbulent Pastor

At midnight the duty officer at Wilhelmstras phoned
Argand. *The Brabanter* had received a note from an
organisation calling itself Green Force. Green Force
claimed to be the military wing of the League for Life. It
demanded, in return for the release of Wolfgang Herm,
the cancellation of the Spartshaven Project and the deposit of ten billion gelds with the Wild Life Fund as
guarantee that it would stay cancelled.

Argand arrived at work on Tuesday morning in better
heart, in spite of the wrapped butter at the Louis Bonaparte. It was again a fine blustery day, and four daffodils
had burst their buds in his window box; in the afternoon
he was to have his first meeting on the Euro-Cup tie; he
felt that after a brief and disturbing interlude things
were back on course again. The fact of the matter was
this: the kidnap note meant that the Herm affair
involved a crime – now it was a matter for the Commissioner for Crime. It could no longer be anything to do
with Jan.

Prinz was waiting for him, back to the window, head
held up so that he looked down, or round, his nose; chest
and what hung beneath thrust out like his lower lip; the
whole suggesting the Churchillian persona he was accus-
tomed to assume at times of crisis.

'Jan. You've heard about this threat from these people who call themselves the Green Force.' The voice was measured, deeper than usual, and matched the posture.

'Of course. The night duty officer rang me. I assume that the matter is now out of my hands and I must say that on the whole I'm pleased . . .'

'No. Not at all. I want you to stay in charge.'

'But the Commissioner for Crime . . .'

'Hang the Commissioner for Crime. Oh, heart of gold and works like a Trojan, but no tact, no finesse, and these are qualities in demand now, and in no small measure. Was it you told the editor of *The Brabanter* not to print?'

'It was.'

'Quite right. Can you see Pieter Stent making that decision? No. Nor can I. Now I'll tell you another reason why Pieter would be quite the wrong person in this situation.' Calmer now, confident that Argand's resistance was melting, Secretary Prinz sat on the edge of the desk and pulled out his pipe. 'I've had Christian Kratt on and off the phone since seven o'clock this morning. He too is very pleased that you gagged *The Brabanter*. If he has his way news of this threat will never get out. He's absolutely convinced there's nothing in it, that it's just a stunt put up by these League for Life people, and will blow over in no time. If it gets no publicity, which is all they can expect from it, then no harm will have been done.'

'But we must investigate this threat.'

'Of course we must. That's what I told him. If after all there did turn out to be something in it, and we had been sitting around on our arses, you'd be back on the beat and I'd have nothing to do but watch my wife's roses grow. I put that to him and he pleaded that it should be you who continue to handle it all. I must say you do seem to have impressed the EUREAC crowd and I can tell you they don't impress easily. Anyway, that's it. You're still on the job. Don't worry about old Pieter. I'll square it with him. Let me know how you get on.' Prinz blessed Argand with a smile that suggested fellowship, a shared secret, even that the difference in rank between them was a thing of no importance. Then he squeezed Argand's arm and left.

Argand was irritated by the pungent smoke that hung in the air and even more by a sense that things were again being done against all normal practice and procedure. But so strong was the habit of trust and obedience in him, it did not occur to him to question the reasons given. Possibly too he felt a little flattered, in spite of himself, at the Secretary's easy dismissal of the Commissioner for Crime.

The note, which had arrived at the newspaper offices by post, told him nothing. The original was already in the hands of forensic – the photocopy that he was given laid out exactly the same terms as the phone message had done. The original had been printed on cheap and common notepaper and a children's printing set had been used. Every toy shop in the Province carried them and they were on sale in Holland, Belgium and France too. With no other leads to go on Argand decided to see the organisers of the League for Life.

Spartshaven shocked him: first on account of the tattiness of the place, secondly because of the signs of revolt and repression which everywhere added their own peculiarly ugly nastiness to what was already shabby. The settlement – one could hardly call it a village – consisted of three parallel tracks, each about a kilometre long, extending in a more or less straight line down the spit of shingle to the point where it was no longer wide enough to take them. These tracks had once been concreted over but the surface was now shattered and scarred with potholes. The shanties that lined these three tracks were all constructed out of old railway carriages — the most common method had been to put two carriages side by side, about five metres apart and roof and floor the space between to create one or two quite large rooms while the compartments of the carriages served as bedrooms, kitchens, and so on. Several of them had been painted up quite smartly, even pebble-dashed or covered with cedar weather-boards, yet paradoxically these efforts at permanence and normality only exaggerated the general air of pathetic dereliction, as indeed did the sorry attempts to create gardens and rockeries on a shingle base.

There were slogans everywhere — from sad little messages like 'Why can't you leave us alone?' through EUREAC KILLS to NO TO CAPITALIST EXPLOITATION OF THE ENVIRONMENT, and the anarchist 'A' in a circle had been aerosoled on every surface large enough to take it.

'What sort of people choose to live in a place like this?' Argand asked after a moment or so of lurching at about eight kilometres an hour over what was no more than flattened rubble.

'An oddly mixed bunch,' replied his companion, a lieutenant in the Rural Guard. Since they were beyond the City boundaries, courtesy demanded that Argand should go everywhere in a Rural Guard car with one of their officers as guide. 'Many were retired people, some of them very old, who had lived here for twenty or thirty years and naturally didn't want to move now. Then quite a few houses are second homes, summer places kept by shopkeepers, better paid workmen in Brabt. They were usually left empty during the winter. Well, those two groups, the retired and second homers, for the most part accepted the EUREAC offer and got out, though I'm afraid several of their places have now got squatters in them — louts and layabouts attracted by this confrontation with big business. But there's a third group, not

49

large, but the most troublesome of all, sort of adult drop-outs I suppose you could say, and they are the ones, about thirty families all told, who won't budge.'

'I don't understand what you mean by "adult drop-outs".'

'Well, there are two ex-schoolteachers, one now scrapes a living as a writer, the other does odd jobs, two or three ex-businessmen who sold up, a doctor who now goes in for nature cures – people of that sort, in their forties or older, with families, respectable educated people who have, for God knows what reason, chucked their jobs and decided to slum it here. There are also quite a few real workmen, I mean men who held down well-paid skilled jobs in factories, engineering and so on, who've also packed it in, and now run tiny little businesses of their own – welding, decorating, plumbing and so on, from these crazy bungalows. You know it's this group, not the hippy squatters, who are the real trouble. Here we are. The man you want is usually here or hereabouts.'

The car pulled up outside a shanty with a higher roof, covering a larger space between the carriages than most of its neighbours. Boards flanked both sides of the door. To the left the notice read: 'Church of Inner Salvation – the City of God is in Your Heart or it's Nowhere. Pastor: the Reverend Martin Kant'. To the right: 'The League for Life: Please come in – all welcome'.

Argand approached with mixed feelings. His father had been a member of the Church of Inner Salvation, which thirty years ago had been a sect with very strict principles. He had died when Jan was eighteen, a year or so before Jan had given up the church – but Jan recognised that he owed a lot of what he felt and believed about life to its teaching. On one side he now feared he would discover that it had decayed into a weak and sloppy caricature of its former self; on the other that it had remained unchanged – in which case he would find hostility or resistance from its pastor, this Martin Kant who doubled as local convener of the League for Life, difficult to cope with.

He and the lieutenant went up the two wooden steps and through the open door. The room where they found themselves was a mess. Large and dark, it resembled a chapel and indeed at the far end there were four or five short rows of collapsible chairs facing a plain deal table with a plain unpainted Cross on it and a Bible – Jan recognised the austere arrangement that had dominated every Sunday of his childhood. The foreground had been converted into a makeshift office – there were tables with two old typewriters on them, an ancient hand-operated duplicating machine, filing cabinets, and boxes of stationery. A woman was using one of the typewriters. Argand recalled the kidnap note.

'I shall want this place sealed off,' he said. 'Nothing, not a scrap of paper must go out of it until the forensic unit has gone through it. In fact I'd like to get that organised before we go any further. Is there a telephone here?'

'There may be, but if there is, it won't work. These people reckoned it would hinder EUREAC if they pulled down the line so that's what they've done. I'll use the car radio, and meanwhile I'll get a couple of Rural Guards to watch the door.'

The lieutenant turned to go out again but as he did so the woman stood up. She was large, blond, about forty, and dressed in a darned heavy sweater and patched jeans. She had a scarf over her head with the ends tied at the nape of her neck.

'You'll need a warrant from an Examining Magistrate before you do that,' she said.

Argand faced her. She was a type he instinctively disliked – a busybody, bossy, probably a feminist.

'I don't think so.'

'Well I do.'

'Madame, there are two reasons why I do not need a warrant. First, because I am sure Pastor Kant will be quite ready to co-operate when he knows why I am here. Secondly, I am investigating a crime that is classed in the Code as one where material risk to human life is involved. In such cases, as I am sure you are aware, I have discretionary powers to act without warrants. Please carry on, lieutenant.'

'I don't know what you're talking about. What crime? The only crimes committed here are by you people and the EUREAC Health Guards.'

'Madame, I don't have to explain myself to you. Could you tell me where I might find Pastor Kant?'

'I don't have to tell you that, nor anything else you may want to know.'

'Oh, for goodness sake, let's not be childish. I am investigating a case of kidnap, and it is necessary that I should see the Pastor.'

For a moment she bit her lip, then sat down to her typewriter again.

'If you want to know, he's up at the barrier with other members of the League.'

'The barrier?'

'Yes, the barrier. It's a barricade guarded by armed bullies, and its sole purpose seems to be to stop bird-watchers looking at birds. They stole my husband's field-glasses the other day and roughed him up quite savagely.'

'If there is any truth in what you are saying, I hope you have filed a formal complaint.'

'Oh it wasn't your lot that did it. It was our friends and good neighbours, the EUREAC Health Guards.'

Argand felt the now familiar anger and at the same time bewilderment.

'Then if there were witnesses you should bring an

action for theft and battery against EUREAC, or the individual guard who did it.'

She had been making a show of sorting through papers on her desk. Now she looked up with an expression of bitter scorn on her face. 'Either you are a joker,' she said, 'or you come from cloud-cuckoo-land.'

Argand was relieved when the lieutenant returned to say that two Rural Guards were on their way. Five minutes later they were in the car again. The track above the chapel was smooth, newly surfaced, though aerosoled with 'EUREAC = FASCISM'.

'They dug this up, and the other two tracks when the first contingent from EUREAC went through. We have to keep ten men permanently on patrol to make sure they don't do it again.'

Shortly the three tracks converged into one as the spit narrowed, and the shanties petered out. To the left they could see the sea, deep blue, the tide in, a good swell running with the March wind, white breakers. It looked fresh, clean, vigorous in the spring sunlight. To the right there was a narrow irregular belt of sand-dunes covered with coarse grass and then the marsh. Because the tide was high it was two-thirds covered with water whipped into spumy wavelets by the wind. The third that was uncovered was broken up into large patches of bog rosemary growing on the more elevated mudflats. Argand supposed that some would find it a featureless, bleak landscape: to him its emptiness and simplicity were attractive – especially in the bright light of a March day.

In front the scene was different. A kilometre ahead rose the white towers of the EUREAC Plant on the other side of the narrow tidal entrance, a gleaming insolent cluster soaring into the blue and white of the cloudswept sky; in the immediate foreground there was a three-metre high chain-link fence, topped with barbed wire, running clean across the spit from sea to marsh. In the middle was a high gate, red and white, set where the track passed through the fence. Beyond it were prefabricated transportable sheds and huts, stacks of timber, two bulldozers and other impedimenta and *matériel* associated with construction sites.

A small crowd was gathered at the gate. As they drew up Argand realised that those on the far side were all EUREAC Health Guards, those on the near side were a more motley group, five or six only, two women amongst them. One man stood out on account of his height. Two metres tall but stooped, he was wearing a trilby, a loose muffler, and a long tweed coat of good quality. He turned at the sound of the car, and Argand noted, in spite of the muffler, a clerical collar above black.

As he opened the car door, the group parted — Argand had a swift impression that the men were all bearded, all wore duffle coats or anoraks, and all carried field-glasses — and this tall man came through, holding out his hands in a theatrical gesture of submission.

'Ah,' he called, 'I suppose you have come to arrest us then, is that it? What will the charge be? Breach of the Peace? Public nuisance? Interfering with people in the pursuit of their legitimate occupations?'

Argand looked up into a face ascetic and healthy, though he supposed the breeze, which was brisk, even rough in this unsheltered spot, was responsible for the pinkness of the high cheek bones. The eyes were deep blue, hard, unsmiling, fanatical. He got out, straightened. The Pastor's face still seemed a long way up.

'I am Commissioner Argand, from Brabt. I take it you are Pastor Martin Kant.'

'I am. Well, Commissioner — I believe I should say "Excellency", should I not? — what is the charge to be?'

'There is no charge, Pastor. And I am to be addressed as "Excellency" only in the circumstances where you would be called "Reverend". I am not here in connection with whatever it is that's going on here. But I do need to ask you some questions relevant to another matter and ask for your co-operation.'

'You do? What other matter?'

'Wolfgang Herm, Vice-President of . . .'

'I know who Herm is.'

'Well, he has disappeared. We have good reason to believe that he has been kidnapped by a group closely connected with your League for Life, perhaps even actual members of it.'

'Poof! Rubbish! This is some ruse to get us all locked up under suspicion so that this obscenity can be carried forward.' He waved a gloved hand at the fence and chimneys behind him.

Argand felt again the frustrated anger rise in his chest. 'It is nothing of the sort. Perhaps you should read this,' and he thrust the copy of the ransom note under Kant's nose. He took it and read it.

'This is nonsense. My people would never do anything like this. Well, certainly not kill a man; and I doubt if they would keep a man incarcerated against his will. We are principled you know, and this is where our strength lies. We will not use the tactics of the enemy. An essential element of our cause is its dignity, and we will not stoop . . .'

'Pastor Kant, I'm not interested in hearing you put your case at this moment. Whatever you may think, your League *is* implicated by this note and I would be failing in my duty if I did not question you and your associates most closely about it.'

Something in this appealed to the Pastor. Possibly the note of sincerity with which it was delivered, possibly the word "duty". His head went on one side and he looked down at the Commissioner.

'All right. I may answer your questions if I find there

is nothing in them that is against my conscience. But first you can establish your good faith by helping us.'

Argand's high-arched brows lifted yet higher, and he waited.

'We have been asking these oafs here to let us through their fence. All we want to do on this occasion is walk a short way along the dunes and look through our field-glasses. We shan't touch a thing, or interfere with what-ever they are up to today, nor take photographs. Just a stroll. Did I say an hour? Twenty minutes will be enough. If you would speak to them, offer yourself as guarantor of our good behaviour, then they might give way. And then I, as I said, will help you as far as I can.'

'There must be a purpose to this stroll.'

'Oh, there is. But I doubt you will understand it. The Chief Oaf here thought I was mad when I put it to him and he is convinced it is a ruse to cover some dissident ac-tivity.'

Again Argand waited.

Pastor Kant shrugged and went on: 'We wish to see if the little terns are back yet, and, if they are, if they are nesting. That is all.'

Argand went up to the EUREAC Health Guard who ap-peared to be in charge, explained who he was, and said he would accompany the Pastor and his friends. The gate was opened. The little group made its way to the marsh side of the spit, the bird-watchers in front, the pastor and the policeman following. Argand felt some of the tension that had built up in him leak away as the wind whipped round his ears and gusted fine sand round his ankles; the marsh covered in water had taken on an indigo hue with white-capped wavelets, and looked huge from this low position. The land on the other side, the fen between where they were and Brabt, was a brown and blue line two kilometres away at the nearest point, broken only by a church steeple and a clump of skeletal diseased elms. Two gulls flew alongside the group, keeping station, riding the wind effortlessly, watching them with beady black eyes; then three duck, large, white, green and russet, wheeled up from a mudflat still uncovered by the water and circled over them before flying off purposefully to the other side of the marsh.

'Shelduck,' said Kant. 'One of the few species that stays with us all the year round. Much loved by the fowlers on account of their size, but I'm happy to say they can only be poached now, not shot legally. No luck, Vic?'

One of the bearded, anoraked men had turned and was walking back to them. His companions had stopped, seemed not to want to go further. 'No Pastor,' he said. 'No sign of them yet.'

'But it is early.'

'Oh yes. They have been back as early as this in the past, but usually it's in the first week of April.'

Kant nodded. 'We must return then in a week's time. I hope, Commissioner, you will be able to return too to vouch for us.'

He was about to retrace his steps, when a sudden cry from the group in front held him, then, aware of excitement, of raised field-glasses, the three of them hurried on over the thirty metres that separated them.

'What is it?' cried Kant. 'Are they here after all?'

Another answered him, identical to the first except that he wore a duffle not an anorak.

'No, Pastor. Not the terns. But look in the gap there. Here, take my glasses.'

They had now reached a point from where they could see the very end of the spit and the narrow space, not wider than two hundred metres, where the tide flooded in and out of the marsh. The EUREAC Plant on the other side looked very near.

'Good gracious,' cried Pastor Kant. 'Can it be?

57

Well, that is marvellous, that's really good. Here Commissioner, take these, and be one of the few to see a sight that has been very rare on these coasts for a decade or more.'

'Where am I meant to be looking?'

The Pastor pulled his sleeve. 'There, there right in the gap. Can't you see the white where the water breaks, right there in the middle?'

Jan found the slash of white, fiddled with the focus, and then drew in his breath quite sharply as a little stab of delight surprised him; the hair on the back of his neck rose with it.

What he was looking at for the first time in his life apart from in a tank in a zoo, was a seal, a grey tubby seal, frisking for the fun of it in the tide-race. Then: 'Goodness, there are two of them.'

'Better give the glasses back to the owner. Poor chap has hardly seen them yet.'

They waited, taking it in turn to watch for another five minutes, and then the seals moved into the marsh and disappeared behind a mudflat.

Back at the barrier, the EUREAC Health Guards and the lieutenant of the legitimate police were equally puzzled by the blessed expression on their faces.

'We saw two seals,' said the Commissioner.

The relaxed feeling among them remained as the Rural Guard drove them back to the chapel, and Jan hoped that having done Kant a favour and perhaps earned a little respect, he would have no more difficulties. He was quickly disillusioned.

As they entered the large blond woman rose. Clearly she was in a foul temper.

'Pastor, thank goodness you are here. I have never been so badly treated. These two bullies', she gestured at the Rural Guards they had left there before going to the barrier, 'would not let me out of here. Not even to go to the lavatory. And when I said I had to go and made a move to go, they pushed me so I nearly fell over. That man', she pointed to Argand, 'will now tell me to file a complaint. Well this time I will . . .'

'All right, Maria. I understand. You have been badly treated. Now if you still have to go the lavatory, please go.'

'Thank you, Pastor.'

She reached behind her and unhooked a woven shoulder bag from the back of her chair. The lieutenant looked warningly at Argand who was already feeling put out because Kant had told her she could go without first checking with him.

'She can leave the bag,' he said. 'My people may want to look at it.'

'Maria is a diabetic. She wants to go to the lavatory for an insulin injection. The apparatus is in the bag. Please go along, Maria.'

The lump of frustrated anger rose.

'She must take out what she needs and leave the bag.'

'For goodness sake, Commissioner, what do you imagine it is that Maria is taking out?'

Argand's voice rose to something not far off from a shout: 'A child's printing set. Now please take what you want and leave the bag.'

Looking a little startled now, Maria fished about and came out with a small box. She showed him the label. It said it contained a disposable syringe of insulin.

'Go with her,' said Argand to one of the guards. 'And see she comes back here when she has finished.'

Of course there was no printing set in the bag and he felt ashamed to be rooting through it, especially beneath Kant's scornful gaze.

The rest of the interview went badly. Argand wanted a list of the members of the League for Life. Kant would not agree that the League had members.

'We are not an organisation. We are not even a group,' he said. 'We are friends. We come together, we talk about what concerns us, go on talking until we are all agreed on what should be done and who will do it, then we go our own ways.'

'You must meet regularly.'

'No, not really.'

'Then you must have some way of convening each meeting, you must have an address list. After all you have already said there are over two hundred ... friends.'

'Yes, there is an address list.'

'Then that is what I want.'

'And that is what I am not going to give you.'

'I'm afraid you have to.'

'Commissioner. Those addresses were given to me in confidence and good faith. I simply do not have the right to divulge them to anyone, not even from one friend to another, without first getting permission. A man's address is a private ...'

'Pastor, none of these people has anything to fear from me at all, unless they are involved in the extremely serious crime I am investigating.'

'I should like to be able to believe you. But I think the time has gone when you could make any such claim with confidence. It could be a serious matter for some of these people if it were known that they are part of the League for Life. Suppose, I am not saying it is so, but suppose there are some employed by EUREAC. It is likely that there would be, since EUREAC is the chief employer in these parts. Or suppliers with contracts with EUREAC ...'

'But I'm not going to let these addresses and names get anywhere near EUREAC.'

Kant looked at him, head on one side.

'You know, Commissioner, I almost believe you are

sincere. But these things are not in your hands, whatever you say. Your colleagues will know you have the list. Your superiors and those under you. I cannot imagine that you will keep it so closely that they won't have access to it. I am sorry but I would not be acting responsibly if I gave you that list.'

'Then I shall get an Examining Magistrate's warrant for it. And you will be charged under section twenty-three of the 1977 anti-terrorist law with obstructing a police officer investigating a case where human life is at risk.'

'So be it.'

Argand used the car radio to get in touch with the appropriate official and made arrangements for Kant to be taken to the nearest station and charged. He knew there would be no question of an arrest; bail would be set at a very low figure. By the time he had finished and knew the warrant was on the way his forensic team had arrived from Brabt.

They went through the office and chapel with minute particularity and found a stock of paper identical to that used for the kidnap note. Since it was the brand of cheap paper most commonly sold throughout the Province this had little immediate significance. However, there was a chance that dust, a mote, a hair, a flake of skin might appear in the packet and match a similar crumb in the kidnap note or in its envelope.

During this search the address book came to light; Argand leafed through it, then on a whim turned to the "S"s.

'What do you know of this Emil Schneider?' he asked the Pastor.

Kant had remained silent for most of the time since his return, being only as co-operative as was necessary to prevent the use of violence on him or on the filing cabinets or other objects the police wanted open or moved.

61

'He's a good person. A fine painter.'

'He's also a good friend of Wolfgang Herm.'

Kant hesitated a second.

'Is he?' he answered in a voice completely neutral, devoid of surprise or curiosity.

Argand left with the idea in his mind that Kant knew of the connection between the Vice-President of EUREAC and the artist, a man who, it now seemed, figured in the list of more or less avowed enemies of the Company.

6

Deviant Artist

The Commissioner arrived at Schneider's flat a little after six. He was now definitely out of temper and tired too. He had been late for the meeting on the Euro–Cup tie, and it had not gone well – he had been unable to resolve an argument between the chief of the ambulance services and the chief of the riot police: both wanted to use the same side road near the stadium for parking their vehicles.

The artist's apartment was in one of the older parts of the town, in a tall block with a decayed stucco façade and wrought iron balustrades in front of the shutters. With its cagelift set in the stair-well and polished brass fittings it was not unlike the building where Argand himself lived, but in a very different quarter. Following the rebuilding of the university in the middle of the nineteenth century this area had become the students' and artists' corner of the town and it bordered on the red light district. Argand remembered that the room where Victoria Herm had lived, perhaps still used, was nearby.

As he got out of his police car he was irritated to see a large black Peugeot illegally parked on the curb in front of the entrance. A EUREAC Health Guard leant with his back to it and smoked, his perspex-visored helmet resting on the car roof by his elbow. Argand discovered a second on the top landing – still with his helmet on so the tinted perspex hid his face – apparently guarding the artist's door.

'I'm afraid you can't go in there just now, sir,' he said as Argand reached for the bell-push. Angrily Argand pushed his Commissioner's card at him. The guard shrugged and stepped aside.

Schneider answered the door. He was tall, thin, but in good condition – not athletic but one felt that unclothed he would have an attractive body, muscled but not obviously so, flat-stomached, narrow-buttocked. Only thinning black hair, grey streaks in his neat beard and a slightly pinched look about nose and eyes showed that he was older than one would have at first thought, perhaps forty or more.

'Who are you?' he asked. 'What do you want?'

He spoke with an accent and Argand recalled that he had come from East Germany in the late fifties. Argand still had his card in his hand.

'Oh goodness. This must also be to do with poor Wolfgang's disappearance. You had better come in. I already have one guest in this connection.'

Argand followed him down a narrow passage and into a large room, larger than he had expected – probably a wall had been taken down to create it. The end near the door was a living-room furnished for comfort rather than appearance; the other half was a studio lit by tall windows and a built-in skylight. From a chair somewhere in the frontier area between the two, Christian Kratt unfolded his untidy height.

'Commissioner. Well, you work late, I see. And no doubt on poor Wolfgang's behalf. I imagine you have spent some of today with that eccentric priest and his eco-freaks. I hope you have not been wasting your time, though I fear so.'

'That may have been the case. Kant was hostile and

64

unhelpful. Look, if I'm disturbing you I can wait, come back later.'

'No, you are not disturbing us. We had finished our business.' Kratt put his head on one side and his eyes blinked behind his thick spectacles. A finger, nicotine-stained, smoothed the stringy grey hair on the back of his head. 'In fact I had come to persuade Emil to undertake some of the design and so on for the marina we are planning for Spartshaven. Of course that stage is a long way off yet, but we'd like to get it right and *give* whoever is to work on it plenty of time. What we actually have in mind for Emil is a piazza with a centre piece – a sculpture or a fountain or a combination of the *two*, you know the sort of thing. It would be a big commission and I hope he's interested.' He looked at the artist and lengthened his thin lips in what was intended to be a pleasing smile.

Emil gave a slight shrug, looked non-committal. 'Commissioner, can I offer you a coffee or something?'

Argand, who was preoccupied with the fact that he felt sure Schneider had said that Kratt was there in connection with the kidnap, broke his usual habit in such circumstances, and nodded without thinking.

'What about you, Kratt?'

'No thank you, Schneider. I really must be off in a moment or so, and I am sure the Commissioner would prefer me not to be here when *he* talks to you.'

'Excuse me then while I make it.'

Argand thought of calling him back and cancelling the order but then realised that it was a long time since he had had anything to eat or drink, and let him go. He turned to Kratt.

'Why do you think I am wasting my time with Pastor Kant?'

'Oh I am sure they have not got Wolfgang. Kidnap is not their style, and violence certainly isn't. They are taking advantage of his disappearance. I tell you one reason I am sure they have not got him is that if they had, Wolfgang himself would have told them that their demands are quite *impossible* to fulfil. As I was just saying to our artist friend, only a third world war could stop the Project going ahead now, and probably not even that.' Kratt was now talking with some intensity, and unconsciously he twice inched the gold cigarette case in his side pocket into view and twice let it drop. 'Once these things reach a certain point they are *irreversible*. A momentum is built up, and the whole company and many other companies as well, contractors and so forth, are committed. It is not a question of their survival depending on the Project – their existence, our existence *is* the Project. Really, as I said to Schneider,' here acknowledging the brief return of the artist who took a cup and saucer from a cabinet and returned to the kitchen, 'the whole board of EUREAC could be put up against a wall and *machine-gunned*, and it would not stop the Project'. He paused, slapped his bony knees and then pushed on them to unfold his gangly height. 'I must be off. But first tell me, I ask out of idle curiosity, what *does* bring you here?'

'Mrs Herm told me that Mr Herm is friendly with Mr Schneider. He is therefore a possible lead – and has to be checked out.'

'Of course. And no other reason at all?' Kratt's eyes, cool and expressionless, disconcertingly caught and held the policeman's for a fraction of a second. He hesitated, remembered the Pastor's fears that the address book would end up in the wrong hands.

'No. No other reason.'

Schneider now came in with a coffee which he handed to Argand. The cup rattled in the saucer as he did so and the policeman realised that something was disturbing the artist. Then, for a moment he was on his own as Schneider showed Kratt out to the front door of

66

the apartment. Still holding his coffee he moved into the studio area, and there, just as he was sipping the hot drink he nearly choked on it, nearly let it drop to the floor. In front of him, on the large easel which was so angled that he could not have seen it earlier, was a painting, not quite finished, but nearly so, of two naked men kissing each other on the lips. It was done with a fine sensual naturalism and it was clear that the embrace was not a chaste one.

'My God, you are spying on me already.' Schneider rushed past him, took the painting from the easel and turned it to the wall. 'Well. This too is a commission. And one I am less ashamed to be doing than anything that evil man may ask of me. In fact I am not ashamed of it at all. Why should I be?' He now rushed back to the canvas, turned it to Argand, almost thrust it at him. 'See, what do we have here? An act of love, that is all. Just an act of love. But it offends you. Good. I am glad. You should realise that acts of love offend you.'

Argand was indeed deeply upset by the painting and was finding it a quite disproportionately difficult matter to get his mind back to functioning in a cool, responsible, objective way. His first instinct had been to smash the stretcher, rip up the canvas, then beat the artist with the timber.

'Never mind the painting, never mind the painting.' He drank off the coffee which was still too hot, and set the cup and saucer down on the mantlepiece. 'What you paint is your affair. It does not become mine until you exhibit it publicly . . .'

'And no doubt you advise me not to. Pretty pictures of birds, of the sea, yes? They are all right. But they are natural too you know. And what this picture shows is nature. . . .'

'Never mind the painting.' For the second time that day Argand's voice was nearly a shout. 'I have come to ask you a few questions relating to the disappearance of Wolfgang Herm. Nothing else.'

For a moment the artist looked at him, then put both hands to his face – Argand could not help noticing that they were long, thin, but strong, and that in other ways too Emil resembled one of the men in the picture. The face of the other was hidden in the embrace, but he was fair – that was all one could say.

Schneider rubbed his eyes, then with his hands still resting along his cheeks he said: 'Oh God, today has been a nightmare, a nightmare.' He looked hard at the Commissioner and added, also in a near shout: 'And it still is . . . I need a drink before I answer your questions.'

Argand's distaste rose again as Emil not only poured himself a half tumbler of whisky, but used the first gulp or two to wash down what seemed to be a handful of pills taken not from a bottle but from a pill-box. It is not unlikely that had Argand been asked to describe a thoroughly evil person he would have said 'a drug-abusing, homosexual drunk'.

'You are a friend of Mr Herm?' he asked in as even a voice as he could manage.

'Yes.'

'And have been for some time?'

'That is so. Is it three or four years? I painted a portrait of his daughter. He came to see me. I showed him some bird studies I was doing at the time and some seascape sketches. He commissioned a large mural for the foyer of the EUREAC building.'

'I have seen it.'

'It is an awful painting. A lie. If I had the money I would pay twice what they paid me to have it back and destroy it. One day perhaps, when I have had enough of these,' he waved the glass and slopped some, 'I will go down there with an aerosol and I will write all over it . . .'

Argand sensed that obscenity was on the way. 'I am *not* interested in your paintings.'

'But you are interested in me and I am my paintings. All right. Yes. My friendship with Wolfgang. It is closer now than it was. He is trying to be a good man now, we both are. Better than we were.'

Argand did not think it necessary to hear whatever intimacies were in the air.

'When did you last see him?' he interrupted brusquely.

'When did I last see him? That is a good question. A very good question.'

'Please answer it.'

Schneider put one long index finger against the side of his nose and tapped it. 'What would you say,' he said, 'if I told you that I saw Wolfgang on Friday evening?'

'Did you? Did you?' Argand moved a step towards the artist and quite unwittingly clenched his fist. The gesture was not lost on Schneider.

'Hey there,' he cried. 'There is no need to resort to police brutality. Pray do not give me an excuse to express your tidily repressed libido in such socially acceptable forms as beating up deviant artists. I will tell you *everything*.'

Stung by the shrill mockery in this, Argand waited.

'On Friday Wolfgang rang me up in the afternoon. I do not know where from. He asked me to take my car – it is a small DAF – and park it in the service road behind his house and wait for him there at six o'clock. I brought him back here. We had a drink together, and he told me he was going out of the Province for a time, he would not say for how long. At seven o'clock exactly he went to this window,' Argand followed him down the long room, past the offensive picture, and so to the large casement at the end, 'opened it and went down the fire-escape. At the bottom he gave me a wave, and then he went out through the service area and I suppose into the street. I have not seen or heard of him since.'

Argand looked down the iron stairs into an area at the bottom. It was empty save for three cats and seven large black plastic bags — those provided by the City for the refuse collection.

'And he said nothing to you to indicate where he was going or how long for.'

'Just that he was going out of the Province. But I think he expected to be away for some time. Or perhaps he thought he was putting himself in some danger.'

'Why do you say that?'

'He kissed me as he went. Normally he did not do that at parting.'

At home Argand rang up Secretary Prinz.

'I wish to resign from the Herm case.'

'Oh no, Jan. That is quite impossible.'

'I insist.'

There was a pause, then: 'Jan, the only way you can resign from this case is by resigning from the force. Now what is it that's worrying you? What has cropped up?'

'I have a good reason to believe that Wolfgang Herm was having a homosexual relationship with a painter called Emil Schneider.'

Again a pause. 'Commissioner, I don't have to tell you that such relationships are no longer illegal.'

It was Argand's turn to think.

'You are not shocked then. Not even surprised,' he said at last.

'Whether or not I am shocked is immaterial. I am not surprised. There was gossip about to that effect.'

'Which you did not see fit to tell me.'

'No, Commissioner. It did not seem immediately relevant. If it turned out to be so I felt you would discover it yourself. You have, so I was right. Now, am I to assume that your distaste for such liaisons is the reason why you wish to resign from the case?'

Argand remained silent. The Secretary went on: 'Well, I am sure that on reflection you will see that such an attitude is unprofessional to a degree. I think you have always prided yourself on your professionalism. Certainly I have found it to be one of your most valuable and characteristic traits.'

Argand remained silent and the Secretary rang off. An hour later he rang back.

'Jan. Have you seen *Slik Stien* this evening? They have just brought out one of their cursed specials. They have the full text of the Green Force's ransom demand. They accuse us of suppressing it and there are a further two sheets arguing the ecologists' case against the Project. They also say that the ten billion gelds the Green Force want deposited with the Wild Life Fund is exactly equivalent to the sum EUREAC keeps permanently on account against a new liquidity crisis. I've had Kratt on the phone and he is a worried man. He wants to see you tomorrow.'

'Well. Since I am still on the case I had already decided that I would call on him. I still have not seen the minutes of the Inner Board meetings I asked for. I suppose Kratt is now afraid there is someone in EUREAC who dislikes the Project and has leaked all this to *Slik Stien*. I hope he doesn't want me to catch his rebel as well as find Herm.'

'I'm afraid that may be the case. The editor of *The Brabanter* is an angry man as well. He says this is the third time in a year we have asked him to suppress news only to be scooped by *Slik Stien* a day or two later. I have said we will try to keep him more up to date with things as they happen from now on, so if you can think of any-

71

thing to pass on to him tomorrow please feel free to do so — subject to your admirable sense of discretion, of course. Jan. I'm glad to hear that you think of yourself as still being with the force.'

7

Company Practices

Two reports were on Argand's desk the following morning – Wednesday. The first detailed the discoveries of a team of three detectives who had spent the afternoon and evening of the previous day questioning the people who lived at the first ten addresses in the League for Life address book. In some cases they had searched the premises too. Four households they felt would repay further visits. One of the dropped-out teachers was running what he called a 'free' school for the children of neighbours who had rebelled against the state system of education and could not or would not pay fees to private schools. The detectives felt this renegade could be prosecuted under fire and sanitation laws and the children got back into the state system with the minimum of fuss.

The second case was even more interesting, involving the home of an electronics engineer who worked for EUREAC. This man lived not in Spartshaven but in the estate built for EUREAC workers to the north of the Plant and his bedroom window overlooked the estuary of the River Flot and the nuclear power station on the other side. They had discovered a radio transmitter in this man's loft and believed they had stumbled on someone the State Security Police had been looking for for some time.

73

Once a month radioactive waste was shipped out of the power station to be dumped in the North Sea. An ex-trawler called *Fingal's Cave* and registered in South-ampton by an organisation called the Friends of Life had interrupted its usual activity of harassing whalers and seal culls to intercept these shipments. They had seri-ously, even dangerously interfered with the dumping. Clearly the trawler had had inside information about the times the nuclear waste was loaded, though these had been varied as much as was possible within the schedule allowed by the power station. The detectives believed that their man had been watching the power station across the estuary and contacting the trawler by radio when he thought a shipment was about to leave.

At a third address an illegal brewery was in operation and at the fourth the owner was growing and selling compost-fed vegetables without a market-gardener's licence as required under Community regulations.

None of this was in any way relevant to the disap-pearance of Wolfgang Herm. Argand felt uncomfortable – Kant's prediction that the address book would bring trouble to those whose names appeared in it was coming true.

The second report was more pertinent. The man who had been looking into Herm's personal accounts had dis-covered that some shares had been sold by his bank two weeks previously and the money, a quarter of a million gelds, had been handed over to him in bills, the numbers of which the bank had on record. There had also been a small box in the safe deposit which he had taken out on the same day. Mrs Herm did not know exactly what was in the box, but after going through all his holdings they discovered that others were missing and they thought that the certificates had probably been in this box. Refer-ence to the firms who had issued the missing certificates showed that they were still in Herm's name. Sums in excess of five million gelds were involved, about a quarter of Herm's personal fortune.

Argand suffered another bout of revulsion with the whole business and asked to see Secretary Prinz. Prinz was out. After a few minutes' thought he drafted a memo instead, the gist of which was that he was now completely convinced that Herm had disappeared in a planned way and entirely voluntarily. He went on to say that the only evidence that suggested that he was in any sort of danger was the eco-freaks' notes and he believed these to be spurious. In short he did not believe that he had any real evidence that a crime had been committed and he believed that continued investigations would only lead him into further unjustifiable invasions of private citizens' privacy.

Then his sense of duty got the better of him. He remembered that he was expected by Kratt, left instructions for the memo to be typed and delivered to Secretary Prinz as soon as he returned, and took a car down to the EUREAC offices.

Lena Herm and Hector Macher arrived together a moment after him. From the foyer where he was waiting while his identity was checked by the duty Health Guard he saw the personal assistant handing his employer's wife out of the Ferrari he had driven down in, and with his face turned away from the building, but his quiff still visible, Argand remarked again how easily Macher could be mistaken for Herm. Then the assistant straightened, faced about, and the similarity disappeared — Macher was a slighter person in physique, in personality, in presence. The likeness was no more than a matter of a fashionable hair-cut and a fashionable suit.

Another Health Guard drove the Ferrari away to the underground car park beneath the building, and the one who had been keeping an eye on the Commissioner saluted smartly as Lena Herm and her escort came through the electronically-operated plate-glass door.

'Commissioner, how are you?' Again, the alabaster fingers touched his with royalty's cool condescension. 'Have you found my husband for me yet?' She barely paused in her stride, moving on towards the private lift. To answer her at all Argand had to follow. The Health Guard took a step towards stopping him but Macher waved him aside.

In the lift she went on: 'That clever boy you sent round yesterday has made a stir though hasn't he? Hector, did you know Wolfgang has been siphoning off quite substantial sums of money in the last few weeks and stacking it away somewhere? We have yet to find where.'

'No, Lena, I did not. If I had, I should have told both you and the Commissioner as soon as he disappeared.'

'Yes, I'm sure you would. You're a good boy.' She patted, perhaps stroked his cheek just as the lift door breathed open again. She moved briskly into the room. 'Poof, it's stuffy here. Is there no air-conditioning?' Macher pressed a button by the light switches and a soft hum could be heard. Almost immediately the temperature of the room dropped. 'Mind you, Hector, I'm a little surprised at you. After all you are meant to be his private and confidential assistant, and I thought you were good friends too. Yet he slips a small fortune out from under your nose and you notice nothing. Well never mind. See if Christian is here, will you?'

But the door through which Kratt had entered during Argand's first visit had already slid open and the Company Secretary walked in. Lena embraced him perfunctorily – royalty admitting an intimate into her presence.

'Christian, you look tired. I hope you are not letting my absurd husband get you down. Are the others here yet?'

'Only de Merle. Dax would not come.'

76

'Well, we can manage without him. I take it my dear daughter has not turned up yet?'

'No, Lena, I'm afraid not.'

'Well that was to be expected too. Christian, I think you had better put the Commissioner in the picture while Hector and I keep my noble cousin entertained. He does not expect to be left alone.'

She swept away through Kratt's door, and Macher followed her. Christian Kratt tapped a cigarette on a gold case, then as an afterthought offered one to Argand. The sour odour pricked Argand's nostrils.

'You don't, do you? Never? Lucky man. I am trying to *give up*, was succeeding too until this infernal business cropped up. Well now, I mustn't keep you long – you have important things to attend to, and so have I of course. Secretary Prinz told you that I wanted a word with you?'

'Yes.'

'Well, that was early last night. After that absurd rag came out. Yes. *Slik Stien*. You know, Commissioner, many of us feel that the time has come to put that thing down. Oh, I know it's a safety valve, people who would be more mischievous than they are feel they've done their bit to bring on the *revolution* if they read it, and so on, but it really can be quite a serious nuisance. In this instance it's clear to me that they are giving space to some crank in the firm; well, not to put too fine a point on it, some *traitor* . . .'

Somewhat to Argand's surprise, Kratt almost spat the word out, then turned on his heel, found an ashtray and stubbed out the scarcely started cigarette. As he went on the gold case appeared again in his hand, and soon he was unconsciously tapping another cigarette on the lid. Argand, with a non-smoker's sensitivity felt slightly sick at the acrid, strong stench of expensive Virginian.

'Well we have suspected there was disloyalty. There

77

have been earlier leaks, and once or twice things have gone wrong – an important delivery not met because of a clerical error, a particular process messed up because a storage tank had been refilled with the *wrong stuff*, that sort of thing, and now this. The common factor is *ecology*. All the instances have been to do with processes which these freaks have for some reason or other taken against. Why, heaven knows. We are already so screened and hemmed in with rules, guidelines and regulations from everyone from the World Health Organisation to the Spartshaven Rural Council that if one of our day labourers *spits* we are liable to a fine.' The grey head that had been thrust forward throughout all this, pecking from side to side as he spoke, now sank back between the gaunt shoulders, then tipped to the left. 'Anyway, there is someone in our organisation who is on their side, the eco-freaks, I mean. I wish you would root him out for us, Commissioner.'

'Really, Mr Kratt, this won't do.' Argand was irritated, near anger yet again. 'This is really most irregular. In the first place I am not sure that this is a police matter at all. If it is, it is nothing to do with me and my department . . .'

'Dear me. Secretary Prinz was so *right*. He said that would be your reaction. But consider, Commissioner. Poor Wolfgang may after all be in these people's hands. This insider who is betraying us is surely one of them. By tracking him down you may find yourself with a very useful line to Wolfgang's whereabouts.'

'Mr Kratt. Yesterday at Emil Schneider's, you were very firmly of the opinion that the kidnap note from the Green Force is a hoax. I should like to know why you have changed your mind about this?'

At last the second cigarette went into Kratt's mouth and a lighter flared behind cupped hand. Through the smoke the thin lips lengthened into a smile, the tall stoop took on a shambling apologetic look.

'Well Commissioner, you are right, of course. And I shan't pretend to you that my opinion has changed at all. I remain quite sure in myself that the note is a hoax. Look. Apart from anything else, if they have told Wolfgang what their demands are he will have told them that they are impossible. The Project simply cannot be *cancelled*. Even superficial modification would be very difficult. Wolfgang *knows* this, and would have explained it to these people, if he were really with them. They are asking for *precisely* the one thing we cannot do. But you, Commissioner,' the smile became yet more wheedling and apologetic, 'you have to follow up this letter as if it were real. So all I am doing is giving you *every possible assistance* by helping you to follow up a very promising lead. And if on the way you find our traitor for us, then something will have been achieved — even if poor Wolfgang remains missing.'

'Well, I suppose I must look into it.' Argand felt the speciousness of Kratt's arguments but also suspected that further objection would be pointless. He remembered that by now his resignation from the case would be on Prinz's desk.

'Splendid.' Kratt looked at his watch, stooped to stub out the second cigarette, made as if to go.

'Mr Kratt?'

'Commissioner?'

They spoke together.

'Commissioner. I was about to ask what you made of these movements of funds, securities and so on.'

'To me they clearly indicate what I have said before. That Mr Herm's disappearance was, in the first place at any rate, planned and voluntary.'

'Quite. In fact, further evidence that the note is a hoax.'

'Yes. But don't worry. Professionally I must continue

to act as if it were not. I will investigate your leak.'

Kratt smiled again and inclined his head so it hunched between his shoulders, simultaneously he gave an odd and indecisive flap of his hand. '*Touché*, I suppose is what I should say to that. But at the risk of giving you too many lines to follow at once, may I put to you Mrs Herm's view of it; of the movement of money I mean.'

'I should be obliged to hear it.'

'You heard her ask if we had heard anything of Victoria, her daughter.'

'I did.'

'If there is one point in Wolfgang's life where he is vulnerable, it is there. He worships her and feels *guilt* about the way she has . . . grown up. Or failed in that respect. It is her mother's belief that she is in the hands of the Red Spectre again. Either as a member or as a victim, kidnapped or in some other way in their power. That through her Red Spectre has been *extorting* these funds from Wolfgang. His disappearance too, she thinks is connected. Either they have used whatever threat they have over Victoria to get him to fall into their hands, or he has elected to disappear so that he may track them down, without putting his daughter at risk which he would if he publicly revealed what had been happening. That, broadly, is Mrs Herm's theory of the business. What do you think? He has a quixotic streak, you know.'

Argand shrugged. 'It is a hypothesis. It is not impossible. But there is no real shred of evidence yet.'

'Of course, you are right. But it's worth bearing in mind is it not? Lena Herm is a clever woman and *not* to be underrated.' He looked at his watch again. 'Well, I really have to go. The others will be wondering what can have kept us chatting. And I mustn't keep you.'

'Mr Kratt. Before you go.' Argand clenched his fists into balls thrust deep in his jacket pockets. 'I think I heard you say that Baron de Merle is waiting to see you and Mrs Herm. That will make a quorum, with you, of your inner board, your cabinet.'

'That is correct. And it is as such that we are meeting. We felt it essential we should convene following the *Slik Stien* report. It would be surprising if we did not, I think?'

'Mr Kratt, would you please add to the agenda my earlier request for minutes of recent meetings of the cabinet? The ones which Mr Herm attended.'

The eyes narrowed, the thin smile returned.

'Well of course, Commissioner, I will put it to them. But I fear it's a question of *company practice*. I think they will say the full board only will be able to open the minutes of the inner board. Hector is the expert in company practice and we will consult him. Perhaps you should simply leave it to us to go through them. I'm sure we shall not find anything useful. Recent meetings have been very dull, routine affairs. But *extrapolation* of items you might be interested in might be in order, I don't know though. Anyway, I assure you I'll bring it up and see what can be done . . .'

But Argand had already turned back to the window and appeared to be concentrating his attention on the interweaving traffic flows thirty storeys below.

8

Confusion

At midnight Argand's phone rang again.

The duty officer at Wilhelmstras said: 'Excellency, I have the editor of *The Brabanter* on the line. This time he insists on talking to you personally.'

'Can you switch him through to me from there?'

'Yes, Excellency.'

'Do that then. And keep recording.'

'Certainly, Excellency.'

All incoming calls to Wilhelmstras were automatically recorded as a matter of course. Argand did not want the editor to discover his private number; as a senior police officer he felt it was prudent to have conversations with newspapermen on record.

A moment later a new voice, brisk, even impatient, came on the line.

'Commissioner Argand?'

'Speaking.'

'Klaas Visser here. We have had a new note about Wolfgang Herm. I think in the public interest, and in Mr Herm's interest, we should print it. I have just enough time to do that.'

'Describe it to me.'

'It starts . . .'

'No. Describe it to me. The paper, the writing, and so on.'

The editor heaved an audible though still brisk sigh.

'The letters, and occasionally whole words, have been cut from old copies of *The Brabanter* and pasted on to what looks like good quality typing paper. It starts . . .'

'The envelope.'

'What? Oh yes. If you must. Ordinary business manila. Address typed. Postmark, same day in-City delivery, handed in at eight, reached us two hours ago.'

'Two hours ago? Why are you ringing me only now?'

'I rang Mr Kratt of EUREAC and . . .'

'My God. Well never mind. Now Mr Visser, no doubt it has already been handled by you and your staff, nevertheless I should like you not to touch it again but simply read it to me . . .'

'Commissioner, we know and have followed the procedure your people have laid down where such notes are concerned. What I have before me now is a photocopy. Now, may I please read it to you? We go to press in half an hour.'

'Go ahead.'

'It begins: "To the Directors of EUREAC, to the Editor of *The Brabanter*, to the People of the City and Province of Brabt, to the Oppressed and Poor everywhere – Greetings. One of the arch-enemies of the people, Capitalist, Reactionary, and Destroyer of Human Principles, Wolfgang Herm, Director of EUREAC, has been taken into custody by the armed forces for Freedom through Revolution, known as Red Spectre, has been tried and found guilty on various charges of offences against Humanity, some of which carry the Death Sentence. Sentence has been delayed and may be commuted if the following terms are met.

'"Hans Punt, Susan Jansen, and Pier Jansen, at present illegally held in Brabt prisons, are to be released under circumstances to be negotiated with the prison and police authorities. EUREAC is to pay two hundred and fifty million gelds to be used at Red Spectre's discretion to forward the fight of the People for Liberty, Power, and Peace.

'"If these terms have not been approved and carried out by midnight between Wednesday and Thursday, 2nd and 3rd of April, then sentence on Herm will be carried out, as above.

'"Long live Liberty, Long live Peace, Long live the People."'

'That's all.'

'I'll try to have someone round to pick it up before you close down.'

'Of course. But may I print it?'

Argand thought of Secretary Prinz's instruction: "Give *The Brabanter* anything you can."

'Print it.'

'Thank God for that.'

Secretary Prinz blew thick smoke across the desk on which he was sitting. Behind it Argand tried to keep his head beneath the cloud.

'You're right of course,' said the Secretary, 'and I've already put the whole thing in Commissioner Gapp's hands. Not Pieter Stent's you understand — Red Spectre may be, indeed is, profoundly criminal, but their avowed intention is the subversion of the State so it's a job for the Commissioner for State Security. I know you'll give him all the help you can, keep him fully informed and so on. In fact, to be blunt, Jan, I would like you to think of yourself as under him for this exercise. I know you won't mind, this once. He's a good man, has tremendous respect for you, and so on.'

Argand stabbed his ballpoint pen at the blotter in front of him.

Secretary Prinz watched him. 'I felt sure you wouldn't mind.'

Argand looked up, eyes narrowed against the smoke, the arch of his eyebrows flattened by a frown.

'I don't mind working with or under Commissioner Gapp. Of course I hardly know him. He was in Special Branch after he left NATO and I doubt we have met three times outside official functions. No, I've nothing against the man. But what I don't understand is just why I have to remain in touch with the case at all.'

'We-e-ell,' Secretary Prinz was expansive, 'you don't really. But the thing is this. We now have two kidnap notes. We are all convinced, morally certain, that the first is a hoax, and the second a genuine and very serious threat. But Jan, you know the form. Until we are absolutely certain, one hundred per cent certain, we have to go on investigating the first. Now you already have a jolly good team doing just that. It seems silly to break them up and stretch Commissioner Gapp's resources by handing that side of the case over to him, when your people are doing so well. And they are, Jan, they are. Their reports on the eco-freaks make fascinating reading, don't you find? What these people get up to, eh? Anyway, that's the score. I want you to leave all the real work to Gapp, that is the Red Spectre side of it. Meanwhile your team can go on methodically checking out the League for Life just in case, and you keep a fatherly eye on them and look into anything they might turn up. That way we're covered on all fronts. And you'll be able to get back to your proper job. Preparations for the football match going all right, are they? I'm sure they are, but they'll be all the better now you have time to add the personal touch.'

To escape the smoke Argand moved to the window. The chestnut leaves were already further out, impertinently easing fronds of vigorous green through sticky cases. Such pushing life made him feel ill at ease.

'You are ignoring my memo, my resignation from the case.'

'I never ignore anything from you, Jan. But shall we just say that it's staying in the pending tray, for the time being?'

'And of course if my men uncover Kratt's leak for him, their time will not have been wasted, will it?'

In the silence the traffic noise of Wilhelmstras became insistent, in spite of the double glazing. Secretary Prinz stood up and knocked his pipe out into Argand's immaculate white bowl. The filthy ashes continued to smoulder.

'Well, I'm glad you see it my way, Jan,' he said at last. 'Very glad. It would be awfully inconvenient if we didn't see eye to eye on most things, wouldn't it, old chap?'

Argand decided to see the chiefs of the riot police and the ambulance service separately, since he now suspected that the source of their differences lay in "personality incompatibility", or, as he preferred to call it, "bloodymindedness". It was while the chief of the ambulance service was with him, late in the afternoon, that his secretary reported that the bright young man who had been investigating Herm's private finances was on the phone with an urgent report.

'Put him through.'

The young voice was excited, happy even.

'Excellency, I think I'm on to something.'

'Go on.'

'I'm at the offices of Bach, Ellman and Klutt. They're an accommodation agency with offices in Leopoldstras, but they also do a lot of rent-collecting for big property firms and they bank with Herm's bank, the Brabt City Bank. Well, the end of the month is their busy time on the rent-collecting side and this morning they banked a lot of money, most in cheques, some in notes. One note, a thousand geld note, had a serial number from the sequence paid out to Herm a fortnight ago when he sold those securities. The cashier, a bright girl I must say, at the Leopoldstras branch of the BCB, spotted it when she was cashing up and was able to work out that it had been paid in by Bach, Ellman and Klutt. Well, they've been very helpful too, and their records show that cash was paid by only eight tenants. Now shall I read the list?'

'Yes please.'

The fourth name was Emil Schneider, but Argand let him read on to the end.

'You've done very well, very well indeed. I'll see to it now that these people are checked out.'

Argand allowed his neglected duties as Commissioner for Public Order to occupy him late into the evening and it was nine o'clock before he left his office. He knew that he should have found time to organise the investigation of the people on the rent collector's list, he knew that he should have pulled in Schneider and questioned him, himself, but he remained reluctant to do so. On his way home, walking through the brightly-lit streets, past shop windows glowing like treasure caves (all that power burnt up uselessly), and cinemas advertising with thighs, bums and breasts erotic delights he had never even dreamed of, he rehearsed in his mind the excuses he would use if this dereliction of duty ever came to be examined.

He was under-staffed; he had had a mercilessly busy day; it was now firmly believed that whatever Wolfgang Herm had been doing before his disappearance, and even just after it, he was now in the hands of Red Spectre — and Schneider could not be connected with them, even if he was one of the League for Life. Of course, and Argand was quite ready to admit this to himself, none of these was the real reason why he had postponed, perhaps would continue to postpone seeing Schneider. The real reason was that he had done enough prying into areas where a policeman had no business to be, done enough interfering with private citizens' private lives, encroached on freedoms that were, when all was said and done. . . .

So he argued to himself, and tried to brush from his mind the recurring image of two men embracing, and the recurring sound of Schneider's voice: '. . . it offends you. Good. I'm glad. You should realise that acts of love offend you.'

9

Culpable Negligence

Throughout the working hours of Friday things went well for Argand. The Herm affair receded into the background: the three men working on the League for Life address book sent in reports similar to the first one; the bright young man discovered that some of Herm's shares previously thought to be unsold had been transferred to a jobber in Amsterdam, and was delighted when Argand told him to get in touch with the Dutch police and follow the enquiry across the border; Secretary Prinz agreed with him that investigation of the eight people, including Schneider, on the rent collector's list could be left until the three working on Kant's address book had finished.

The preparations for the Euro-Cup tie progressed well. The chief of the riot police agreed to forget his differences with the chief of the ambulance service. A representative of Kirkshield Wanderers flew in and seemed ready to accept all the restrictions on the sale of tickets to his supporters that Argand, advised by the manager of Sports Union Brabt, put to him. He had not expected the Scot to be so co-operative. However, he was a little unsettled when at the end of the session, the Scot had said: 'Of course y'ken it's finally no possible at all to say *any* of our supporters can be relied on not to do a berserk if y'have a bent referee. With a referee as bent as the one at Barcelona, then, mon, I'm guaranteeing you nothing, nothing at all.'

For once Commissioner Argand left Wilhelmstras at six o'clock precisely and with a lighter heart than he had felt for a week. With luck, an hour or so in the morning checking that routine matters were ticking over as they should be would leave the rest of the week-end free, apart from his routine visit on Sunday at four to the psychiatric clinic where his wife played out the time until he should pre-decease her. In her more lucid moments she would say that she was happy to stay there for thirty years if need be, but stay there she would until he was dead. Notwithstanding this, and the fact that more than half his salary was swallowed by the clinic's fees, he knew it was his duty to see her, and he knew it was pointless seeing her more often than once every three weeks. The prospect of this duty did not depress him. Uncomplicated duty, however unpleasant in itself, never did. Only in morally confused areas did he become uncertain, distressed.

At the corner of the road where he lived, a magenta van with *Slik Stien* painted in vermilion letters on the side was just off-loading a pack of newspapers on to the pavement beside the kiosk where he normally bought his morning edition of *The Brabanter*. On the top of the pack he could read the headline, in bold crimson print: WE DON'T HAVE HERM — RED SPECTRE, OFFICIAL. With pulse beating uncomfortably fast Jan bought a copy as soon as the vendor had undone the bundle, stuffed it into his coat pocket, and hurried up the last hundred metres to his block. It remained in his pocket as he climbed the four flights of stairs round the caged-in lift shaft – he believed his arteries would remain in good shape if he avoided lifts – and pulled out his latch key. To his astonishment the door opened before he could get the key into the lock.

'Mrs Esslin! Dear me, you gave me quite a surprise. What are you doing at this hour?'

The widow from the floor above, who "did" for him, looked equally put out. She was a plump woman with a grey, shiny face, an exaggeratedly apologetic way of talking, and small eyes that stared coldly and with distrust at whomever she was talking to.

'Oh Commissioner, you did give me a turn too. But really it is my fault, I promise you. What happened was this. My younger sister's boy, Josef, you know I've told you about him, well he was bad again last night, and she's already missed at the shoe shop where she works twice this week and didn't want to miss again, so she had me over to look after the poor mite. Well, I say poor mite but there wasn't much wrong with him that I could see, a case of anti-schoolitis if you ask me. Anyway I was there all day and I've only just had time to get round and clean up for you. I'm just taking the rubbish out for you, Commissioner,' and she pushed past him carrying a kitchen bin with a lid.

'Why not put it in a plastic bag and leave it on the landing for the porter?' he asked. This was the usual arrangement.

'Well it doesn't really seem worth it, Commissioner. I mean they tell us not to waste things these days, like they did in the war, and my bag upstairs isn't full so I thought I'd put yours in with mine. I'll bring your bucket back in a second.'

He let her go, took off his coat, pulled the copy of *Slik Stien* from the pocket and took it into his sitting-room. There he sat in the lace-curtained window at the round oak table with its beige tasselled cloth, and spread the paper in front of him.

"Today, at our offices in Vaterloostras, an envelope was delivered by hand," he read. "The porter who took it has little recollection of what the carrier was like, apart from the fact that he was fair and wore a workman's blues. The envelope was addressed to the editor, *Slik Stien*, and we print below the text of the letter that it contained, without cuts or additions or alterations of any sort. Photocopies of the original may be seen at our offices, in fact they will be found fixed to our windows in Vaterloostras. To see the original, however, you must apply to Commissioner Gapp, in charge of State Security, in Wilhelmstras, and we must warn our readers that we think he will keep it to himself."

'There we are then Commissioner. That's your bin back where it belongs.'

'Thank you, Mrs Esslin.'

'There's a nice casserole in the oven for you. But it might have too much pepper in it. I'm sorry if it has.'

'Thank you very much, Mrs Esslin. I'm sure it will be delicious.'

'I'm sorry if I disturbed you, Commissioner.'

'That's all right, Mrs Esslin.'

With relief he heard the outer door shut again, and then he wondered absently that it was Friday and she had not asked him to settle up with her. Usually she came down exactly ten minutes after his return home and presented her accounts for the week. Then he turned back to *Slik Stien*.

"Dear *Slik Stien*," he read, "you will have seen in yesterday's edition of *The Brabanter* a letter that purported to have come from Red Spectre, which said that Red Spectre has Wolfgang Herm in its custody, and made certain demands which must be met if Wolfgang Herm is to be released unharmed. That letter is a forgery. We, the action committee of the first brigade of Red Spectre, based here in Brabt, would be pleased if you would publish our categorical denial of everything in the letter that

The Brabanter printed yesterday. Furthermore we would be pleased if you would inform your readers that a similar denial to this one was delivered to the offices of *The Brabanter* yesterday evening. That denial was not published in today's paper, and was not even acknowledged. Finally we would add that our sympathies lie with whatever group does have Herm, and especially with the Green Force and the aims set out by them in Tuesday's edition of *Slik Stien*. If what was said on Tuesday was true then we extend our hands in friendship to them, and add our voice to theirs and to those of the people and the unborn children of the people, in begging EUREAC to cancel the Spartshaven Project and secure the release, unharmed, of Herm. Signed and dated, the Action Committee, etc., etc. . . . ."

There followed a long piece of editorial that Argand ignored. He knew it would insist on the authenticity of this second letter, would hint that Wilhelmstras was as rotten as a wormy apple, would reiterate its support for the League for Life's case against the Spartshaven Project. But he did read the letter through again. Then in his brief-case he found a copy of the letter *The Brabanter* had published two days before and he tried to remember which one more closely resembled in style letters received in the past from Red Spectre. He did not feel certain but he rather thought the rhetoric of the first letter was overblown.

At last he did what he had been steeling himself to do almost since he had seen the headline on the pavement outside: he phoned Commissioner Gapp.

The Commissioner was still at Wilhelmstras. A dry meticulous voice brought to Argand's mind the image of a pale fair man, a man with a thin streak of yellow hair for a moustache, a military man, but military in a modern sense. He was not the sort to lead a cavalry charge, or poke his head out of a tank turret, but a man who knew how to deploy tactical fission weapons, nerve gases, and fighter-bombers that could go twice the speed of sound and pattern the ground with napalm, a man who knew how to interpret the computer print-out that would predict the results. Such a man was Gapp, late of NATO.

Commissioner Gapp admitted that he did have the original of the *Slik Stien* letter in his hands, he did apologise coldly when Argand asked him why he had not been told of the letter's arrival, let alone allowed to examine it.

'But you see Commissioner, we are virtually certain that this letter has no relevance at all to the central problem,' Gapp went on. 'It is nothing to do with the disappearance of Herm. We are treating it as a ruse, as a further interference from your eco-people, what are they called, a League or something?'

'But you had a first letter from them yesterday, the one delivered to *The Brabanter*. I take it there was such a letter, I mean *Slik Stien* is not inventing when it says an earlier one was sent?'

There was a pause.

'No, Commissioner. You are right. There was a first letter.'

'And you instructed *The Brabanter* to suppress it?'

'Yes. Clearly it was spurious. And after consultation at a very high level it was decided that it was, and indeed is, in the public interest to suppress it. Already there is a small but growing interest in your league's case against EUREAC and the Spartshaven Project. It was felt that anything which strengthened the idea that Herm is not held by Red Spectre but by these eco-people would add confusion to an already dangerous situation, would put Herm's life at greater risk, and unnecessarily complicate on one side attempts to discover the man and Red Spectre's hiding place, and on the other EUREAC's attempts to negotiate with them.'

'But I should have seen that letter.'

Gapp sighed. 'Yes. I'm sorry about that. I suppose you should have seen it. But Secretary Prinz was of the opinion that you had a lot on your plate and . . .'

'Commissioner. There is still a possibility, however remote, that it *is* the League for Life or Green Force that has Herm, and not Red Spectre. If they have, and if they finally kill Herm, I am going to be answerable . . .'

'Yes, yes,' Gapp now sounded testy. 'I see your point. Look, I'm quite sure you have done everything you should have done, have left no stone unturned, and if, as you say, the incredible happens and Herm is found to be in the hands of these madmen, then I'm sure that no one will be able to say that you have been negligent in any way. Now I shall see that copies of both letters are on your desk in the morning and an authorisation to go to forensic and see the originals. Will that satisfy you?'

Although far from satisfied Argand hung up. He now had a definite sense that he was being manipulated, that someone somewhere had fitted him, like a cog, into a piece of complicated machinery whose purpose was a mystery to him. With this feeling came a first intimation of danger, of risk, though as yet he could conceive of no risk greater than that of failing to do his duty. He decided that in this case the trouble was that he was not quite sure just what was expected of him — but a life-time of taking certain assumptions for granted still left him incapable of asking himself why this was so, of asking why it was his superiors were not being as frank with him as he would always be with them.

For half an hour he mooched around his flat, attempting to read the papers but finding *The Brabanter* obscure, somehow veiled in its reports — except in its foreign columns where everything that happened to the west of Brabt was shown to be crude and vulgar, greedy and grasping, while everything to the east, to the east of West Germany that is, was shown to be brutal, dull, repressive and ultimately wicked. On these points *The Brabanter* was certain and lost no opportunity to press them.

Slik Stien did not amuse him at all. He found it nihilistic, reductive, plain silly. It was stupid, he thought, to throw so much muck at so many different targets, self-defeating for it was plainly absurd to imagine that more than a tiniest grain of truth lay anywhere in its pages. Its campaign to make it legal for a man to refuse dehumanising work he thought to be particularly nonsensical. He always got angry when socialists went on about workers, the dignity of labour and so on. He was a worker, wasn't he? And his work was often nasty, clearing up after the wild indisciplined excesses of his fellow workers. They should see some of the things he had seen after a football match, or one of their absurd anti-nazi demonstrations, but you wouldn't catch him trying to dodge his duty by claiming it might be dehumanising.

He flung the rag away and turned on the television. A speakerine was announcing the programme for the evening. She turned to camera two, putting her face and bust into profile and her breast and nipple, covered only with a film of gauze, were silhouetted by the pink light that bathed her. Commissioner Argand switched off.

In his kitchen he spooned stewed beef from the casserole on to the plate Mrs Esslin had laid up for him on the formica table. He ate abstractedly at first and then with a little enjoyment, for the gravy was tasty with caramelised onion and carrot, herbs and spices. It was not too peppery. The meat was tender, almost falling apart, yet he knew that when she did present her account, it would be shown to be one of the cheapest cuts. He often said to her: 'Mrs Esslin, I don't know how you make such marvellous casseroles out of such cheap ingredients.' Had she once explained that long and gentle cooking was the secret, it's possible that things would have turned out better for him and Herm than they actually did.

His meal did not last more than a quarter of an hour and by the time it was finished he knew what he must do. However reassuring Gapp had been, Argand knew that they had both been negligent. Whatever Gapp might say, the letter, the *two* letters refuting the first that purported to be from Red Spectre, materially increased the chances that Herm was after all in the hands of the Green Force.

He had been explicitly ordered to continue to investigate the League for Life – that way at least the path of duty was still clear. He knew he had been wrong to leave the investigation entirely to subordinates right round the clock, through twenty-four hours. He stacked his dishes in the sink, folded his napkin and put it in the table drawer, and looked around. Certainly Mrs Esslin had made a good job of things, in spite of not being able to come in until the evening: the place was spotless.

He put on his hat and coat, locked up, descended to the street and caught the bus which would take him nearest Emil Schneider's flat.

The night was drawing in, most of the street lights were on. Nevertheless there was some daylight left and the harsh white light of arc-lamps in the service area at the bottom of Schneider's fire-escape seemed excessive. Argand pushed his way through the small crowd that had gathered in the street outside, and showed identification to one of the policemen who were holding them back. He then had to squeeze past the ambulance that almost filled the entrance, its blue light slowly turning. Beyond the area was a garishly lit cave in which five or six men orbited methodically with the various instruments of their trade – measuring tapes, fingerprint powder, cameras with complicated lenses. In the midst of them, the centre of their attentions, lay Emil Schneider. His legs rose in a 'V' over black plastic bags of rubbish, one of which had split beneath him spilling peelings, coffee grounds, and tin cans on to the concrete around his head and shoulders. It was clear that his neck was broken and that he was dead.

Powers of Observation

'I'm treating it as murder, though it's too early to rule out either suicide or even accident. First let me show you how we think he went over the rail.' Inspector Laruns of the homicide squad, which was of course part of the crime department and came under Commissioner Stent, was still quite young for his rank and felt both pleased and nervous that a Commissioner of Police, albeit from another department, had arrived on the scene of a major crime only an hour or so after it had happened, less than an hour after his own appearance on the scene. Yet he felt he had done well in the time, carried out the proper routines, laid the foundations for a properly scientific enquiry, had begun to formulate hypotheses though maintaining a properly professional open mind. He led Argand through the studio part of the flat and out on to the top landing of the fire-escape.

'He went over here. Almost certainly. An ordinary magnifying glass picked up fibre from the sweater he was wearing snagged in the rust.' He indicated without touching the top rail. 'Then his head caught the second rail down when he was already travelling at a considerable speed, his body having turned through ninety degrees. The back of his head actually, which would have created a whip-lash effect between the weight of his body falling and the interruption of the fall on his head caused by the rail. That whip-lash broke his neck, and was almost certainly the cause of death. The rail I'm talking about had hair in it just as this one had fibre. I shall be very surprised if it turns out not to be his hair.'

'And so you think he was pushed?'

'It's not certain by any means. One thing seems certain. He didn't jump. I don't think suicides ever go over a rail head first using the rail as a fulcrum, if you see what I mean. No. If it were suicide, then we have interpreted the wool and the hair wrongly. And of course that's possible.'

Argand frowned. 'I can't visualise someone pushing him like that, nor him going over by accident in that way.'

'No. Nor could I at first. But come and look at these.'

The inspector led the way back through the studio and into the living area. On the low table, on either side of which Argand and Kratt had sat three days earlier, was a collection of sealed and labelled transparent polythene bags. 'These are all things we have found in the flat. First a whisky bottle, as you see half gone. One glass. Then these. Just look at these.'

Argand stooped, put his hands on his knees and peered at the two bags indicated. He drew in his breath, almost let it whistle out. In the first bag were three glass ampoules, the ends filed off; in the second, a hypodermic syringe.

'Do you know what was in them?' he asked.

'No, not yet. But if he was drugging himself and if he also drank that amount of whisky tonight, then perhaps it would not have been very difficult to tip him over the rail head first, for he would have been in no state to resist. And equally it's just possible that he might have leant over it, been overcome with dizziness and tipped himself over. Well, we shall see. The autopsy will tell us a lot. But until then there is sufficient evidence for me to act as if it is a murder case.'

'Oh certainly. Certainly. You have acted quite correctly I am sure.

Inspector Laruns looked pleased.

'One thing you have not asked me, Inspector, is why *I* am here.'

Now the inspector looked disconcerted.

'I . . . I took it for granted that you were passing, saw my men here and came in to see if you could help.'

'You should know better than to take anything for granted in a case like this. You may know that I am investigating certain aspects of the disappearance of Wolfgang Herm. I was on my way to ask Schneider a few questions in connection with that, and I find . . . this.' For a moment Argand looked confused, distressed, then he pulled himself up. 'Obviously I shall want to be kept fully informed about everything you find. And at the moment I am particularly interested in the serial numbers of any bank-notes Schneider might have had here.'

'Of course, Excellency. Excellency, if you will excuse me I think I had better get in touch with Commissioner Stent. I . . . I had not realised that the case might be so . . . so serious.'

'Yes. I think you should. Tell Commissioner Stent I am here and will wait for him if he decides to come.'

Laruns hurried away, using the lift to get out to the radio patrol car that had brought him. He was sensible not to use the phone, Argand thought. Forensic often finds quite a lot in the interstices of the mouthpiece.

He wandered slowly through the apartment, not touching anything, keeping to the long sheets that had been rolled out over the floor. Things were much as he remembered them. The obscene picture still stood against the wall, exactly where Schneider had put it down. It looked as if he had not touched it in the last three days. He heard the voice again: 'You should realise that acts of love offend you', and he winced away. How could there be any love in an act like that? People did not know what the word meant any more.

He padded into rooms he had not seen before. First a kitchen. Nothing special there, except yes, an ashtray turned upside down on the draining board, propped against two glasses. Schneider had not been a smoker, so that might be important. He put his head into the bath-room, and wrinkled his nose. The room seemed spotless, but there was an odour, an unpleasant one. Not too long ago, Argand thought, a man – or a woman, let us take nothing for granted – has been ill in here, has vomited. And then someone, someone else? cleaned up afterwards.

Argand followed the sheeted path into the bedroom, to the foot of the large bed. On either side of it two chairs had been pulled away from the walls and were now stationed near the bed, awry, clearly in nothing like their normal positions. Argand speculated. It looked as if two people had sat on either side of the bed, facing the pil-lows. Like visitors in a hospital. This was borne out by the state of the bed-clothes. The bed was neatly made, yet down the middle there was a deep indentation as if someone had lain on the silk bedspread. Finally, above the bed, a framed drawing of terns was askew. Schneider, thought Argand, had been a tidy man. He would not have left the chairs thus, nor the picture tilted.

'Commissioner Stent is on his way.' Laruns, a little breathless, was behind him. 'He'd like you to wait here for him.'

'Of course.'

Argand walked back to the living-room, feeling a little pleased with himself. It had been a long time since he had been involved in detective work. He wondered how much of what he had noticed Laruns would miss, even the forensic team perhaps.

'Just let me be sure I have things right,' he asked. 'No one actually saw Schneider fall.'

'No. But a lady opposite heard him, and the man on whose rail he hit his head. That was at five past six.'

'Then what happened?'

'They both ran down the fire-escape, then the man went back to his flat by the lift to get to his telephone.'

'The lift was on the ground floor?'

'Yes. Yes, that is what he said.'

Argand nodded. They were back in the studio area now and he picked up a sketch-pad that was near the offensive painting.

'May I?'

Laruns shrugged. 'Go ahead.'

Handling it as little as possible, using a clean handkerchief, Argand slid the pad on to a table, turned back the cover and the succeeding leaves. The first four had bird studies on them. The fifth sheet was difficult to make out: it appeared to contain three varied studies, very freely done, of a square or piazza. Each study had in common with the others a background of chimneys and cooling towers, and a figure crouching in the middle of the piazza, where one would expect a statue or fountain.

The sixth sheet, the last one used, made quite clear what the fifth had been about. There was one sketch, finished but crudely done, as if for a newspaper cartoon. Again the piazza, again the stacks and towers behind, but this time the figure in the centre was clear and boldly drawn. It was a fierce caricature of Christian Kratt, done as a Greek (Argand supposed) statue, naked, muscular, and in that setting, three times life-size. The figure was crouching forward, knees bent, bottom in the air, and the face, spectacled like Kratt, had a look of deep meditation. Between the feet was a pile of steaming fecal matter. The sketch was titled: KRATT'S LAST KRAPP.

Argand did not recognise the cultural puns. His disgust would not have been lessened if he had.

Two hours later, after an exhausting session with Commissioner Stent whom he did not like and who did not like him, Argand returned at last to his home. He poured himself a thimbleful of plum-flavoured dry gin and sat down in his father's chair; then, still feeling shaken, stood up and went to the window. He told himself that he did not feel unduly upset that Schneider was dead, nor troubled by the thought that if he had got round earlier the painter might still have been alive. At such times the Commissioner thought of himself as a realist – one had to face up to these things if one was a policeman, otherwise one would not be able to carry on.

The light behind him, a reading-lamp, was dull; the street lights below were bright. A girl came out of the café on the other side of the road, looked up at his window, and crossed. She was wearing an anorak and jeans and she had long blond hair. Argand moved into the middle of the room and waited for the bell to ring. He knew she was coming to see him. Who else in that apartment block could Victoria Herm have business with?

11

Parti Pris

'I rang your bell about an hour ago. There was no answer. Then the lady on the floor above leaned over the banister and said that you had gone out at seven o'clock, so I went to the café over the road and waited for you.'

'Mrs Esslin seems to keep an eye on me.'

'The lady upstairs? Yes, I think she does. But I suppose she has nothing much better to do than watch her neighbours. I don't suppose she has any meaningful occupation, does she?'

'She has money of her own.'

'You mean society has given her the right to live off the surplus value of someone else's labour.'

Jan Argand began to feel that his first impression of Victoria Herm had been hastily favourable. She was tall, well-built, healthy, with a pleasant freckled face. Although her clothes were functional, they were neat and clean. Her manner of announcing herself had been firm and confident, but not pushy. She seemed a very open sort of person. But easy dismissal of an elderly widow's right to the little capital her grocer husband had left her, Argand found callous, as well as politically repugnant. He sat down in his chair and indicated that she too should sit. She chose an upright chair, taking it from under the table in the window.

'What can I do for you, Miss Herm?'

'I would rather you called me Victoria. Or just Herm.'

'I'm sorry, but I don't think I'm capable of doing either.'

'Very well. Never mind.' This was said with sympathy as if Argand's refusal to be other than conventionally formal and polite was a failing for which he could not be held responsible: he felt patronised and did not like the feeling. She went on: 'It's quite simple. I've come to tell you that my father is not with Red Spectre.'

Argand thought for a moment.

'You seem a sensible sort of person. Not given to hysterical imagination, at least. So you must have good grounds for saying that. Which implies you either know where he is, or you know Red Spectre well enough to be sure they have not kidnapped your father. Now, if the latter is the case . . .'

'I should be careful of what I say because Red Spectre is a proscribed organisation, and association with it is a criminal offence. I know. I'm taking a risk. But I assume you will hear me out before arresting me.'

'Yes. But the decision is yours, and if I decide that action against you is necessitated by what you say I shall not hesitate to take it.'

'I should not have expected otherwise from a policeman. Well, having got all that out of the way, shall I begin?' Argand nodded. She leant forward a little from the hard-backed chair, and began to talk more quickly. 'First, I *don't* know where my father is. Second, believe it or not, I don't much mind, but actually I am not a member of the Red Spectre cadre. I don't think they would have me even if I wanted to be. It's not that I dismiss violence as a possible or even necessary weapon in our struggle, I don't; it's just that at the moment I don't think I could act violently. I would be unreliable in a situation where violence was called for. Still, they trust me enough to ask me to come directly to you, knowing that you would listen to me because I am who I am. And they have asked me to tell you that they do not have my father, and they did not send the letter which says they do.'

Argand put his fingertips together. Many thoughts were in his mind. He wasn't sure where to begin.

'Well that's that,' Victoria said. 'I mean, is that it? I suppose you believe what I have just said.'

'For the moment I am not even sure in myself that *you* sincerely believe what you have just said.'

'Do you have to be so suspicious? Are you so suspicious of everyone and everything all the time?'

'Come on Miss Herm. You can't have thought that I would simply take your word and leave it at that. Any more than I accept *any* of the letters we have so far received on the subject of your father's disappearance. You want to convince me, so why not start by telling me exactly how you received this instruction from Red Spectre, who it came from, what made you so sure that it really is Red Spectre that is in touch with you, and so on. Wait a moment. I will tell you why you will not tell me these things. You cannot answer those questions in a way that would satisfy me without compromising Red Spectre. So you won't answer them. Now, look at the case from another point of view. An organisation calling itself the Green Force has also claimed to hold your father. You must convince me that you are not acting for them. Miss Herm. Not too long ago you passed your baccalaureate. Unless our schools have fallen into even worse decay that I thought they had, you will remember that it is impossible in logic or by scientific method to prove a negative, except by an excluding positive. There isn't one here. You can belong to as many organisations as you like.'

'Do you go on like this with everyone you question?'

A vision of Schneider spread-eagled and broken on black plastic rubbish bags.

'No. No, I don't. I'm sorry Miss Herm, but I've had a long and disturbing day. What I am trying to say is this. If you want me to take you seriously you must find a way of being convincing. I have tried to indicate that this will not be easy.'

There was silence. Then: 'Commissioner' and 'Miss Herm' sounded together.

'Sorry, you go on.'

'I was going to ask why Red Spectre is so concerned to show that they do not have Mr Herm?'

'Right. I'll try to explain that. You know who Roman Punt is?'

'I believe he is the criminal, the murderer who runs Red Spectre.'

Victoria Herm flushed. 'We are not going to get anywhere if you say things like that.'

'Miss Herm. The man is an admitted criminal and murderer, and he claims to run Red Spectre.'

'Listen. Roman admits to taking money from banks. He has killed enemies of the people. It is you who call those acts crimes and murders.'

'This is ridiculous. It is I and every other decent respectable Brabanter who is afraid to walk the streets at night or even in daylight because of this criminal and others like him, it is the law of the land, it is plain simple common sense that calls this man a criminal and a murderer. Now go on. What were you going to say about him?'

'I don't think I can go on. There isn't going to be any point.'

'Miss Herm, it can't have come as any sort of surprise to you that I call this man a murderer, an enemy of society, who, if I had my way, would be guillotined as soon as he is caught. Having said that, I remain interested in

108

what you have to say about him.'

'Well I will try. There is too much at stake to allow myself to be riled by you. But please try to keep your abuse to yourself.'

Argand looked up at her. Until then he had thought Victoria took entirely after her father – in appearance and build, and from what he knew of Wolfgang Herm, in the sort of openness she characteristically displayed. In the last remark it was Lena Herm who had spoken.

'Roman Punt's brother, Hans, is serving a life sentence. The note purporting to be from Red Spectre asks for his release as one of the conditions for the release of my father. Not only of Hans but of the Jansens as well. Since Roman did not send the note, he naturally wonders who did, and why. One possibility he fears is a plot to make his brother and comrades "disappear" – in fact allow them to be quietly done away with. Shot resisting re-arrest after a fake release, something of that sort.'

'Miss Herm, these suggestions are absolutely absurd, the products of a diseased mind . . .'

'You are being abusive again.'

'I am not. I simply will not take seriously allegations of this sort. People of the utmost respectability would have to be involved for such a plot to come to fruition, people of very senior standing in the Province. It is unthinkable that it should be so, and as I said, anyone who can think like that has a twisted mind.'

Victoria breathed in very deeply, closed her eyes, and began again. 'All right. You already think Roman Punt has what you call a twisted mind . . .'

'True.'

'So it will come as no surprise to you that he believes the rulers of the Province, having foolishly done away with the guillotine, are capable of this sort of plot. So. Please accept that I am here in the first place because Roman Punt sees serious danger to the lives of his comrades if the public continues to believe that they are to be exchanged for my father. There are other factors — of less importance personally to Roman, but perhaps of more importance to the movement as a whole.'

Talk of "movements" never improved Argand's temper, but he restrained himself.

'Go on.'

'It is possible that the first note, the one from Green Force is genuine. Now, the League for Life is not Marxist-Leninist. It does not see itself as having a revolutionary role. One of its chief spokesmen is even a priest.'

'A Pastor. Reverend Kant would reject the title "Priest".'

'Yet in so far as their aims are directed at bringing down EUREAC, or at least at humanising EUREAC's operations, they are revolutionary, whether they like it or not. As was said in the letter *Slik Stien* printed, Red Spectre supports and approves their actions against EUREAC. And clearly whoever is behind the spurious letters does not, and whatever else happens the aims of both the League for Life and Red Spectre will be hindered if you and everyone else go on believing that Red Spectre has my father. Whether or not that spurious letters is part of a plot to take the lives of Hans and the Jansens, to execute them in a less clumsy way than the Germans used on Baader, Ensslin, and Raspe remains to be seen. But one thing is certain, and that is that that letter is the work of a reactionary group, is part of a reactionary conspiracy.'

Argand suppressed his own reaction to this sort of talk.

'There is one other aspect. Kidnapping Wolfgang Herm, my father, threatening his life, and possibly killing him is seen by the committee as being counterproductive. The workers at EUREAC know of him as a well-intentioned person who has often acted in their interests, as he sees them, to the best of his ability. Oh I know they haven't much time to waste on him, but more than on any of the other bosses there. Now Red Spectre is a guerrilla. And a guerrilla cannot operate in a countryside or conurbation that is hostile to it. It depends on the support, however passive, of a large part of the proletariat in the area it operates in, and action against Herm might well alienate a fairly substantial number of those who give it this passive support. In petty bourgeois areas too my father has a certain sort of popularity as a glamorous and attractive figure, and attitudes to us, to Red Spectre would harden in that area as well if people thought he had suffered through us. I'm sorry. I continue to use the first person. I repeat, I am not a member of the Red Spectre cadres, but it would be absurd to pretend that I am anything less than extremely sympathetic towards them. There. Does all that do anything at all towards convincing you that Red Spectre does not hold my father?'

Argand was surprised at the intensity of this last appeal.

'Miss Herm, are you fond of your father?'

The hesitation was fractional. Argand guessed that it arose out of her doubt as to where the question was leading.

'Yes. Yes, I am.'

'So you have a personal reason for trying to secure his release. Or reappearance.'

'Yes. But my feelings are qualified. I would reject him utterly if I thought he were a willing part of the sort of plot Roman Punt thinks may be behind all this. I think my father is a naïve man. Clever as a scientist, clever later as an organiser, even as a financier. But really rather simple-minded. He believes the System delivers the Goods. He used to say there are always enough men around with what he calls "good will" to make things work for the good of the greater number rather than not. He believes in technology, in progress. He was so happy when the Americans landed on the moon. I remember him saying, "You have to hand it to them for doing a thing like that – you have to respect them in spite of Vietnam." I was only thirteen then, but I remember it. Well. He was a good father, generous, fun. And well-intentioned. As a daughter I can forgive him a lot. As a realist, less. But if he has gone completely over to the pigs he works with, gone over to them body and soul yet seeing them for what they are, then perhaps I could kill him.'

'I assure you there is no plot of that sort in this business. It's simply not possible.' Argand stared for a moment at the electric fire which glowed rhythmically behind a simulated log. His son's wife had bought it for him when the zone was declared smokeless. He hated it. 'And even if it were possible I don't think your father would be part of it. There are some things I have found out about your father and some things I was aware of before I began this investigation, that I view with . . . distaste. But from what I've learned of him, he doesn't strike me as being capable of lending himself to a deception of the sort Punt fears. No more than I am.'

The silence grew between them as the fact sunk in that Argand had, by implication, accepted the girl's sincerity. Not only that: in saying that he thought Herm was incapable of subtle and evil deception he had offered her a sort of gift – of reassurance if nothing else.

It was natural that he should now withdraw.

'I should say this though,' he was brisker again, 'it would be dishonest of me to let you believe that you have convinced me that Red Spectre do not have your father. You have suggested the possibility of a complex and subtle plot involving EUREAC and the authorities. It seems to me far more likely that if such a plot exists, it stems from Red Spectre. You say you are not part of their inmost counsels. How can you be certain that you are not a dupe yourself, and achieving something quite different from what you imagine by coming here and saying what you have said?'

Victoria shrugged. 'I'm certain of it. But I know the people I have come from. I know the standards they share and the ideals they fight for. To you they are criminals. I know them to be heroes.'

Whatever sympathy Argand had felt for the girl quickly leaked away. He stood up, ready to bring the interview to an end. She stood up too, but hovered, would not move to the door.

'Just now,' she said, 'you suggested my father might "reappear". As if this were an alternative to being released. What did you mean?'

'I don't think I should go into that. I spoke carelessly.'

She gave a little puff of impatience. 'Well, the implication is there. That he was not kidnapped after all, but has simply disappeared, presumably voluntarily, and that *all* these ransom notes are spurious. And yet you say he is not a willing part of a plot against Hans Punt and the Jansens.'

'Certainly I stand by that.'

'Well, if that is the case and you want to find him, the person you ought to see is Emil Schneider. The artist. He has been closer to my father in recent years than anyone else.'

12

Mortal Part

Disturbed by Victoria's visit, disturbed particularly by
her last remark, Argand found that any wish he had had
to go early to bed had gone. He paced about his flat for
half an hour or so, called to mind again and again the
broken body of the painter surrounded by refuse, and
tried again and again to fit the signs he had observed in
the studio into a pattern that would reveal what had
happened. He recalled that if he had pursued his enquiry
as diligently as he should have done, the artist might well
still be alive, though possibly in police custody. At this
thought he pulled a face – aware that his recent visitor
would not agree with him that police custody was at least
safe. And so his mind went back to Victoria. He would
have to report her visit to Commissioner Gapp. For reasons he preferred not to consider too closely he felt uncomfortable at the thought of doing this. Then back
again his mind went to Schneider, and bit by bit the
desire to know more, to have in his hands all the pieces of
that particular area of the puzzle, became intolerable.

He rang up the duty officer at Wilhelmstras. The
doctor doing the autopsy was Jean-Paul Dael, a friend of
many years standing. A further call discovered that the
autopsy had been under way for only half an hour –
there had been delays – and Dr Dael would be delighted

to have him there. It was nearly midnight when Argand descended the concrete stairs in the basement of the Wilhelmstras building, and was admitted to the mortuary.

Argand was not upset by the place. He never had been. In the earliest days of his training when his fellow cadets had been sick and even fainted as the basic principles of autopsy were demonstrated on derelicts, victims of street accidents, and in one case on an infant who had swallowed undiluted bleach, he had felt nothing much except a sort of cool peace. This rose, he thought, from the clinical detachment of what went on, from the calmness with which the surgeon unfolded and revealed the passions, failures and stupidities that had deposited the cadaver in question on his marble slab; and all this without pain, without pain of any sort to anyone, least of all the subject, who, probably only hours before, had suffered wretchedly.

Since then Argand had not haunted the place or even felt tempted to, but on the rare occasions when a visit had been necessary he had not hesitated to go down there again.

Jean-Paul Dael was a brisk, round, red-faced, jolly little man, with a pointed white beard and spectacles. He stripped off his gloves as Argand entered the chilly white, brightly-lit room, came to meet him, put an arm round him.

'Well, Jan. How are you? Is this one of yours then? I thought you did nothing but public order now. Well there has been disorder here right enough, but on the whole private mayhem, I should say, private mayhem.' He gestured to the figure stretched out on the narrow, waist-high bench. What was mortal of Schneider was brilliantly lit and reduced to a neat demonstration of anatomy. The neck had been opened to reveal the wrenched and cracked vertebrae, the abdominal cavity gaped, and the stomach, itself opened, lay with the upper intestine still attached, on the edge of the bench.

'I'm not directly in on the investigation,' Argand replied. 'That of course is being done by Commissioner Stent's people. But this man is connected with something I've been asked to look into, and it would be useful to me to know as soon as possible what happened.'

'Oh very hush-hush, I see. Well I won't probe any more, not into you anyway. Doesn't do to get notions about a customer before I've made up my own mind. In fact this is an interesting one. Very interesting. If it comes to court, and I should think it will, from what I've been able to make out, there's going to be a lot of very interesting argy-bargy about this one.'

'Why? Why do you say that?'

'Well. In the first place it's about as tight a thing as you can imagine between deciding whether his neck got broken before he was dead or after, and, even if it was before, it will be hellishly difficult to say that the neck breaking killed him, or whether it accelerated what was already well begun, or whether he might not, without his other very considerable troubles, have survived the neck injury.'

'What was wrong with him then?'

'When he sustained that neck injury he was already far gone. Unconscious probably, on the verge of a very deep coma out of which I doubt he would have ever emerged.'

Argand looked down at the body. In the areas unmarked by the anatomist's knife, the skin was very white, very clean. It had been a well-proportioned body, well-kept.

'I know you want to tell me all about the causes of this coma, and I want to know. But first, tell me, was he so far gone that it would have been impossible for him to have walked ten metres immediately before he sustained the neck injury?'

'Probably unconscious, I said. Under cross-examination, on oath, that is all I will say. What I can say for sure though is that if he wasn't already unconscious he would have been within minutes, seconds even. Out cold, and within half an hour quite probably as cold as he is now.'

'All right. Now tell me why.'

'Yes. But first Jan, statutory warning. What I am going to say is based on preliminary tests, made on small samples, with techniques of analysis not as reliable as the laboratory will use tomorrow as soon as it is open. My final report will be based on those.'

'I've never known your first report to differ much from your later full one.'

'It's five years since you were involved in anything like this, Jan. Science does not stand still. There have been some very interesting new techniques developed in that time in this line of business, I can tell you, but there, I've made my point. Right then. In my opinion our friend here had drunk twenty-five ccs of alcoholic liquid, thirty-five per cent alcohol by volume, and good quality Scotch whisky by the odour. He had been injected with, or injected himself with, a dose of sodium amytal sufficiently large to bring on a coma on its own without the alcohol, and on top of that he was full of d-lysergic acid diethylamide tartrate – how much I can't say for sure, but it would have done nothing good for him with the rest. And all this within two hours of death at most. So you see why it's going to be devilish tricky forming even an opinion as to the relative effects of all that lot with the fall – I suppose it was a fall, with the abrasion on the back of the head it looks like it – and so making an exact statement about the cause of death. Of course if it was all self-administered, including the fall, then I suppose it doesn't much matter.'

'Could it have been anything other than self-administered? The drugs I mean?'

'Oh yes. Even the alcohol could have been got into him without his consent, though I doubt it was. There would have been bruising round the mouth and throat if that lot had been got down him without his wanting it. But the LSD could have been in his whisky without him knowing it, and, as I say, the odd thing about the sodium amytal is that it went in through a needle. Usually, as you know, it is taken orally.'

'What effect would that have had? I mean what difference would the needle have made?'

'Much quicker effect. And a much quicker primary effect, before drowsiness and eventually coma set in.'

'And what is this primary effect?'

'With this barbiturate, in this sort of dose, first a very pleasant relaxed euphoria, garrulity, desire to giggle and so on. For a time he would behave and feel as if he had drunk twice the scotch he did drink. And I might add, that with the LSD too there would be a space of about five or ten minutes when he would be like a baby, he would do anything you wanted, as far as his limbs would allow. You could probably tell him to jump out of a window, and he would.'

They both looked down at the cadaver. Dael then spoke more slowly, in a more even-toned voice than before.

'I recall a paper I read some years ago. I can check it when I get home. It said that experiments with barbiturates and LSD used together had shown the combination to be remarkably effective as a truth drug. Does that interest you, Jan?'

'Yes. That interests me. And the sodium amytal could have been pumped into him, or it could have been self-administered?'

'That's it. Nothing I'm going to find here is going to

tell me which way it was.'

Argand nodded, slowly, then his eyebrows went up and he scratched his large nose and sighed.

'Well. What else? What else have you come across?'

Dael rattled away more briskly. 'Subject had vomited perhaps as little as twenty minutes before death . . .'

'Just a moment. How well controlled would that have been? I mean if he was going comatose he would have made a mess, wouldn't he?'

'Not necessarily, but I would have thought so. The vomiting was too late to do him much good. It would have been very different if the sodium amytal had been taken orally, then it might, I only say might, have saved him. But the onset of drowsiness and collapse would be quick in these circumstances and I would say that if he was still at a stage to be able to vomit he would still have enough control to direct it.'

'What about washing-up after? Cleaning out a lavatory bowl, wiping away traces, spills?'

'That would be unlikely. Quite unlikely I'd say.'

'Go on.'

'No signs of recent sexual activity. None really of sexual deviance either. None I could swear to anyway.'

'You have something in mind.'

'Well. The anus is slightly and permanently enlarged. But that could come from chronic constipation. But he didn't look the sort to suffer from that — I should say he had been something of a food-freak and they tend in the other direction. Mind, that can cause an enlarged anus too. And finally, no sign of habitual drug abuse.'

'Really? Are you sure?'

'Well, nothing serious, I am sure. He wasn't taking heroin or cocaine or any of their derivatives as far as I can tell. No doubt he had the occasional pick-me-up or put-me-down, but don't we all? I know I do. Anyway. I should say this . . . this experiment with barbiturates and acid was the first and last. Yes, well. One thing you won't find my final report contradicting is that it was the last. Oh very definitely the last.'

Argand was back in his office at nine o'clock on Saturday morning and feeling oddly alert, even light-headed through missing nearly four hours in bed and sleeping badly once he had got there. No doubt I'll suffer for it later, he thought.

First he went through his usual Saturday routine, checking that no new indications of civil disturbance had appeared on the horizon over the weekend, checking that preparations for those already expected were complete. This week-end looked a quiet one. Sporting Union Brabt had an away match; there would not be more than five thousand at the other local team's ground. They were second division and part amateur. Picketing would continue at the docks against a shipment of arms to Chile, but it had been peaceful so far and anyway the rifles had been got out under the dockers' noses three days earlier in containers marked motor car parts for England.

Then, Argand rang up Commissioner Stent. To his surprise the crime chief was ready to be very co-operative. Yes, forensic had finished in Schneider's flat. Yes, Argand could go over it now if he wanted to. No, there was no report from forensic yet, but he didn't think they had much to report, though that would depend on how it fitted in with the autopsy. There had been visitors to the flat sometime during the twelve hours before Schneider died. Probably two, one of whom smoked. There were no readable fingerprints but this was not surprising if their visit had been a short one. And someone, presumably Schneider, had cleared up after them, washed the glasses and ashtray and so on. There was really no reason to connect these visitors with what had happened, though of course efforts were being made to identify them. Schneider's prints were on the ampoules and the syringe, though blurred. No, he hadn't heard anything about vomiting in the bathroom, but then he hadn't had a full report at all. Yes, he'd let Argand have the serial numbers of all bank-notes found in the flat. Meanwhile there was still a policeman on the door and he'd let Argand in.

13

Immortal Part

The artist's flat was very still, very silent. It was almost as if all the objects he had brought there, placed in positions that were idiosyncratically right for him, and then used, eaten with, drunk from, played with, worked with, had died with him. For a time they had been informed with a part of Emil Schneider — now they stood around waiting for someone else to take them up, give them a new life, or throw them away. Argand spent more than an hour amongst them, and perhaps learned something from them — and not all to do with the case.

First he put the chairs back round the bed as they had been when he first saw them, and then he paced deliberately and carefully through the flat from bedroom to studio window and fire-escape and then back again, several times. Ineluctably a scenario developed in his mind. To begin with, different phases came in the wrong order, had to be juggled with, pushed about until they made sense, but in the end he felt there was only one sequence that would fit, only one sequence that took in all the facts.

Two visitors had come who wanted Schneider to tell them something. Don't worry about what, yet. By guile, perhaps by intimidation, perhaps by force they filled him with whisky, sodium amytal, and LSD. He became garrulous, then began to lose the power of his limbs. They put him on the bed, sat beside him, questioned him, listened to him. He was going out too quickly. They got him up, made him vomit, but they had injected the barbiturate and vomiting did no good. The artist became unconscious, looked bad, might die. At the least he now clearly needed medical attention, a hospital even. But then if he survived he would be able to say who had questioned him and why. Perhaps the plan all along was to kill him, but question him first. Perhaps the overdose was not a clumsy mistake but intentional – make him talk briefly, but not for long, for what they wanted to know would not take long to tell. But after all he hadn't said enough, so they made him vomit.

Then what? He was unconscious, comatose. Quickly they went through the flat, carefully wiping out most traces of their visit, but not all. Why not? They were in a hurry, perhaps? Or perhaps sophisticated enough to know that they could never wipe out all traces – fresh tobacco ash would linger, an unnoticed area fingerprinted and left unwiped, so they concentrated on removing signs that connected them with the whisky, the LSD, the sodium amytal, the vomiting. They forgot the chairs by the bed but at least one oversight was to be expected. After all a man was dying in front of them. Then. When all was ready they moved quickly, gambling, but gambling sensibly. Drag him to the fire-escape. Perhaps he was still just conscious, could take a little weight on his own feet, "would do anything you wanted". 'Come on, old chap, what you need is fresh air.' Open the tall window and the shutters. Step over the low sill. 'There we are, lean against the rail, breath deeply and you'll feel better,' and they took his ankles and tipped him over.

Then straight down the passage, out on to the landing, and into the lift – probably they had called it first and held it there by jamming the door – and down to the ground floor and out into the street while anyone who had heard Schneider fall was out on the fire-escapes, going down the fire-escapes as they naturally would. Even so the man downstairs had moved quickly, but nothing like quickly enough to see the two visitors leaving, just quickly enough to find the lift still on the ground floor.

Argand sat in Emil Schneider's armchair by the bookcase and music centre. What was it they had wanted the artist to tell them? Well, there was no proof but it seemed pretty certain they were saying over and over again – where is Wolfgang Herm? And who knew or suspected that Schneider had the answer to that question? Well, me for a start, thought Argand. I knew about the banknote, I knew Wolfgang Herm came here after he left his house. And by extension, the rest of the police department, the authorities generally, EUREAC. Obviously that is not a line worth pursuing. Who else? The eco-freaks, assuming they did not have Herm, and Red Spectre assuming they didn't. Which, Argand reflected, is awkward – for it seems most likely, in spite of Victoria's intervention, that Red Spectre do have him, yet the eco-freaks on the whole seem less likely candidates as murderers. Though certainly there are acid-droppers and barbiturate-takers on the fringes of the League for Life.

And beyond that one cannot for the moment go. But Argand felt pleased with his hypothesising, felt he was on the right lines, at least about the mechanics of what had happened, and he wondered how far Commissioner Stent had gone down the same road.

There did remain one question. Had Schneider indeed known where Herm was? If so, was there still anything in the flat that would give a clue? Well, no doubt Stent and his men had been thorough, but still there was no harm in repeating the process. They might have missed something. They might not even tell him about everything they had found. This consideration, prompted by Gapp's earlier suppression of the second Red Spectre letter, brought back the feeling of bewildered frustration, the sense that all was not right, that he was not trusted by his superiors and colleagues, but Jan pushed it aside and his eyes moved slowly over the book shelves trying to decide where to start. His glance fell on the record deck. There was a record on it. Mendelssohn's *Scottish Symphony*. Side Two. Two concert overtures as fill-ins: *The Hebrides Overture*, and *Calm Sea and Prosperous Voyage*. Jan Argand was a tidy man, punctiliously tidy. Almost without thinking he went through the record rack and found the empty sleeve. It looked new and on it, written in fine felt-tip was a message. 'This might remind you of me, play it if you feel lonely! Wolf.'

And that was the only indication Argand found in the whole flat that there had been any sort of relationship at all between the two men. There were no letters, no photographs, no sketches, nothing that could tie them together. He had been pre-empted. Someone had been there before him and removed it all including, he discovered as he moved into the studio area, the obscene canvas and the sketch-book with the obscene caricature of Christian Kratt. No doubt Commissioner Stent and his men had it all. Well they would have to let him see what they had taken, and it was to be hoped that they wouldn't make a fuss about it when asked.

But he did find one thing which pleased him, even moved him. This was a large portfolio of gouache bird and animal paintings, each labelled, and the whole en-titled: *The Wild Life of Spartshaven Marsh*. The work was lively, well-finished, and ready for printing. The colours and vigour, the naturalness of the paintings seemed to enliven the dead rooms as Jan went through them. There were the little terns, of course, but Jan was surprised to find how much more: the sandpiper, the redshank and the ruff (portrayed by two males in their ceremonial dance); then smaller sandpipers, tubby and a little comic on their short legs – the dunlin with a sooty tummy and the sanderling. There were plovers and scarlet-beaked oyster-catchers. There were geese and ducks – brent and barnacle, greylag and pink-footed scaup, pochard, and the shelduck Pastor Kant had pointed out to him. And finally herons, like bishops on one leg, or flapping heavily across a grey sky.

The folio closed with a smaller section on mammals: water-rats, voles, field-mice peeped through the rushes and bog rosemary at the edges or scampered across the mudflats. The very last picture of all was of a family of seals – a baby on the mud, white and tubby, its mother bringing it a sprat, while whiskered father wallowed in the tide-race, just as Argand had seen them, when was it? Tuesday? It seemed a long time ago.

There was a letter at the beginning of the folio, paper-clipped to the cover. It was from a firm of publishers, Zart and Millan, and it said that they were delighted with Emil's first sketches, hoped that the rest were coming on as well, reminded him that 31st March was the dead-line. Today, thought Argand is the 29th. It looks as if he would have made it. It would, he thought, be a kindness to tell Zart and Millan that they could go ahead with their book; he would ring them first thing on Monday and tell them where it could be found.

Back in his office he found another letter, or rather note, from Secretary Prinz. He read: 'Dear Jan, just a quick word to say that Kratt and Commissioner Gapp are now definitely in touch with Red Spectre and negotiations for an exchange – Herm for the younger Punt – are under way. It's a tricky business, you can imagine just how tricky, but that's our worry not yours. In fact that's the point of this note – we really are sure now that it's Red

Spectre who have our friend, so you can ease off your pursuit of the eco-people and have a pleasant and relaxed week-end. I envy you — think of us sweating away trying to get these obscene psychos to see some sort of sense. Yours ever, Wotan Prinz.'

There was no hurry then about reporting to Gapp that he had seen Victoria, no hurry at all. Clearly she was deluded, a dupe after all. She would be an irrelevance to his colleague at this point, an irritation, a distraction. Monday would do. Of course this news finally dished his favoured hypothesis that Red Spectre had killed Schneider in an effort to find where Herm was. Well, never mind. Schneider's murder, if murder it was, was not his business either and no doubt his part in Herm's disappearance, the bank-note he had paid his rent with, and everything else as well which still puzzled Argand would all be cleared up when Herm was finally released.

The main thing was that the rest of the weekend promised to be quiet after all — and that was a relief.

14

Family Practices

Every third Sunday Jan Argand visited his wife in the Hearts Haven Clinic, and that Sunday was a third Sunday. Each floor, consisting of fifteen rooms, had its own sister. On the way in Argand stopped to ask how his wife had been, just as he always did.

'Much as usual,' the sister replied. 'About a week ago we had a little trouble with her. The voices first, then she was sure Doctor Liszt was plotting to kill her, and the pills were poison, so a little sedation was necessary for a few days. She's coming out of it now, though you will find her a little sleepy perhaps. Try not to upset her. I'm sure you won't. And how are you, Excellency? You look as well and as sane as ever.'

She always said that.

His wife had a small but pleasant room to herself, though normally she took her meals with the other patients and spent most of her day with them. Now though, she was alone, waiting for Jan, sitting in a basket chair in front of her window, with a sampler, needle and silks on her knee. She was a big woman, in her fifties like her husband, but pale and empty looking, not exactly unkempt, but the greying hair pulled back in a bun was straggly, her dress hung baggily, and the cardigan that she had put round her shoulders had slipped on one side and gave her an incongruously raffish air. As Argand stooped to kiss her, he adjusted it. Impatiently she shrugged and it fell back again. He settled himself in the spare chair beside her, looked at his watch, and mentally adjusted himself to the sixty minutes of boredom that lay ahead of him.

'How have you been then, Maria?' he asked.

'All right,' she squinted down at her embroidery. 'Doctor made another attempt but nurse spotted it in time and gave me an anditote.'

'Antidote.'

She raised her eyebrows at him, as if he had said something silly or naughty, and then went back to her sewing.

'And how have you been, Jan?' she said after a time.

'Quite busy, really. Busier than usual. For a time I was involved in trying to find this Wolfgang Herm who has been kidnapped. I expect you have seen something about it on the news.'

'Oh yes. He's a skiier or something, I believe. Well no doubt you all have to pull together at times like that.'

'Yes. Anyway, while I was working on that I met a Pastor of the Church of Inner Salvation. I had quite believed they had all disappeared by now, but he was still going strong.'

'The Church of Inner Salvation. You belonged to that, didn't you? Or your father did.'

'Yes. And your family did too.'

'Did they?'

'Yes. We were married in a Church of Inner Salvation.'

She lowered the sampler again and fixed him with eyes of very pale blue, spectacles forward near the tip of her pointed nose.

'Were we?' she asked. And continued to stare at him. 'That was a very long time ago.'

'Yes. I suppose it was.'

'I don't suppose this pastor had much to say to you. Nothing complimentary anyway. I mean it must be fifteen years since you went to church.'

'Well. That was because our church was knocked down for the supermarket. You know that, Maria. That's why we stopped going.'

'Didn't stop me from going to the sumer-sumer-s-supermarket though, did it? Ah well, I suppose it's all for the best. Mrs Esslin has been looking after you properly, has she?'

'Oh yes. She left me a delicious casserole the other day. Friday it was.' Argand felt a tiny *frisson*; there was something wrong connected with the casserole. He couldn't think what.

'She's after you, you know. She plans to have you when I'm gone. But you can tell her from me that I don't plan to go before you. What's more I plan to get out of here as soon as you're gone, but you know that, don't you? If I'm clever enough to outwit Doctor Liszt, you don't think I'm not a match for you and Mrs Esslin, do you?' Her eyes narrowed. 'Got you in her bed yet, has she? No? Well I don't mind if she has. Precious little of any use she'll find there, I can tell her.'

Occasional outbursts of obscenity, usually directed at his sexual ability, had become a recent feature of his visits to his wife. They angered Argand, made him feel very bad indeed, but he somehow managed to conceal this.

He reached towards the sampler.

'What are you doing now, Maria?' he asked, in as even a tone as he could manage.

'"Like a crab I walk sideways",' he read, in ornamented gothic letters. Underneath she was now filling in a crab in scarlet and blue silks.

'Very nice,' he said.

130

'I knew you wouldn't understand,' she said complacently.

In a way he would have been hard put to explain, he felt he understood only too well.

Shortly there was a knock at the door and the sister came in.

'Licentiate Piet Argand is downstairs,' she announced.

'Send him up, send him up, the more the merrier,' crowed Mrs Argand.

'He asked if he could have a word with your husband first. Just a short one. You wouldn't mind that, would you Mrs Argand?'

'Oh no. Fine visiting Sunday it is when all my visitors chat with eachother and leave me alone. No. I don't mind. They only talk to eachother if they are here, so it makes no difference to me. Don't lend him any money though, Jan; if that's what he wants, don't do it. You'll never get it back.'

As he went downstairs, following the sister's starched uniform and her black-stockinged legs with rounded calves, Jan thought: that'll be the day. That'll be the day. His son had never taken a penny from him, had learned from him only too well that you are expected to pay your own way in this world.

They shook hands perfunctorily in the hall. His son was tall, just thirty, with fair hair that was already thinning, and he always wore a blue suit and carried a mackintosh over his arm. He was Lecturer in Social Engineering at the new Advanced Technology College on the outskirts of Brabt.

'Let's walk in the garden,' he suggested.

'All right.'

They paced down gravel paths, through laurel shrubberies. Here and there, in sheltered sunny spots, wooden seats had been left inscribed with names of past patients, but they ignored them, paced on round, Argand with his hands clasped behind him, Piet Argand with his mac over his arm.

'How's Mother?'

'Much the same.'

'She's always going to be the same if we leave her here.'

'She's all right.'

'She's not all right. She wouldn't be here if she were all right.'

'She's all right here.'

Ten paces.

'Look, Father, she's been here six years now, with virtually no change. It can't go on like this for ever.'

Argand said nothing. As far as he was concerned, and he believed his wife would agree, it certainly could go on for ever.

Eight paces.

'I've been making enquiries. We could get her into Brabt State . . .'

'What Piet? In a public ward?'

'Hear me out, Father. They have just opened a new psychiatric wing. They have all the new therapy there. The wards are bright, open, pleasant places, and the staff are properly trained. The great thing is this. They'd cure her. In a few months, perhaps less, she'd be out again and able to take her place as a properly useful member of society.'

Ten paces. Argand felt confused, threatened, thought carefully though and tried to find the right thing to say that was not dishonest either.

'But I don't see how you can be so sure she wouldn't be happier staying as she is.'

'Oh that's nonsense, Father. Nonsense. A day or two of sanity, though very drowsy sanity, then the delusions come back, worse and worse, till they knock her out by increasing the dose of chlorpromazine, and she's back to square one again. That's no sort of life. And even with biperiden as a back-up there's an increasing danger of parkinsonism, with each new bout. You must have noticed she's getting speech difficulties.'

'Very slight. Hardly anything.'

'It's a beginning.'

Ten more paces. Then together: 'I don't see why . . .' and 'What do you mean . . .' Childhood training won and the younger man gave way.

'What do you mean, 'socially useful''?' asked Argand. 'Do you mean she should get a job or something? At her age?'

'I mean socially adjusted. To be adjusted to society is to be useful. It doesn't necessarily imply work. Society functions properly to the extent that each individual is adjusted to it. That's how you quantify the success of a society. It's one way, anyhow.'

'What a wretched society we live in then,' said Argand, thinking of the vandals, the dope-pushers, the football hooligans, the demonstrations he had to deal with – not to mention deviants, Red Spectre, Schneider's painting of men embracing, and Schneider with his neck broken on a split bag of garbage.

'Not at all. I can imagine what you are thinking of.' And his son could, pretty accurately. Perhaps he had become a social engineer in response to his father's jeremiads about society, borne all through his childhood and youth. He went on: 'We've reached a position where the ways in which maladjustment expresses itself are narrowed down to a very few types of outlet, partly because more and more forms of behaviour which used to be socially unacceptable are now acceptable, but more probably because socially unacceptable people are fewer in proportion to the rest of society, so feel more threatened, and take more violent ways of revealing their maladjustment. Of course mass society and its effects is another factor, the anonymity of the crowd no doubt provokes a more violent reaction from the maladjusted. In a society where people tend to mind their own business you have to make a big noise to draw attention. Of course it's difficult to be certain in areas like this. A lot of work has yet to be done, and better directed work than what has gone before. But by and large I would say the best indicators show that western European society, towards the end of the twentieth century, compares favourably with almost all its contemporaries and predecessors. Anyway. This has little to do with Mother. I think she should go to Brabt State, where they'll cure her, slot her back into the niche that is hers. How much is it costing you to keep her here?'

'Nearly half my salary.' In fact it was nearer two-thirds.

'Well then.'

'Oh good gracious, I don't grudge the money. They pay me too much anyway. I don't know what I'd do with it if . . .'

His voice died away. The unspoken, the unspeakable – that he considered it money well spent – hovered between them. Moreover his son recalled to himself that *his* wife wanted to see her father-in-law's surplus safely invested in EUREAC.

Six paces.

'The trouble is, her place in society was looking after you,' the older man went on. 'When you left home to go to university that was it. It's no secret that there's very little between her and me to keep her going. Oh, we get on well enough. We're decent people. We wouldn't do otherwise. But she knows I can look after myself, and you've got Liesbet now . . . How is Liesbet? Well? Fine, I'm glad to hear it. Give her my love. But anyway. This is all silly. She's psychotic. She's been diagnosed as such.

134

She has schizophrenia, paranoid schizophrenia. When we were first told that, we went into all this, you know, you as well, and we decided that since I could afford this place ... .'

'Oh yes, Father, I know all that. And at that time I admired you for making what appeared to be great sacrifices for Mother.' (And at that time Liesbet had been very happy to see her mother-in-law locked away, but he didn't say so.) 'But you yourself, you just said, you don't know what you'd do with the money if ...'

'Exactly. So why can't we let things be?'

'Because ... that's what I'm trying to explain to you ... because,' and here Piet Argand spoke carefully, spacing the words out as if it were his father whose understanding was impaired, 'I believe she would get well in Brabt State, with the new psychiatric team they have there, and the new therapies available.'

'You mean E.C.T. or Insulin. Neither of those is new. I discussed both with Doctor Liszt five years ago. They weren't new then either. He won't use them and I won't have them used on your mother.'

'You know why he won't use them? Because he'd lose half his patients if he did. His recovery rate would go up by thirty per cent and he'd be out of business. Father, this place is a racket.'

'You should watch your tongue, my boy. Doctor Liszt is a fine man, and you are slandering him.'

Ten paces.

'Father. Electro-convulsant therapy is very different now from what it was even five years ago. There's no pain now. No pain at all, the patient is anaesthetised ...'

'The pain has nothing to do with it. Both your Mother and I were brought up to think very little of pain. We were taught that pain is an inevitable part of this life, an inevitable consequence of our fallen natures, and something to be borne with courage, and ... well, it's not the pain. I'll tell you what it is. In cases where E.C.T. is successful it seems there is a personality change . . .'

'Father, this is mumbo-jumbo. How can you quantify a personality change? What is personality change? The words are jargon. The only personality change is the change that takes place when a person who was psychotic ceases to be psychotic. Of course they change.'

'Your mother has a personality, a soul if you like. It's part of the destiny of that soul to spend part of this life with this suffering that she has. Just as it might be part of my destiny to have cancer . . .'

'Father, you're talking nonsense, you really are. Do you know what I think? I think you don't want her back. You don't want her out of here.'

'Do you think I haven't thought of that? Do you think that I haven't wrestled with that temptation again and again? I am not a fool. And I still believe that I am right to keep her here, *for her sake*, until she gets better in God's good time, than mess about with her soul. Listen Piet. You started talking in that infernal jargon you use about the socially useful, the socially adjusted. You are saying it is right to use these "cures", these "therapies" to change people into socially adjusted morons. No. Wait. Don't you understand that's what they are doing in Russia?'

'Oh rubbish, Father. There's a world of difference between a schizophrenic and a political dissident.'

'Is there? Is there? Look. In my job I have to know a bit about this sort of thing. I have to know what a paranoid schizophrenic is. The condition is primarily characterised by unrealistic, illogical thinking, delusions of being persecuted, and so on. The Russians don't call their dissidents dissidents. They say they are people who think unrealistically, illogically, and when they take them to hospital, and they get fears about the doctors and the treatment, they say they have delusions that they are being persecuted; now where's the difference? I'll tell you what it is. There isn't one. They adjust their sick people to their society, and we do the same. And use the same methods of treatment. No, Piet. Mother stays here until she gets better in her own way and as herself. And she will. Oh yes she will. And she knows she will. Ask her if you don't believe me. Go on, ask her.'

The younger Argand had never seen his father so disturbed. Now he looked at him he saw that he was very tired as well as angry, and it dawned on him that he had chosen the wrong time to bring up the question of moving his mother. Hadn't one of the papers connected his father with the Herm case? Well, it was silly of him not to have remembered that. After a time he tried to apologise, tried to withdraw a little.

'Yes, yes. Go on,' replied the older. 'Go and see your mother anyway. She's waiting for you. I'll sit here. Tell her I'll be up presently. Don't worry about me.'

Even after his son had gone Jan remained disturbed. He had come near to saying right out what he knew to be the truth of the matter, the truth as far as he was capable of seeing it, and, put the way he would put it, a truth that would be quite unacceptable to his son. Indeed it was only just bearable for him. As Commissioner Argand saw it, there was no such thing as madness, not at any rate considered as an illness, an unavoidable affliction. As far as he was concerned madness was always self-inflicted, self-induced, often with good reason, though more usually out of self-indulgence. He knew why his wife inflicted madness on herself, and he believed she had an inalienable right to do so if she wanted to. The fact was that *he* was the reason why she was mad, madness was her chosen form of escape from him, and knowing her beliefs about the sanctity of marriage and of bearing the cross that has been laid on you, madness was probably the most sensible escape she could take. He almost respected her for it. At any rate he was convinced she would get better as soon as he was gone, and meanwhile she could stay in Hearts Haven for as long as he could carry the expense.

Argand never re-entered his apartment, not even on a Sunday when there was no postal delivery, without opening his mail-box at the street entrance. At six o'clock, when he came in, he followed his usual routine and found a note on a leaf of exercise paper, folded once. He read it in the hallway, holding it in his gloved hands.

'Mrs Esslin tells me you have gone to see your wife, and that you will be back at six o'clock. Please may I see you? I will be in the Wilhelmspark near the big pond until seven o'clock and I will prove to you then that what I said on Friday was true. Please, please come. Victoria Herm.'

15

Breach of the Peace

Since the big pond was less than a twenty minute walk away, Argand went on foot. He didn't bother to go up to his flat, there was no point – he put the note in his pocket and set off through the wide, Sunday-quiet streets towards the park.

It was a cloudy evening with the prospect of an angry sunset and rain. The gusty wind which had tossed the daffodils and the chestnuts in the public gardens and blown along the boulevards all day was dying away, but would no doubt be back after dusk.

Argand's route took him through what had once been the wealthiest part of the town – before the land on the far side of the hill where the Herms lived had been developed – and it had not decayed at all, simply changed its function. The high stone-faced mansions of the bourgeoisie that had created the town and gathered to themselves the wealth of the Province were still there, Byzantine, neo-classic, and second Empire rococo façades facing each other across the double carriageways – which really had been ways for carriages when they had been built – and looked as if they would easily outlast the plane trees and chestnuts that nodded between. Now most of their upper storeys were offices, merchant banks, the surgeries of exclusive doctors, trading agencies with expensive furnishings in the latest style and receptionists who looked like very high-class whores, agencies where the phones never seemed to ring and no business was ever apparently done.

The ground floors were now shops – shops where the same Turkish carpet remained in the same window for a year or more, galleries where a Tiepolo sketch in oils glowed in a massive frame protected by bullet-proof glass and space-age electronics, jewellers who put none of their wares on display, and furriers to be seen only by appointment. Nearer the river there were cafés and Argand thought of a cup of coffee – but it was nearly twenty past six, and in any case he felt a hundred gelds for a coffee was a felony that Commissioner Stent's department might reasonably look into.

He paused on the bridge, looked down the wide river, grey, flat, apparently unmoving, though its surface was just broken enough to convert the reflections of the first lights into traceries; and then from the river towards the high-rises, the cranes, the masts, derricks and funnels of the docks that had made the first of the fortunes behind him, and those over the hill as well. It was an area that had changed. Bombing, blitzes from three different air forces, had flattened it in the war. For a time it seemed it would never recover, but with containerisation and dredging it had. Wharves that had coped with twenty vessels at once now handled one monster at a time, and where a work force of thousands had once toiled in filthy holds, now a few hundred pressed switches, giant chair-like hoists ran smoothly down oiled rails, and the huge rectangular containers were slotted on to the backs of juggernauts. It was, of course, all for the best. Argand turned his face to the hill.

At the top, a kilometre away and a hundred metres above him was a fairy castle – towers with steeple roofs clustered above an unreal confection of flying buttresses, gargoyles, portcullises, and drawbridges, but all on an oddly miniature scale which left you with the impression that you were looking at a toy. Which is what it was. In the Middle Ages it had been a sound enough fortress not easily taken and ugly too; in the eighteenth century it became even uglier, for Marshal Vauban had flattened the turrets, dug huge moats, thrown out redoubts and built up a glacis on principles meticulously rational — but by eighteen-seventy the same rationality had spawned the military machine of Bismarck and the technology of Krupp and Nobel. The then Grand Duke, Wilhelm XXIII, correctly decided that his home had lost all military significance and, following the example of his Bavarian cousin, made the fairy palace of it that still stands. Unlike his cousin's, his wealth was built on solid foundations, and he was not really mad either. The palace was small and did not ruin him. However it proved impossible to live in and the Grand Duke's modern successors prefer Monaco and more recently Sardinia, returning only for royal weddings and funerals, and the Opening of the Moot which takes place regularly, following the Constitution, once every five years. The palace now houses a collection of mid-nineteenth-century paintings that no one visits — though there are signs that the period may become fashionable again.

Below the castle, between it and the river, the Grand Duke's ancestors had kept a hunting-park. Wilhelm XXIII converted this, using money willingly subscribed by the rich merchants who were building the streets Argand had passed through on the other side of the river, into a park where the burghers could drive their carriages as if they were noblemen — and indeed many of them soon were — and their ladies nodded at each other from inside their crinolines, from beneath their parasols, for all the world as if they were in a *real* place like Paris or Antwerp.

There were gardens in the English style, gravelled walks, bandstands and cafés, and a cascade modelled on the one at La Granja which drained into a large pond near the river. Downstream a lunapark was built – a considered move, since the new working classes had to get through it if they wanted to use the Wilhelmspark and gardens, and most of the proletariat were content to stop beneath the big wheel, amongst roundabouts, side-shows and beer gardens, spending their money on less refined if more robust pleasures.

Round this large pond or small lake Argand briskly strolled, glancing past leprous stone maidens at the slopes of rhododendrons and pines towards the castle or along the walks by the river, wondering from which direction Victoria Herm would come. Quite soon he saw her, and nearer too than he had been looking. She rose from a stone bench by the side of the dry cascade where water flowed only on public holidays in summer.

A river god whose trident had bled green streaks down his venous forearm for a hundred years had hidden her from view. She was dressed as before, but now a red scarf kept most of her straw-coloured hair out of the wind.

'It was good of you to come,' she said. 'Are you alone? I think you are. I've been watching you for at least ten minutes and I'm sure no one has been following you.'

'Of course they haven't.' Jan was annoyed. She spoke as if he was on some clandestine affair, or part of some absurd spy thriller. Nevertheless as he looked around he had to agree that she had chosen the spot and the time well. There was almost no one about, they were sur-rounded by open spaces except up the hill above them, and she would have been able to see him right from when he first went on to the bridge on the other side. The near-est people were some workmen at least three hundred metres off. They were digging a hole in an asphalt path. Unusual for a Sunday evening but their equipment was painted yellow and their plastic top-coats were yellow too – the colour used by the Municipal Water Authority. Without really thinking Argand supposed some minor emergency. There were three of them. No four. It was difficult at this distance to be certain how many.

'What do you want to see me about?'

'Haven't you seen or heard the news today?' She was striding away from the cascade at an angle, up the grassy slope where a few daffodils tossed restlessly in the breeze. A Province which exports millions of daffodils to the rest of Europe from late January to April may allow bulbs to come through the grass without fear of them being vandalised.

'I have seen no news. I was working this morning. This afternoon, as you know, I have been with my wife. In a nursing home thirty kilometres away. I have just got back.'

'I'm sorry about your wife. Mrs Esslin said she had been bad for a long time, is not expected to recover. I'm sorry if that's true.'

'Never mind.' He thought: Mrs Esslin really does seem to pay far too much attention to things that are not her business. 'What's this about the news?'

She turned to face him. She was very slightly out of breath from the slope, and colour glowed on her cheeks. If one didn't know, one would judge her to be a really nice girl, Argand thought. A sensible head on her and no flashiness.

'Christian Kratt was interviewed on the lunchtime news. He said negotiations were going ahead with Red Spectre. That the authorities approved, because of the importance of my father as a public figure and because the success of the Spartshaven Project depended on him. That final details were still to be fixed but he hoped my father would be exchanged for Hans Punt on Tuesday, twenty-four hours before the deadline.'

'Yes. Though I have not heard the news I heard some of this in the office before I left yesterday morning.'

'But it's not true.'

'My dear, it is true. I can assure you. It is true. You should be pleased at the prospect of your father coming through this unscathed. As you know, few people in his position are so lucky these days.'

'I know it is not true. I know it can't be true because Red Spectre has not kidnapped my Father and we, they, are not negotiating with Kratt. But Kratt may know where my Father really is. Emil knew. I told you that. And now he's dead, and you must have known that when I told you. You knew he was dead. Did Kratt kill him? Did Kratt kill him so he wouldn't say where my Father is?'

Argand's head swam. He struggled to put these fantasies aside, to get through to the girl how mistaken she was. 'Listen. You told me yourself that you are not really a member of this ghastly gang, but only, and God knows why,' the disgust in his voice was palpable, 'a sympathiser. Now do you think these people, to whom lying must come even more naturally than killing, are going to allow you to believe that they have kidnapped your father? That they are threatening his life? You may only be a sympathiser, but you are a valuable one. Of course they tell *you* that they don't have your father. But they do, you know. They really do.'

She lifted an arm slowly, till the palm was level with the top of her head. For a second Argand thought she was going to strike him, then he realised it was a signal. A man appeared in the trees fifty metres behind them, and walked down the steep grassy slope. He was wearing a grey raincoat with the collar turned up, a scarf that covered his mouth, and dark glasses. He looked to be in his late twenties or early thirties. Argand's skin chilled as he came closer, adrenalin gave a bitter flavour to the saliva in his mouth.

'Commissioner Argand?' The young man stopped in front of him and took off the scarf and glasses. He was pale, with deep-set eyes and a long, hollow-cheeked face. His wrists and fingers were long too, giving the impression that the sleeves of his raincoat were too short. One would have supposed him to be a visionary, but a rationalist too – a mathematician, perhaps, or a philosopher. 'I think you know who I am.'

For a moment Argand just looked at him, as if a fatally poisonous snake had crossed his path, or worse – the Devil perhaps. Argand's adult soul was not quite free of the belief in the Principle of Evil that had haunted his childhood.

'Yes. I believe you are Roman Punt.'

'Shall we sit down?' The terrorist gestured to a nearby bench.

Shall we? thought Argand. Surely I should leap on this monster, crush him. Arrest him anyway. He is very sure I won't. Why? He sat as far as he could from Punt, pushing his back against the wooden arm of the seat. Victoria moved behind them, stayed standing behind them. Punt turned in his corner to face him, stretched a long arm along the back of the seat towards him.

'You must be able to guess why I have arranged this meeting.'

'No. No. I have no idea at all.'

The terrorist frowned. 'You have been speaking to Victoria.'

'Yes.'

'And she has told you that Red Spectre does not have her father.'

'That's what she said.'

'And you don't believe her.'

'No.'

'I hope you will believe it from my lips. I assure you we do not have Wolfgang Herm.'

'There is nothing that I know about you that encourages me in any way to believe anything you may say.'

The silence lengthened between them. Below them one of the three workmen – it seemed now that there were only three – began to wield a pick. They were far enough away for the percussion to reach their ears a moment after the pick hit the asphalt. It crossed Argand's mind that they might be terrorists too, that they might be the reason why Punt was so confident that Argand would not manage to arrest him.

Almost it seemed as if Punt had read his thoughts – something surely not beyond the powers of the Prince of Darkness.

'I'm taking a very considerable risk in seeing you like this. You might arrest me. In a struggle you might overpower me. No, it's not impossible. You might carry a gun. If you did you would be applauded by your people if you simply pulled it out and shot me dead, no questions asked. At least ask yourself why I should take such a risk.'

'I don't need to. You will give me the same story as this woman did. That you fear some absurd plot against your brother's life.'

Punt's eyes narrowed, then widened, and he hit the back of the seat with his fist to emphasise his words.

'How can you say "absurd"? Why should you say "absurd"? Is it so long since Andreas Baader, Gudrun Ensslin, and Jan-Carl Raspe were murdered in Stammheim Prison? Why should I imagine that the Brabt SS are any softer or more law-abiding than the German SS . . .'

'Be quiet. Stop saying these things. If you want me to stay here in your filthy presence then you must not slander my colleagues either here or in the Federal Republic. They are decent, brave, hard-working men, and what they face daily because of rats like you . . .'

'Oh. I see. You really believe the suicide story. The pistols ludicrously smuggled in, and all that.'

'Yes.'

'Then you must be the only person in Europe who does. You and the Prime Minister of England. Well, Victoria said you were a decent person. Indeed it is because you have a reputation for honesty, shared by none of your colleagues, that I decided to make this approach. And I am not sure how to deal with *decent* people, people who sincerely believe . . . well, all the things you no doubt say you believe in.'

The distant pick fell, and the thud reached their ears. It was no surprise to Argand that this pale, gaunt fanatic had difficulty talking to a decent man.

'Listen. I will try hard to put myself in your place,' Punt went on. 'You firmly believe that Red Spectre has kidnapped Herm. You know me to be what you call a leader of Red Spectre. And I am trying to persuade you that we do not have Herm. At least ask yourself just why I should want to do that. In your place I should be curious to know why this charade had been put on for my benefit. Tell me, Commissioner, what ideas have you on that? Just why in your opinion am I here?'

Argand looked at him with hatred that incredibly intensified.

'I don't know what evil trick you're up to. I'm only sure that it is an evil trick.'

'Come Commissioner. That's not worthy of you. You may be a sincere man, but you are not a fool all the way through. Your intelligence still works at some levels, at the mechanical day-to-day level of doing your duty, and so on, and you hold a senior position. Evil tricks are not in any case our style, I think. We have been direct and sudden in bringing the war home to the class enemies of humanity, and I don't think we can be accused of being over-devious or subtle about it. I beg you again, Commissioner, ask yourself what possible motive I could have for being here, other than the one I have given you.'

Argand felt harried. He twisted away and the words that came out of his mouth sounded strangled. 'How, in Heaven's name do you imagine *I* should be able to work out what *you* are up to?'

'Well think about it, please. I know you will report this meeting to your colleagues and your superiors. Tell them what I said, qualify it as you will with your own judgements, but at least report me accurately. Red Spectre does not have Wolfgang Herm. I have taken the risk of telling you this out of fear for my brother's life. Moreover I fear for Herm. Since he is not in our hands, it is possible he is in danger elsewhere. Following the murder of his friend Emil Schneider he might be in great danger. Now tell your colleagues these things. And do one other thing. If they ignore you, or convince you of what you already believe, that what I say is part of some plot, then still I beg you do one thing. Keep faith at least with what you know to be true. That is, that this meeting did take place, and that I have said these things. Whatever they say to you, whatever pressure they put on you to deny it, at least hold to that.'

Roman Punt got to his feet, and wrapped his scarf about his mouth again. Then he took out the dark glasses and it was as his hands went to his face with them that the top of his head flew apart spattering bone and blood over Argand. The sound of the shot, no louder than the sound of the distant pick, came next, but from behind, high up in the woods behind, perhaps even from the battlements of the fairy castle. The terrorist lurched forward, then plunged headlong down the slope, landing on what was left of his face, crushing and staining the daffodils.

The workmen ran towards them, fanning out below them as if to cut them off. They carried pistols. But Victoria Herm did not move, perhaps could not. Her face was transformed, ashen now, the eyes wide and staring, the mouth bloodless, and it was at Argand she looked, not at the dying man. Argand looked back at her as he wiped away at the mess on the side of his face, and it seemed to him that she must believe that it was he who had wittingly led Punt into the trap. He longed to tell her that he was innocent but the words would not come.

16

Reprimand

At State Security Headquarters Argand rather expected
to be confronted with his counterpart, Commissioner
Gapp, but this did not happen. He was questioned, very
courteously, by an inspector, asked to wait while a statement was prepared for him to sign, and finally ushered
to the door and invited to go home. But first, while they
were waiting for the typist to bring his statement, he was
told that Roman Punt had been under surveillance since
negotiations for the release of Herm had been opened,
that a conversation he had had earlier in the day with
Victoria Herm had been heard on an eavesdropping
device, and that they had gathered from it that Punt
was to meet an important official in the park between
six and seven. The device had not picked up who the
official was. Naturally, State Security were intrigued, in
fact worried. No one should be seeing Punt unknown to
them. They put men in the park in the gear of workmen
for the Water Authority, and had Punt covered most of
the time by a skilled marksman. But the light had not
been good and the distance had been four hundred
metres – the marksman had seriously thought that
when Punt raised his hands to put on his dark glasses,
he had a gun in them, was about to shoot Argand. The
standing orders relating to situations of this sort, which

had been reformulated to comply with the Euro-agreement on anti-terrorist Laws, left him only one choice in that situation. 'Imagine, Commissioner, you would now be dead if Punt had had a gun. You should be grateful to Sergeant Mand – he acted swiftly, accurately, and quite properly.'

Argand went home. There Secretary Prinz reached him on the phone. He had nothing but sympathy for his Commissioner, was full of praise for his courage and presence of mind throughout a terrible ordeal, insisted finally that Argand should have the following day off, absolutely must have, that is an order old chap. 'And you are to stay indoors. We don't want you harassed by the press and the media, and you surely will be if you poke your head out. In fact we'll put a couple of men on the door to keep things quiet for you, and when you come in on Tuesday we'll send a car for you. By the way,' he concluded, 'there really is no need to bother with the League for Life any more. We're closing that file and returning the men you had on it to normal duties. All right? All you have to worry about now is your football match on Sunday. God bless, Jan, have a good rest, you must need it.'

Argand understood from all this that he was under police protection in case Red Spectre should decide that he would be the ideal target for a swift reprisal for the death of Roman Punt. Tired though he was, and in shock too, he still found the monotony of a whole day shut in his flat almost impossible to support. His only relief was the newspapers and the television.

In the morning *The Brabanter* reported the shooting of Punt accurately enough, though it did not state why Punt and Argand had met. The implication was strongly there that the meeting had been part of the negotiations for the release of Herm. A leader regretted the incident, while offering no criticism at all of the State Security

Police involved – they had acted quite properly. Punt had clearly made a gesture which could be interpreted as a threatening one, and the marksman had been right to shoot. What was regrettable was that there would clearly now be a setback in the negotiations for Herm's release.

A separate item reported that Victoria Herm had been charged under the new laws with consorting with a man, knowing him to be a terrorist. The maximum penalty for this crime was ten years in prison.

The lunchtime news on TV added only that Mrs Lena Herm had approached the magistracy asking them to set a figure for bail for her daughter. 'Whatever figure they set, I will meet,' she said. 'Already the strain of this terrible time is taking its toll on me. I cannot bear to think of my daughter in prison on top of everything else.' A spokesman for the police said he thought bail would not be opposed. It was understood that in this instance Miss Herm had been acting as go-between in the very sensitive negotiations, and could hardly be blamed for acting out of her deep concern for her father.

All this left Argand disturbed. Nowhere was there any hint that his interview with Punt had been on quite other lines. He did not waver in his belief that Punt had been deceiving him, but he began to feel unhappy that his account of the meeting, made in his statement, had been completely ignored, or at any rate kept from the reporters.

At six o'clock *Slik Stien* challenged the official version with an interpretation of the events that came very close to one that Punt would have approved. 'Let us just for a moment assume,' the editorial began, 'that Red Spectre do *not* have Wolfgang Herm, that Green Force has. What then would have been Roman Punt's motive in arranging this meeting with Commissioner Argand? The answer is plain – he wanted to say personally and forcefully that whoever purports to be negotiating in the name of Red Spectre for an exchange involving his brother Hans Punt is a liar, a fraud. And why did Roman Punt risk and lose his life to make this plain to the Commissioner? Because he could foresee a situation potentially dangerous to his brother. Someone, he did not know who, was, and perhaps still is about to take Hans Punt and the Jansens out of prison and cause them to disappear. Who? It is not our policy to speculate blindly and we will not hazard a guess. But there are many people, of the extreme right and of the extreme left too (for rivalries, ideological differences, are not unheard of between terrorist groups) who would like to see Hans Punt dead.

'At all events,' the writer continued, 'we believe that our reconstruction has more of a ring of truth about it than the official version. Is it really possible that even our Security Forces would bungle negotiations like these to the point of shooting the other side's spokesman? Were they really so ready to invite the inevitable consequence, the murder of Herm in reprisal? Or can it be that Commissioner Gapp and his men saw no risk to Herm in this killing because they know that Herm, wherever he is, is not in the clutches of Red Spectre?

'One man can shed light on all this, one man so far silent or silenced. We refer to the honest commissioner, Commissioner Argand. In the past he has been no great friend of ours. Three times he tried to close this paper. His ideas are anathema to us, and in some respects he is a silly old fuddy-duddy. But in our dealings with him we have come to respect his sincerity and his honesty. Perhaps it was these very qualities that led Punt to approach him. At any rate it is now up to the honest commissioner to come out with the truth, and tell us just what passed between Roman Punt and him in the moments before our gallant police blew the top off a defenceless man's head. For how long will Jan Argand's self-respect allow him to remain silent?'

Although this question gave Argand an unpleasant evening the answer was never really in doubt. He would keep silent for as long as his superiors wanted him to, and in the morning they made their feelings clear.

After making his own coffee — and finding it as good as the Café Louis Bonaparte's — he was driven to Wilhelmstras, where he was told, even before he reached his office, that Secretary Prinz wished to see him straightaway. The Secretary was not at ease — already he was puffing almost feverishly on his pipe. In contrast, Commissioner Gapp who was with him was composed, cool, distant. Prinz sat Argand in a high-backed chair in front of his desk, took refuge behind it with Gapp then began.

'Now Jan,' he said, 'I'm afraid this is an official, indeed a formal occasion. Yesterday morning Commissioner Gapp placed a formal complaint against you. In line with the procedure laid down I have investigated it and duly found that there is a case to be answered.'

Argand looked up at the large blond figure of the Chief of State Security. Gapp's eyes were fixed on the window beyond, his only reaction to the Secretary's remarks was to pass a pale tip of tongue along his lip, beneath the thin line of his yellow moustache.

Secretary Prinz shuffled some papers in front of him, put his smoking pipe in an ashtray and went on: 'In your statement regarding Sunday's incident you say that you twice had communication with Victoria Herm. Once personally, at your house, on the night of Friday last, then by a note, then personally again on Sunday — the occasion which led up to the shooting of Punt. Commissioner Gapp's complaint is that you failed to report the first meeting to him, and your receipt of the note. It is his contention that you should have done, and his work on the Herm case has been very seriously compromised by your failure to do what was clearly your duty on these occasions. Jan, I must say I feel inclined to agree with him. But it is now your right to make an explanatory statement if you want to.'

Argand rubbed his eyes with his open palms. He felt more wretched than at any other time in the case, for he knew what would follow. He thought back. Why had he not reported the girl's first visit? He had been going to, then something had happened, what was it? He had gone to the mortuary, then slept badly. Then back to Schneider's flat. Then in his office, yes, that was it, a note from Secretary Prinz himself, telling him that Gapp was already negotiating with Red Spectre, a note which made nonsense of Victoria's visit, which made her seem at best a dupe, at worst a hysteric with illusions about Red Spectre that could only be irrelevant, could only get in Gapp's way. Well, that had been his reasoning at the time. At the time it had seemed sensible. But then why had he not reported the note, why had he gone off to meet her a second time, again without telling anyone? He shook his head in disbelief at his own stupidity, his negligence. Had he anything to say? What was there to say? It was not his way to plead strain, tiredness, shock. At last he looked up and simply shook his head again.

'In that case it is now my duty to reprimand you. This reprimand will be recorded in the official documentation of the Herm case and in your own dossier; and with it you automatically lose a year's seniority. You have the right to appeal to a tribunal, but not until the Herm case is closed.' Secretary Prinz sat back in his chair and took up his pipe again. 'Well that's it Jan, that's the worst over. I trust you bear no ill-will to Commissioner Gapp on this account. I don't think he could really have done other than he did. I hope you won't take it to heart. I know your record was clean up to now, but you know very few officers come right through a lifetime in the service without putting up at least one black somewhere along the line. Still, you're off the case now and I blame myself for putting you on it in the first place. Not your pitch at all, eh?'

Argand stood up. He said nothing. There seemed to be nothing to say. Commissioner Gapp continued to stare out of the window.

'There is just one thing before you go.'

'Secretary?'

'This . . . this rag.' Secretary Prinz held up the previous evening's edition of *Slik Stien*. 'You saw it, did you?'

'Yes, Secretary.'

'Now you don't have to assure me that you will ignore the personal appeal made to you. I know you quite well enough to be certain that you will rise above cheap blackmail of this sort. But Commissioner Gapp knows you less well than I and I think he would like to have an assurance to that effect from you in person.'

Argand pulled himself up straight. He was angry now as well as wretched.

'There is not the slightest chance that I will communicate anything at all, on any subject whatever to any journalist at all, except on the explicit instructions of this office.'

Gapp at last turned to him.

'Would you put something in writing for me to that effect?' he asked.

Argand fumed. 'Draft it yourself. If I feel I can sign it without exposing myself to further indignity, I will.' Then at the door he turned again. 'Everything seems to have become a matter of record as though no trust existed amongst us any more. That being the case, I should like it to be clear that I still stand by every word in my statement of Sunday night. Punt did insist to me that neither he nor Red Spectre have kidnapped Herm. Now I did not believe him then, nor do I believe him now. But

156

that *is* what he said to me and he must have had some reason for saying it. And the fact that he said it might turn out to be of importance to you, to your case. So let *me* protect myself. I want to be sure my statement of Sunday night also remains unaltered on the Herm file.'

Gapp answered. 'Of course, Commissioner. Your implication that a statement of yours could disappear from the file surprises me. But of course it will stay there. And, Secretary, I think we may waive a written declaration from the Commissioner in the matter of *Slik Stien*. It was silly of me to press for one.' He turned back to Argand whose hand was still on the door. 'I must though share with you, Commissioner, your bewilderment that Punt should have denied my negotiations with him, even though, up to the point where he was shot, they had all been conducted through intermediaries. I really do find it very puzzling. If you come up with an explanation or a theory that might lead to one, I'm sure you'll let me know.'

'Of course. And in writing. But I doubt if I shall. I simply cannot conceive what end he thought he was serving by telling me this . . .,' he hesitated and was himself surprised at the note of doubt in his voice, ' . . . this lie.'

There was a pause. Then Gapp said, very dryly, very coldly: 'I take it there is no doubt in your mind, Commissioner. I mean *you* believe Red Spectre has Herm, and it is with Red Spectre that we are negotiating his release. I assure you it is so. If it had not been so we would not have been able to find Punt and keep him under surveillance. And if he had not been under surveillance, we would not have known of the meeting he arranged with you in the park.'

Argand had had enough. 'I have never in my career doubted my colleagues or superiors, and I am not yet ready to do so now. Now I think I should go back to my office, and back to my own work,' and with that he at last managed to get out of the door.

17

Kant's Last Tape

When Argand got back to his office he found there was very little of his own work to do. In his absence his small team had managed perfectly well without him, the arrangements for Sunday's match were complete, the dock pickets had fallen away and only three men and a dog had turned up that morning. Nothing else in the way of trouble was in sight. There was, however, a substantial amount of stuff on his desk relating to what had been his side of the Herm case, the League for Life side. For a moment he thought of bundling the whole lot up and sending it along to Gapp, but curiosity got the better of him, curiosity not untinged with resentment at the way he had been treated. On the top was a tape cassette labelled 'Pastor Kant: Sermon at Morning Service, Spartshaven, 30/3/80'. Argand slotted it into the recorder that was part of his desk furniture, and listened.

'Friends, the City of God is within you or it is nowhere.' At this, the traditional opening to every sermon given in the Church of Inner Salvation, Argand was suddenly carried back to his childhood in a way that almost frightened him, certainly filled him with a longing for times more austere, more certain. But the voice moved on, a thin voice, not overtly emotional, but nonetheless intense, impassioned. The momentary vision of childhood was replaced in Argand's mind by the tall ascetic figure of Pastor Kant, standing at the plain deal table with the Bible beneath his hand in that chapel improvised out of the roofed space between two old railway carriages. He wondered how many there were. No doubt a supplementary report would tell him, probably with the names listed, but meanwhile the voice went on.

'Friends, as the crisis of our trials draws near, I thought today it would be right for me to take for my text our Lord's words when spies had been sent forth, which should feign themselves just men, that they might take hold of his words, that so they might deliver him unto the power and the authority of the governor. And the fact that there are men among us now, equipped with a recording device, who are also spies, and may or may not be just men, and who will certainly take my words back to Commissioner Argand, is really . . .' At this there was a sound of shuffling on the tape, then a burst of loud laughter, but also a voice saying 'kick them out the pigs'. Then the Pastor's voice again, a little more strongly this time. 'No, no, I am glad they are here. Sorry only that Commissioner Argand is not. Doubly sorry in that I believe he was once a member of our church and I hope will be again one day. At all events I am very happy he should hear what I have to say on my text: "Render therefore unto Caesar the things which be Caesar's, and unto God the things which be God's", for, as I am sure you all know, that is the answer Our Lord gave to those spies, feigning to be just men, when they tried to trick him with the question, "is it lawful for us to give tribute to Caesar or no?"'

'Friends. In the Heavenly City which it is our duty to strive for on earth, first in our hearts and then in all around us, in the Heavenly City, the division between what is God's and what is the State's will not arise, will not exist, for there the will of the State will be the will of

God. I do not need to tell you that we are very far away from that happy existence. How then do things stand now? How far do we owe a duty to the State, and how far do we owe a duty to God?

'My friends, the text I am using has been most horribly abused in the past, to justify the belief that we should let the State look after secular matters while the Church takes care of the spirit, as if there were a duality in man, a separation of spirit and mind, soul and body, of time from the eternal. I do not believe that such a duality exists. I believe that those who say it does seek to repudiate the eternal now; they try to have their cake now and eat it in eternity.

'Our Lord's reply to the question – what belongs to the State? – was unequivocal, the phrasing only was clever, even perhaps a little sly, for our Lord was a clever man, a witty man, and knew how to turn, with wit, a question phrased with ill intention. To Caesar what is Caesar's, to God what is God's. This means – Don't ask me what should be given to Caesar until you are sure you have given to God what is His. Or – How can anything be owed to Caesar before we have given God his due? Or – How can the State demand anything of us that would not be acceptable to God as well? Or – Let us be sure that before we bow our will to the will of the State, that the will of the State is the same as God's will. For, my friends, I would not have you mistake me, even less would I like the worthy Commissioner to mistake me. I do not preach the downfall of the State, I do not believe God wishes us to do without the State. I would go further. I believe that God has created Man as a social being, and that Man cannot do God's will completely except as part of a godly society. I would go further. I believe that a godly society, a godly State is an indispensable part of God's will. That only when the State's will is God's will, when the obedience and tribute that the State exacts from us is the same or part of what God demands of us, only then will Man, as opposed to mere individual men, be saved.

'In the meantime . . . in the meantime, my friends, it is our Christian duty to resist the State whenever it demands from us tribute that would not be acceptable to God himself.

'My friends, I don't think I have to press this point home to you, you would not be here if I did. But Commissioner Argand perhaps needs to be reminded of these simple truths. It is not our Christian duty to pay tribute to, to offer obedience to, to live passively in and without resistance to, a state, or system of allied states, a so-called community of states that destroys what is essentially and eternally human, and therefore divine, for the sake of what is transient, shoddy and spurious. It is not God's will that we should give up *his* gifts in exchange for material wealth beyond our physical needs. It is not his will that we should seek to live long in a world of dull uniformity at best, but more often of foul ugliness, both physical and moral. It is not his will that we should live long at the expense of vast numbers of mankind who are starving, nearly starving, living in squalor that is only in the matter of physical pain and discomfort worse than the plastic squalor that surrounds us.

'My friends, Commissioner, I believe the State has become Mammon. If the spies sent to our Lord had asked what tribute is it lawful to give Mammon, we know what he would have answered — no man can serve two masters: for either he will hate one, and love the other, or else he will hold to the one, and despise the other. Ye cannot serve God and Mammon.

'In a week's time, a week and a day, the earth-movers will come down the street outside and they will start pushing away, like so much rubbish, the community we have tried to build here. They will do this with the full authority of the State, with all the machinery and panoply of the law, they will do it protected by, and no doubt under the eyes of, the armed guardians of the law. Not only our homes will go, but the last area of wilderness left in our Province, left indeed in this part of Europe, will disappear too. What is now fresh and clean and beautiful, what now harbours some of the loveliest of God's creatures from the little tern to the common seal, from the gaudy shelduck to the pert and elegant reed bunting, will become in parts a collection of foetid poisonous tanks, while the rest is to become a blank of unchanging flat grey water. There men whose allegiance to Mammon is more whole-hearted than ours to God will drive ear-shattering power-boats, will drink, and lust, and disport their miserable possessions. And all they will see and feel of God's world, where now there is so much, will be the sun and the wind and the water, and the sun will be veiled with poisonous vapours, and the wind will stink of them, and the water will be dead.

'Friends, it is God's will that you do all in your power, all in the power God gives you, to resist this outrage of God's will. By doing so you will be hastening, perhaps only by a mite, the time when the State's will is God's will, and by rendering to one, men will render to both. I say all this to you, not to persuade you, because I know you are persuaded already, but to give you courage, for, friends, we are going to need courage, and we must help eachother, and we must not scorn any whose courage may be less than ours, and we must be ready to look for love and strength from those around us when our own courage fails.

'Friends, there I was going to end, but we still have guests in the guise of just men among us, with their recording device. They are here because it is possible that a man has been kidnapped by people who support our cause. Now I do believe that if this man Herm is in the hands of those who support us then there still remains some hope for us, for Spartshaven. What I hope and pray for is this, that by living with people who believe in what we believe in, who hold dear the things we hold dear, this Herm, who I have heard is not a man without the power of love in him, may have the courage to declare himself an enemy of EUREAC and this vile Project. And if any of you are anything to do with this kidnap, then let that be your only aim — to win over Wolfgang Herm from the false Mammon that is the State today to the Kingdom of God that is to come. And since we are being recorded let me end, really end, with a message to Commissioner Argand. Commissioner, we pray that you too may one day return to the belief that the City of God is within you or it is nowhere.'

18

Reprisal

With the tape there was, as Jan had expected there would be, a list of names, those his men had identified as being part of the Pastor's congregation. Argand folded this list carefully and put it in his pocket. He did not see what use it could be to Commissioner Gapp.

The next item on his desk was a copy of Doctor Dael's autopsy report on Emil Schneider. It was shorter than he expected, more definite than he expected. After two pages of more or less technical data it came to two conclusions that Argand found surprising. The first was that death had definitely resulted from the broken neck. There was not even the suggestion that the drugs could be considered as an alternative or supplementary cause. The second conclusion was stated a little less certainly, but still in a way that did not invite dispute, and that was that the drugs had been self-administered. The final statement was the most surprising of all. 'In the opinion of this investigator there is nothing in the condition of the deceased, or in the cause of his death to contradict the hypothesis put forward in the report of the forensic department.'

Commissioner Argand went quickly through the documents on his desk, then again more slowly and carefully. There was no forensic report.

He sat back in his chair, put his fingers together, and

164

thought about it. He was no longer officially connected in any way with the case. He ought to drop it. If he tried to get hold of the forensic report he would be blocked, referred to Commissioner Gapp. Gapp would certainly want to know why he wanted to see it. Anyway, there would be an inquest, a public inquest in a day or two, a week at most. He would learn then what the forensic department had reported.

Argand decided that he did not want to wait. He reached for the phone, hesitated, felt a slight sweat break on the back of his neck, then his hand went on and he picked it up. In a moment or two he heard Doctor Dael at the other end.

'Jean-Paul, I have here your autopsy report on that man you were cutting up the other night.'

The silence at the other end continued until the thought was forming in Argand's mind that they had been cut off.

'I'm sorry, Jan,' said the doctor at last, 'I was just surprised that you had it. I understood that you had been taken off anything to do with it. I can't imagine how my report got into your hands.'

'Yes. Well, you're right, I have been taken off it. And I suppose it's a mistake my having your report. I expect someone forgot that stuff would go on coming through to my desk until it was stopped. Anyway I do have it and I'm a little curious about one or two things in it. Just curious, nothing more.'

'Well, I'm not going into it for you, if that's what you want. Honestly Jan, I think you might have told me that it was connected with this EUREAC business, Herm and all that, before coming along to my mortuary and pumping me.'

'I did not pump you. And you told me you don't like to know too much about a customer in case what you know prejudices your findings.'

'Quite. But I had no idea we were in such a sensitive area.'

'Jean-Paul, I'm not quite sure I understand what you are saying. You're not trying to tell me, are you, that there's something wrong with your report?'

Again the long silence.

'Jan, there is nothing in my report at all that in any way conflicts with the scientifically observed facts of the case. I hope you did not mean to suggest that there might be.'

'No, no, Jean-Paul. Not at all. I did not mean to suggest anything of the sort.'

'All right then. Just what is it you want to know?'

Argand thought: What I want to know is why you decided so positively that the fall killed him, that the drugs were self-administered. He said: 'I just wondered what the hypothesis was that forensic had put forward. That's all. I had no intention at all of questioning your report. Far from it.'

'Well. Well then. I don't see that it matters if I tell what they said. Just that all the evidence suggested that after filling himself with barbiturates and LSD the poor man suffered a bad trip and defenestrated himself. It's happened several times with acid-droppers, and everything they found in the flat pointed to that conclusion. And of course there were no counter-indications either.'

'What about the visitors, the two visitors?'

Argand heard the doctor sigh.

'What two visitors, Jan? There was no mention of visitors in anything I read.'

'Oh. Are you sure?'

'Quite sure. Jan. Take my advice now, will you? Keep off this one. They've taken you off it. They're going to be very upset if they get wind that you're still nosing into it.'

Argand replaced the phone and passed a hand over his face, then reached for his handkerchief – he had not realised that a cold sweat had broken out on his forehead, the same psychosomatic symptom that had marked the stress he had felt at the thought that Lena Herm might lie to him. He was now fully aware that he had been excluded, probably from the start, from a vast area of all the tangled events and manoeuvres that made up the Herm affair. But the unmentionable suspicion that he had been excluded because something was happening that ought not to happen remained suppressed – it grew in the dark corners of his mind like rot in the cellars of a house, something he dared not look at, dared not bring into the daylight; and the sweat pricked his forehead and his palms, and anxiety like a dead cold hand squeezed his diaphragm.

His thoughts went back to Schneider. He remembered the folio of bird and animal paintings. He thought of Kant's sermon. What had the Pastor said? What were his words? – 'the gaudy shelduck and the pert, elegant reed bunting'. Kant had had a good word for the artist, had called him a good man. He must have seen Schneider when the artist was doing the sketches for the paintings, seen him and got to know him. Presumably Kant approved, had perhaps encouraged and even initiated the idea for a book *The Wild Life of Spartshaven Marsh*. Well, Argand thought, it would be a pity if the book never came out because the publishers thought that Schneider had not finished the pictures.

It took him some time to get hold of the director of Zart and Millan who had been particularly concerned with the book, and then more time to convince the man that although he, Commissioner Argand was *the* Commissioner Argand, the call he was making was not on police business at all. When at last he did understand that all the policeman wanted was to tell him that the folio existed and could be put into his hands, he became apologetic.

'It's very good of you to take this trouble, Excellency, but I'm afraid it's trouble wasted. You see a book of this sort, with quality reproductions and probably a very limited appeal has to be financed. It has to be sponsored. This book did have a sponsor, but I'm afraid that sponsorship has now been withdrawn. We heard this sad news only two days ago. Of course we will honour our contract with the artist, I should say with his heirs, I mean they will be paid the sum outstanding on delivery of the paintings, but that's as far as it will go.'

'Do you mind telling me who the sponsor was?'

'No. Not at all. It was EUREAC. Well, actually it was Wolfgang Herm, you know this poor man Red Spectre have got their hands on, but he was acting through EUREAC.'

'And now it's cancelled.'

'Yes.'

'But not by Mr Herm.'

'No, no, Excellency. I imaginé he's hardly in a position to take steps like this. No. We had a letter from Hector Macher, his personal assistant. It was he who cancelled the sponsorship.'

How could Macher act for Herm? How could he know what Herm would approve? The dread returned and Argand desperately pushed the League for Life file to the end of his desk and began feverishly to invent work for himself that had nothing to do with Herm, Kant or the two visitors to Schneider's flat whose presence forensic science could not uncover, though Argand had seen the tumblers they had used on the draining board in the artist's kitchen. At eleven o'clock, Argand's secretary announced a visitor he had not expected – Commissioner Gapp. Gapp was wearing a three-quarter length coat of military cut, and carrying hat and gloves.

Again he would not look at Argand, but fixed his pale eyes on a point high up in the window or in the sky beyond.

'I, er, came in to tell you that on a, well, personal level I'm sorry about that scene this morning. I'm afraid our Secretary Prinz made rather a meal of it. There was no need for him to be quite so pompous.'

Argand could find nothing worth saying to this, so he said nothing.

'I mean,' the military man continued, 'that I hope you understand there was nothing personal in it at all. I'm sure you see that purely from the official angle I had to protect myself. One has to keep to the form in these things or one ends up in the shit. Well, that's my experience anyway.'

Argand did not like people who used words like "shit" and especially not when they did it not because they knew no better but out of affectation.

'I understand, I'm sure.'

'Splendid. No hard feelings then?'

'None personal.'

'Fine. I'm just on my way to the EUREAC building. It seems they are in touch with Red Spectre again. For the first time since Punt got himself shot. I wondered if you'd like to come.'

Argand was astounded at this, but took care not to show it.

'Well. You know these people, you were in at the beginning. Anyway two heads are better than one, and if we actually get to a situation where an exchange is to be discussed then I'd value your advice. These things can be the devil to organise. You might see a snag I miss and so on. Will you come?'

'Oh yes, I'll come.' He gathered together his coat, hat and gloves and followed Gapp down the corridors, into the lift and so to street level. At the top of the wide steps down to the street Gapp said: 'Well, it's clearing up again, I think. Very changeable at this time of year, isn't it?' He held open the door of the large State Security Mercedes for Argand to get in. A guard rode with the driver and they were flanked by two armed motor-cyclists.

As they moved off into the traffic Argand speculated, but to himself. What was going on? The chances that the point of the exercise was simply to improve relations between the two Commissioners were so slight as not to be worth considering. Was it then to demonstrate to Argand that negotiations really were going forward with Red Spectre? Or was it really just what Gapp said it was — that he was frightened that he might leave something uncovered when it came to an exchange, something that Argand with his greater experience of such things might notice. Whatever the reason though, it was an odd business to be going back to EUREAC just after he had been told the case was closed to him.

'By the way, did you ever get out of Kratt the minutes of the inner board meetings? I had the feeling he was stalling with them.'

'What they call the cabinet?' As usual Gapp was looking out of the window, but Argand had the impression that the chestnuts, people shopping, hurrying about their business, the traffic, all went by unnoticed. 'Oh yes. They turned up the day I took over. He had them all ready for you. But I can't think why you wanted them. Nothing there at all of any interest to the case. And they were heavy reading too.'

'Yes? But at the time, if you remember, I was working on the assumption that Herm had disappeared voluntarily. And I thought they might provide a clue as to why.'

'I remember you did have that idea. Of course as it turned out there was nothing in it, nothing in it all.

These Red Spectre shits had him all along. Well, here we are.'

The door out to the service road behind the Herms' house, Herm's visit to Emil Schneider, the present of a record, a parting present, all flicked through Argand's mind as he stepped out on to the pavement.

What happened next was confused, but afterwards Argand went through it again and again in his mind until he was sure he had it right.

On the pavement outside the big glass doors were two EUREAC Health Guards, big men in the neat dark green uniform, with heavy automatics and truncheons on their webbing belts. Their faces were of course obscured by the darkly-tinted perspex visors fixed to the rims of their white helmets. They saluted as Gapp came up to them, and at the same time the heavy glass doors swung open. Gapp went through, Argand followed. The doors closed behind them and the State Security Mercedes with its escort moved off leaving the curb clear. Meanwhile, inside, Christian Kratt came across the marble foyer towards them.

'Good of you to come so quickly, Commissioner,' he said to Gapp, and then to Argand: 'And you too, Argand. I'm sure we're most grateful. Gapp told us that he hoped to *persuade* you to come along.' Then releasing Argand's hand, but continuing to hold him by the elbow, he glanced over the policeman's shoulder to the door beyond. 'Ah, here they are,' he said. 'They come most carefully upon their hour,' and he laughed. Argand half-turned and saw, beyond the glass doors, Hector Macher getting out of the Ferrari, just as he had seen him six days before, the previous Wednesday. Macher was doing exactly what he had done the first time. He opened the passenger door for Lena Herm and handed her out on to the pavement. Then he straightened, with the car keys in his hand, ready to give them to one of the Health

Guards, who had come down the step and was at his shoulder. At this moment the glass doors swung open and Lena Herm crossed the threshold into the foyer.

Argand saw Macher beyond her suddenly twist then freeze, saw the gun in the Health Guard's hand. Then the second guard came into his line of vision, also with his gun out, held in both hands and in a straight line as if it was the extension of a pointing finger, a straight line that pointed at the middle of Argand's forehead. Or so it seemed to him. And at that moment Kratt's grip tightened on his elbow.

The gun went off, with an appalling crash in the echoing space, the air between Argand and the guard seemed literally to bend, bulge, then explode into a shower of crystal, and the bullet whined about their heads for what seemed like seconds, screeching when it hit polished marble, and whining off again until at last it fragmented, miraculously without hurting anyone.

A deep, throbbing roar from the street, and the scream of tyres announced the departure of the Ferrari, with both guards in it and, of course, Hector Macher.

Kratt cursed and released Argand.

'He hit the glass door,' he cried. 'The bullet clipped the edge of the door as it shut. I tell you those doors are meant to be bullet-proof. Look at the damn thing, just look at it.'

Argand wiped his brow. 'Yet it deflected the bullet,' he murmured, 'and it would have hit me if it had not.'

Lena Herm, pale with fright Argand thought at first, but in fact with rage, stamped her foot and then stamped it again. 'It's too much,' she screamed, 'it really is too much.'

Only Gapp seemed unmoved. Without speaking he strode across to the reception desk and picked up the phone.

19

Telly Revelation

'Following the extraordinary and dramatic kidnapping this morning of Hector Macher, private assistant to Wolfgang Herm, we have in the Vista studio tonight Mrs Lena Herm and Miss Victoria Herm. Both believe that by appearing on our programme, they will be able to do something to help the man who is the husband of one and the father of the other. But that is for later. We open tonight's programme with a very different guest and a very different topic. First some background film.

'*Fingal's Cave* was once a Scottish deep-sea trawler. Two years ago her time was up and the owners of the fleet she belonged to were ready to scrap her. At this point in time my first guest tonight stepped in. Richard Hurst is a member of an international group calling itself the Friends of Life. They bought *Fingal's Cave*, got together a crew, and put Richard Hurst, of mixed Brabanter and English parentage and holding an English Master's Certificate, in charge. For the last two years *Fingal's Cave* has been used to make practical demonstrations of its owners' beliefs. Sometimes these demonstrations have bordered on the violent, life has been endangered, property has been damaged, and earnings lost. Recently they have been involved with the dumping of waste from the River Flot Nuclear Power Station, but usually they harry whalers and seal cullers. At this moment in time *Fingal's Cave* is in Brabt refitting and tonight we have its captain, Richard Hurst, as our first guest.

'Richard Hurst, what gives you the right to interfere with other men's livelihoods in this way?'

'What gives men the right to hunt and kill whales?'

'Captain Hurst, international law and international agreements give men the right to hunt whales. . . .'

'I think it's pretty well known that most whaling countries exceed their quotas, which were set by the industries in the first place and not by ecologists . . .'

'That's as may be. But why not answer my first question? What gives *you* the right to interfere?'

'The right of conscience. The rights of our children's children who may or may not be born into a world where there are whales. The whales themselves – noble, intelligent animals. On man-devised scales they rate in intelligence only just below the highest primates – on scales devised by themselves they might do even better. These marvellous animals should not be hunted, hideously maimed, cruelly slaughtered to make rich men richer.'

'And what about the men who earn their daily bread on the whalers? Don't they deserve some of your sympathy?'

'I don't think any of the large whaling nations have serious unemployment problems. The tiny numbers employed in the whaling industry could easily be absorbed into the labour market.'

'So you say, Captain Hurst. So you say. Captain Hurst, who pays you?'

'The Friends of Life.'

'But where does the money come from? *Fingal's Cave* must have cost millions of gelds to buy, fit and run. That sort of money does not come from selling flags in the street, from collecting boxes. There must be some very rich men behind you.'

'If there are I don't know them. I haven't met them.'

'Captain, in my experience rich men do not lay out millions without expecting a return. Have you asked yourself what the return might be in this case? Are you not worried that you may be serving ends other than purely beautiful, humane ones?'

'I suppose you mean the vegetable oil and fat industry. Are you saying that is where the money comes from?'

'I am not saying anything, Captain. I'm trying to get you to tell the public. You interfere with the dumping of nuclear waste as well, I understand. Why?'

'Because I, we, think that nuclear power is an extremely unsafe, dangerous, horribly dangerous way of producing energy.'

'I find you must be a very proud man. Scientists, technologists, governments with their experts have gone very thoroughly into this question of radioactive waste. Why are you so sure you know better than they?'

'I am not alone. For every scientist in the pay of the governments who say there is no danger, I can find one who says there is. It is not conceivable that something that can remain lethally active for many thousands of years may not in some distant future escape from the containers it is put in. Scientists can cope with the foreseeable, but no one can foresee the future entirely. There is always the unforeseeable.'

'And the men who pay you think the same.'

'I believe so.'

'They could not have invested in other forms of energy I suppose. They could not be politically interested in preventing the growth of an economically prosperous Europe.'

'I don't think so. I think our backers are disinterested, altruistic people. Every indication I have had about them suggests they are good men and good women prompted by feelings as genuine as those that prompt the thousands of good ordinary people who occasionally put a ten geld piece in one of our collecting boxes.'

'Captain Hurst, that is your belief and I would be the last person to deny anyone the right to his beliefs, however absurd. But in my experience, and I think my programme has demonstrated this often, the rich and the great are cleverer than ordinary mortals, more hardworking, with stronger drives, and that is why they are rich and great. And I don't believe any rich man will put his hand in his pocket to the tune of many millions of gelds with the lack of thought and motive that a housewife drops ten in a collecting box.'

'I did not say that our funds come without motive. I said that the motives were disinterested, altruistic.'

'I don't understand that.'

'I mean that the money is given with care and forethought to promote a good end, often an end that the giver will not enjoy himself.'

'What end?'

'A better, cleaner, safer, less greedy, more beautiful planet for our children to live on, than we have.'

'As I said, Captain Hurst, I am the last person to deny a man his right to his chosen faith, however absurd. Thank you for appearing on my programme. We'll take a break there.'

'Welcome back. This morning at a little before noon, the Herm affair took a new and dramatic twist. As our bulletins have reported throughout the day, Hector Macher, Wolfgang Herm's private assistant and friend was kidnapped by members of Red Spectre disguised as EUREAC Health Guards, on the steps of the EUREAC Building and in the presence of not one but two of our police Commissioners. At two o'clock this afternoon Vista, the programme now coming to you live, and *The Brabanter* received simultaneous telephone calls. The message was brief. Here is a recording of the one the Vista office received.'

'"Red Spectre speaking. Hector Macher, secretary of Wolfgang Herm, was arrested by Red Spectre at noon today. This action was necessitated by the brutal killing, without trial, of Roman Punt on Sunday last. Macher will have the benefit of a trial. If he is found guilty of the offences against humanity with which he is charged, he will be sentenced to death and the sentence carried out at midnight tonight."'

'Mrs Lena Herm, the past ten days must have been a nightmare for you.'

'Too terrible, too terrible for words.'

'We must not add to your burdens. I am sure you will say when you would rather not go on, and we will respect your wishes. I, the people of Brabt, those in other countries, our neighbours, watching now, we all join together in sympathy for your terrible ordeal. Now, Mrs Herm, I am sure there are members of Red Spectre out there who are watching too. Do you have anything particular you would like to say to them at this moment in time?'

'Yes, I do. And I am so deeply grateful that Vista has given me this chance.'

'Go ahead, Mrs Herm.'

'First I must speak about poor Hector. I think there are people nowadays who no longer believe in the idea of "service", who believe the word "servant" is a bad word, a sort of insult. Hector Macher is not one of those. His loyalty and devotion are above reproach and beyond praise. Moreover, for years now he has been a friend to my husband and myself, as well as a servant. So, I should like to say this to Red Spectre. It is so wrong of them, of you, wherever you are, to talk about sins against humanity when you talk of Hector. He is a good soul. He would not, ever, hurt anyone – a gentle, kind, loving soul. So I say this to you. Please, please keep him out of this. I know I speak for my husband in this. If Hector comes to harm then his blood will be on our heads as well as on yours.'

'Mrs Herm, I'm sure I speak for all of us when I say how moved we are that you should make Hector Macher your first, if not your primary concern.'

'As far as my husband is concerned I have this to say. First, I want his kidnappers to believe that the shooting of Roman Punt was a mistake, a horrible mistake. Then in your pamphlets and so on you have, I believe, made much of ideals, of courage, of nobility and sacrifice. I beg you now to think – would it not be more noble to carry on with the negotiations as Roman Punt would have done, if this terrible accident had not happened? Would not that be the noblest course? And now I have this to say. You have asked for two hundred and fifty million gelds for my husband. I am now empowered, by the board of EUREAC, by my cousin Baron de Merle, who himself has been the victim of one of your attacks in the past, to say that we will pay three hundred million gelds if you will now release my husband.

'As far as Hans Punt and the Jansens are concerned, that is not for me to say. But I can say this. I know Commissioner Gapp, know him very well, and know him to be a profoundly honest person. I understand Red Spectre has feared some trap or trick at the moment of change-over. This suspicion is not justified. I do not know what Commissioner Gapp and his superiors in our government have decided, but I can promise you this, with all my heart, that what Commissioner Gapp undertakes he will do, honestly and above board, and with no trick or trap. There, that is all I have to say.'

'Mrs Herm, I am sure I speak for all our viewers in the Province, even may I say, for those in other states on our borders, when I express as I do now a profound sense of privilege at having been with you and seen and heard you make this appeal. And now I have something to tell you, which may bring a little light into the darkness that you are in: we have just heard, from the very highest government sources, that Commissioner Gapp is now authorised to include the Jansens with Hans Punt in the negotiations for your husband's release.'

'Oh that is wonderful news, wonderful, wonderful news, I can't tell you . . .'

'There are times, moving times, when every individual, however prominent, has the right to expect privacy from the media, and so we will leave Mrs Herm there, but we are pleased and proud that we were the first to bring her what may be a real ray of hope in her terrible ordeal. But now it is her daughter's turn to make her appeal for the safe return of her father. And I understand she will also reveal to us now, for the first time on Vista, coming to you live, information which has not yet been released and which may have an important bearing on the case. For Victoria Herm's revelations, join us after the break.'

'Welcome back. Miss Herm, I think before you say what you have come to say we should clear up one or two misconceptions there may still be around about you. First. Are you estranged from your parents?'

'No. I live away from home . . .'

'Could you speak up just a little?'

'Oh yes. I'm sorry. I was saying I do not live with my parents as I am an adult and prefer to be on my own. I am very fond of both my parents. I have perhaps a little more in common with my father . . .'

'All right, Miss Herm. No estrangement. Now what about your connection with Red Spectre?'

'There is no connection. As you know, two years ago I gave lodging to two men, one of whom was Hans Punt, but I did not know who they were at the time, and the charges against me were dropped.'

'On Monday it was reported that you may be charged again, this time because of your connection with Roman Punt, a connection which led to the fatal meeting in Wilhelmspark. But that you were released on bail provided by your mother.'

'I'm glad you brought that up. I was not charged and my mother did not provide bail. I was released on Monday, two hours after the police had any legal right to hold me, because I had done nothing at all which came under the anti-terrorist laws, even allowing for the incredibly wide interpretations those laws are capable of. Roman found out my address, it is not a secret, and communicated with me twice. On both occasions I went straight to Commissioner Argand, as in fact Roman had asked me to . . .'

'Why Argand and not Gapp, who, I gather is the Commissioner in charge of the case, and the negotiations with Red Spectre?'

'That's a good question. But I can't answer it now beyond saying that I think you should ask Argand himself, and also ask him to give a full and accurate account of exactly what did happen in Wilhelmspark, and of what passed between him and Roman before Roman was shot.'

'Miss Herm, are you suggesting that we do not know the full story on that?'

'I am. Not only that. The story that we were there to negotiate my father's release is a fabrication . . . but I don't want to go into that now.'

'Miss Herm, I think I should warn you that what you say on this programme is your own responsibility. We do not attack the police here, we believe them to be, on the whole, a fine body of men doing difficult, dangerous work . . .'

'I meant no criticism of the police.'

'But you say their version of what happened in Wilhelmspark is a lie.'

'Yes.'

'Pardon me, Miss Herm, but that is a criticism, to call someone a liar. Unless of course you have no deep convictions about the importance of truth.'

'I don't understand what you are trying to make me say . . .'

'Miss Herm, it is not my practice to make people say things.'

'May I get on now and say what I came here to say?'

'Yes.'

'Well, it's simply this. Early this afternoon shortly after the kidnapping of Hector Macher was announced, my doorbell rang. I have one of those telephone devices which communicates with the outer door on the ground floor. A voice, male, told me I would find an important message in my mail-box. In the box was a note. It was printed with what looked like a child's printing set and it told me to come here, make a fuss, try to get on your programme tonight, because by the time the programme went on the air I would be in possession of important information regarding my father which it was important should be made completely public.'

'And are you now in possession of that information?'

'I think so.'

'You think so? Ah, I see. You have a tape cassette there.'

'Yes. I think it was slipped into my pocket about an hour ago, just before the programme started.'

'So you haven't heard it?'

'No.'

'And you don't know who passed it to you?'

'No.'

'Don't you think you ought to hand it over to the police first?'

'No. I believe my father wants you to play it on your programme first. After that it can go to the police, of course. My father always spoke very highly of Vista – as you know he appeared here twice in the past. He spoke very highly of your integrity and skill.'

'Very well. I also have a very high opinion of your father, a man of great intelligence and drive and with tremendous charm too. And since you say this is the way he wants it, we will hear some of this tape. I suppose we can find a machine on the premises? We can? I can see my producer nodding his head, but I do foresee a moment's delay. Now, if you'd like to hand the tape to the technician to your right . . .'

'No. You can bring the player here. I shall not give up this tape, unless I am forced, and I warn you I shall fight, until I have heard it.'

'Dear me, we are getting a little paranoid, aren't we, and a little hysterical? Never mind . . . My producer says a portable player is on the way. Well, the marvels of modern technology never cease to amaze me. I think I should apologise in advance for what may turn out to be poor reproduction, playing into a microphone as Miss Herm insists rather than feeding it through our sound system which we would have preferred. There, all is ready. You simply slip your cassette . . . yes, you know, every one knows how to work these things, and press this tab, that's right . . .'

"This is Wolfgang Herm speaking, at the request of Green Force, as these people who are holding me insist on calling themselves. Following earlier events today they are anxious that I should make it as clear as I can who it is that I'm with, and prove if I can, that this really is Wolfgang Herm. So they devised this plan to get my voice on Vista. How are you all, on Vista? I have good friends on that programme, especially the producer, and I hope they will give me a full, fair hearing.

"First – for my family, for Vicky and Lena, I am well, well looked after, and apart from the fact that these people are determined to kill me next Monday unless the Spartshaven Project is cancelled, I find I get on rather well with them. They are not, repeat not members past or present of Red Spectre or any . . ."

'Stop. Stop, Miss Herm, here give me that thing, well, pull the plug on her then, there. Miss Herm, calm down. Please calm down. We will go on with the tape, but first let us just check what we have so far. In a minute. My producer says we will go on. First, just tell me this. Is that your father's voice?'

'Yes.'

'Are you sure?'

'Of course I'm sure. Now are you going to let me go on with it? Is the public to hear what I thought you would agree is their right to hear?'

'My producer is signalling yes. All right. It's upon his head. You know how to rewind and restart . . .'

". . . past or present of Red Spectre or any similar organisation, but a group called Green Force, and what they want me to do is establish beyond any reasonable doubt that I really am Wolfgang Herm, to say something no one else could know or something which no one else could possibly say. After some thought I have decided there is only one thing I can do on these lines. First let me say that there is documentary proof of what I am about to assert and I shall produce it as soon as I am released. The things I am going to say are on record. Here goes then. EUREAC, in common with many other firms of its size, has a slush fund and ways of transferring money or shares clandestinely to people who have helped the firm in more or less illegal ways. One of the recipients of substantial sums from this fund received them for his indispensable help in getting the compulsory purchase order for property in Spartshaven through . . ."

'Stop. We must stop there, Miss Herm, we cannot allow what might be . . . I tell you we must stop . . .'

'Clearly our Vista interviewer tonight could not allow the tape to continue to be played without first clearing it with senior colleagues, and since allegations of a possibly criminal nature were about to be made our legal advisers also will have to be consulted.'

'We have just heard that Mrs Lena Herm, who was already in another part of the building during the broadcast of the tape that purports to be a recording of her husband has now made a public statement. She wishes to say that at this stage she is not at all convinced that the voice on the tape was her husband's, in fact rather the reverse. Allowing for the poor reproduction it is her view that the voice was that of a clever mimic.'

20

Leaders and Reports – 1

THE BRABANTER

   The incidents last night on RTVB's Vista ought not to have happened. So much is indisputable. The sight of a respected interviewer brawling physically with a girl barely out of her teens over a portable tape-recorder, promoted no cause, informed no one, was not even entertaining.

   'One has noted, and in these pages condemned, a growing tendency on TV to sensationalise, and over-dramatise issues and events. In Vista's case this tendency has shown itself with increasing frequency in the form of live interviews, and the presentation of unscripted, unrehearsed material. There is no doubt that this element of the unexpected has attracted many viewers back to the programme. Having said that, it remains that last night Vista and RTVB were playing with fire: it is to be hoped that as a result only fingers were burnt – nothing worse.

   'As for the content and provenance of the tape Miss Herm produced – well, it is not for us, nor indeed for anyone else, to comment on that until the police have fully substantiated or denied its authenticity. Wild and uninformed speculation will do no good at all, and may add to the terrible risks that already face the kidnapped

men. Secretary Prinz was perfectly right to issue a statement to this effect late last night and we applaud his
action in doing so, confident that when the time is ripe,
when such a step can be made without endangering
anyone, then and then only the full truth will be revealed.'

SLIK STIEN
'Late last night a tape, similar in appearance as far as
we can tell to that produced and played by Victoria
Herm on Vista was handed in to us here in Vaterloostras.
The first few feet of this second tape carried exactly the
same message, as far as we can recall it, as that played on
Vista. What we print now is a transcript of our tape beginning at the point where last night Vista's interviewer
cut the programme short.

"Here goes then. EUREAC in common with many other
firms of its size has a slush fund. One of the recipients of a substantial sum from this fund received it
for his indispensable help in getting the compulsory purchase order for property in Spartshaven through the
Moot. I am referring to the Deputy Chairman of the
Moot who devised a programme for the passage of the
bill which made concerted and informed opposition to it
virtually impossible.

"He did this by including with the Spartshaven purchase two other purchases which no one in their right
minds would have disputed or opposed. He then sched-
uled the debate to follow an extremely contentious bill
regarding the implementation of European Community
regulations about the marketing of dairy produce. As
might have been expected this first debate went on till
late at night. After the vote was taken thirty-six out of
the fifty-three deputies who make up the Moot went
home . . . or tried to. However, the Deputy Chairman's

plan had now gone too well since no bill can be passed unless there is one third of the Moot sitting, a point which one of the deputies happened to notice just in time. Fortunately two more deputies were found still on the premises and the bill was passed on the nod. It may be remembered that the Deputy Chairman was criticised in some parts of the press at the time but that he issued a statement saying that the Moot was heavily involved with European Community legislation and that the only way of getting through minor and local bills was to run them together.

"Ten days after the passing of this bill the Deputy Chairman received one hundred ordinary shares in EUREAC, now valued at nearly three-quarters of a million gelds. There is no record that these shares were ever paid for. I, Wolfgang Herm, can and will produce evidence, the day after my release, that EUREAC approached the Deputy Chairman, took his advice, set up the deal, and finally rewarded him in the way I have described.

"Finally, I repeat. I am under threat. I do believe the threat will be carried out if the Spartshaven Project gets under way next Monday. Furthermore, if the police do not issue a denial of the reports that I am in the hands of Red Spectre, and if EUREAC do not cancel the Project I will continue to tape information connecting EUREAC with people who hold positions of the highest trust in our Province. That's it for now. This is Wolfgang Herm. My life depends on your believing that. God bless to all who love me.'"

RTVB NEWSFLASH, 1933 HOURS WEDNESDAY 2/ 4/80. RED SPECTRE CLAIMS HECTOR MACHER DEAD. DETAILS IN OUR BULLETIN AT 2100 HOURS.

'We now go straight over to Wilhelmstras and the Home Department where Secretary Prinz is about to make a live statement on the latest developments in the Herm kidnap case.'

'People of Brabt, City and Province, it is my duty, a most unhappy duty to tell you that we have received a communication from Red Spectre. I am not going to read you this communication. I don't think I could. As you would expect it is couched in dictatorial terms and bristles with the disgusting cant and jargon that organisations like Red Spectre love to affect. But the central points, apart from the callow and violent propaganda, are clear enough.

'First – Hector Macher, employee of EUREAC and personal assistant to Wolfgang Herm, is dead. Apparently he was shot in the back of the neck sometime in the early hours of today. Next – Wolfgang Herm will be shot in the same way if all the demands of his captors have not been met in full by midnight on Sunday the sixth of April.

'And now good people, I come to something which grieves and angers me more than I can say. You all know that last night Victoria Herm caused a tape to be played on a television programme which purported to be a recording of her father's voice. While I do not for a moment condone her actions last night, I believe she was acting in good faith.

'Just how wrong she was will become apparent in just one moment. But what I cannot condone, what I utterly condemn was the action of a gutter newspaper of our town in printing earlier this evening what purported to be a transcript of a second version of that tape. For I believe it was the gross irresponsibility of this act that led to a swift and horrible reaction from Red Spectre. For as well as the news of Macher's death the communication from these gangsters also declared that it had become necessary for them to prove to us that they do have the real Wolfgang Herm in their clutches, and so their message was accompanied by a matchbox containing the top joint of a right index-finger. Good people, it did not take long to establish conclusively that this finger was poor Wolfgang Herm's. His fingerprints are on file here in Wilhelmstras. That is all I have to say now, except that it is my earnest wish, as I am sure it is of every decent Brabanter, that the wilder and more irresponsible journalists and television interviewers amongst us will now learn their lesson and think twice before printing or showing anything, anything at all, which might lead to further suffering for Mr Herm.'

'Secretary, a question or two please.'

'Very well.'

'Do the police have any idea where Red Spectre are holding Wolfgang Herm?'

'I'm sorry. I thought I had made it clear. Our first aim now, our *only* aim is to get Wolfgang Herm out and free before he suffers further harm. Once he is safe then of course the hunt for these foul and deluded criminals will be pursued with every means in our power, that goes without saying. But first our *only* concern is Mr Herm's safety.'

'Secretary, what is your opinion of the tape that was played on Vista last night.'

'I said in my statement last night that I would not speculate on its authenticity until I had heard or seen the reports from our experts here. But surely what I have had to tell you tonight, and particularly the evidence of this dismembered finger, such sad evidence, must mean that that tape was spurious — a wicked, silly forgery which will demonstrate once and for all the wrongheadedness, to put it no more strongly than that, of these life people or whatever they call themselves.'

'If that tape does prove to be a forgery, Secretary, will criminal proceedings be taken against the people who made it?'

'Oh definitely. Very certainly. And in the light of the suffering they have brought on Mr Herm, they may expect the very stiffest penalties the law allows.'

RTVB LATE NIGHT NEWS

'Information is just reaching us of an explosion and fire in Vaterloostras. It is believed that the offices of *Slik Stien*, the newspaper which earlier today printed what purported to be a transcript of the tape . . .'

21

A Matter of Conscience

Looking over a resumé of these reports and events in Thursday's edition of *The Brabanter*, Argand felt relieved. A corner of his mind murmured that this was an unworthy emotion – he should not enjoy the fruits of others' suffering in quite so plain a way, yet still, there it was, the death of Macher, the mutilation of Herm, both so clearly at the hands of Red Spectre. This spelled for him the end of what had become a horrid, obsessive nightmare. The memory, the ghost almost of Roman Punt which had appeared to him every night since the shooting, floating into his mind just as he was dozing off to sleep, the pale face with deep-set eyes, the voice: '. . . at least report me accurately. Red Spectre does not have Wolfgang Herm' would now be exorcised and the memory too of Emil Schneider with his neck twisted and his head cushioned in garbage, surely that too would no longer trouble his dreams. He folded back his paper, sipped his coffee, and unwrapped the cube of butter on his plate. Already he had forgotten the generous, creamy slices of *beurre en motte* whose disappearance had so upset him less than a fortnight before.

As he stepped out of the Louis Bonaparte the waiter remarked to himself that His Excellency the Commissioner had almost smiled at him.

In his office he drew up an agenda for the final meeting concerned with the Euro-Cup tie; briskly rejected an appeal from the Anti-Fascist League to hold an official demonstration against the bombing of the *Slik Stien* offices on the grounds that to allow it would appear to give government assent to the view that fascists of some sort were responsible; and then settled down to read a report from the City Architects' Department on a proposed development of the university campus. His main concern in this matter was that the access roads should not easily be barricaded. The student riots of '68 had inflicted a nervous breakdown and early retirement on the last Commissioner but one, and Argand had no intention of going the same way.

Then his secretary buzzed him.

'I have a Pastor Martin Kant on the phone for you, Excellency.'

'If it's to do with the Herm case tell him I'm no longer concerned with it.'

A pause.

'He won't say what it's to do with, but is very insistent that he should speak to you.'

'Very well. Put him through.'

'Argand? Kant here. Pastor Kant. I have to see you.'

'My secretary told you . . .'

'Never mind. I have to see you. It is a matter of extreme importance that I should see you.'

Argand looked at his appointments book.

'Today I am very busy. If you could call here in the late afternoon, say . . .'

'I should much prefer to see you in your own home. Much prefer it. And it should be this evening at the latest. If you will give me your address I will call at seven o'clock.'

'Pastor, I am not in the habit . . .'

'My dear man. What do I have to say to you? What

can I say to you on the phone? Just that this is a matter of the greatest urgency, that when you have heard what I have to say, you will realise that to have refused me would have been a terrible dereliction of duty on your part. Will that do?'

Argand's high brows rose another millimetre. 'I am not to be coerced, Pastor. I will give you two minutes tonight at seven, and if you haven't convinced me in that time that I should give you more, I shall show you the door.' And he gave his address.

Uneasy apprehension, like the drizzle off the North Sea that spread over the Province during the day, chilled Argand's euphoria, left him irritable and preoccupied.

The Pastor turned in front of Argand, leant forward with his gloved hands on the high-backed chair in the middle of the sitting-room, and looked down at the policeman.

'This morning I saw Wolfgang Herm. He still had all his fingers,' he said.

For a moment Argand felt dizzy, then he took a deep breath.

'Herm is nothing to do with me now. I think you should go straight to Commissioner Gapp. He is entirely in charge of the affair.'

'Do you believe what I have just said?'

'No, of course I do not. You must be the victim of some delusion or hoax. Nevertheless I do not doubt your sincerity, and granted that you believe what you have just said, you should go to Commissioner Gapp.'

'Suppose that for a moment I am right. That I have seen Wolfgang Herm. Suppose that he is in the hands of some people calling themselves the Green Force and that they want to halt the Spartshaven Project, suppose that all this business about Red Spectre and a missing finger is a pack of lies, then do you think Commissioner Gapp would give me any sort of hearing at all?'

'I don't know what you mean. But I reiterate. I would very much prefer it if you took your tale to the right quarters.'

'Will you listen to me while I tell you what I mean?'

Argand shrugged. Faced again with the tall, intense pastor he felt the doubts flood back, the dark fears that had been plaguing him. Kant took off his hat and put it on the table. Rain glistened on it.

'This morning a friend called for me and took me to the place where Wolfgang Herm has been since he disappeared. I talked with him. He is now in fear of his life, indeed feels that his life depends upon it being speedily proved that he cannot possibly be in the clutches of Red Spectre, and not only proved but the proof published. It is now very close to the time when the Spartshaven Project will become irreversible, when the earth-movers will destroy the village and fill in the tidal gap to the marsh. He fears that the day that happens they will kill him. This is what he asked me to say to you.'

'You cannot possibly expect me to believe this. To believe this would mean to believe that Gapp, Secretary Prinz, Kratt, and God knows who else have been duped on a quite extraordinary scale . . .'

'That is not the only possible explanation of what is happening. You asked me what I meant when I asked you if I thought Commissioner Gapp would give me any sort of hearing. What I meant was that I believe he and the others you have just mentioned are part of a conspiracy to protect the Spartshaven Project against the . . .'

'Oh forgive me, Pastor, but you are talking the most absurd nonsense, quite ridiculous. Now I really am going to ask you to leave. And you are right about one thing. I don't believe Gapp will listen to you, but not for the reason you give.'

Kant's cold eyes caught Argand's and the policeman flinched away.

'And if you are going to accuse me of being part of this so-called conspiracy, I can assure you that I most definitely am not, that no such conspiracy exists, and if you persist in saying it does, I shall take leave to doubt your sanity.'

Kant moved the chair he had been leaning on and without asking sat down. He leant across the table towards Argand.

'You say you are now nothing to do with the Herm case. That you have been taken off it.'

'That's right.'

'Do you know what happened to that address book you took from my church?'

'It was sent back to you, wasn't it? I assumed it was sent back to you once it became quite clear that Herm has been kidnapped by Red Spectre.'

'No, it has not been sent back to me. And every household in that book has been searched from top to bottom. Several of the people in it have been taken to State Security Police Headquarters and questioned, sometimes harshly. Several of them complain that they believe that they are under surveillance and that their phones are tapped. In the last two days a second wave of searches and harassment has started and EUREAC Health Guards have been assisting the State Security Police. Do you know why this has been happening? Can you think of a better reason than that someone in Wilhelmstras still believes, in spite of chopped off fingers and negotiations with Red Spectre, that Herm is held by someone connected with the League for Life? That's why these searches have gone on, invasion of privacy, molestation, everything you can think of except outright brutality. There is no other explanation.'

'You are wrong about this. Quite wrong about this. I had no idea that investigations into the people in your address book were still going on, but I am not altogether surprised if they are. The first report I had, showed that various offences had been committed and I imagine that what you are talking about is a follow-up to what was discovered then.'

Kant was sarcastic: 'Ah, I see. Thank you for putting me right on this, Commissioner. The State Security Police, at this time when a terrorist organisation is murdering and maiming prominent citizens, has nothing better to do than investigate an elderly couple who continue to brew their own wine made from gorse flowers in contravention of some new regulation emanating from Brussels; and have held an ex-schoolteacher for questioning for well over twenty-four hours because he has been giving lessons to four of his neighbours' children as well as his own. Tell me Commissioner. Did you ever ask yourself why Emil Schneider was murdered?'

'He was not murdered. He fell off his fire-escape when under the influence of a massive dose of barbiturates and LSD.'

'That's not what Wolfgang Herm believes.'

'You mean I suppose the man who is duping you. The man you say you met this morning, who is impersonating Herm.'

Kant injected a note of assumed patience into his voice, as if he were talking to an obstinate child.

'Wolfgang Herm believes that his friend Emil Schneider died whilst being questioned. He was being questioned by people who believed he could tell them where Herm is.'

For a time Argand had thought much the same. He felt harried, bewildered.

'I knew Emil,' Kant continued. 'He drank occasionally. He took some tranquillizer, a mild one, Librium I believe, whenever he felt under stress. He did not take drugs.'

Kant stood up. He continued speaking and as he did so, he began to take off his gloves.

'Commissioner, do you still have access to the file on the Herm kidnap?'

The answer was yes, he did have access. All the files in Wilhelmstras were available on request to a Commissioner. However he would have to ask Gapp for it, and he felt reluctant to do so. But he agreed he could see it.

'I suppose it will have Wolfgang Herm's fingerprints in it? And a print taken from this finger they say arrived in a matchbox?'

'I should be very surprised indeed if they were not in the file.'

'Then I'd like you to take this down to Wilhelmstras tonight, and compare it with the prints there.' Kant now pulled a card from his pocket and pushed it across the table to the Commissioner.

Argand read: 'I hereby swear before witnesses, including Pastor Kant of the Church of Inner Salvation, that the print alongside this statement was taken from my right index-finger, and that I freely allowed this print to be taken. This was done on Thursday 3rd April, 1980 in the place where the Green Force has held me for the last thirteen days. Signed: Wolfgang Herm. Witnessed: Martin Kant.'

Beside it was a fingerprint in purple ink, the same shade as that used in the first kidnap note.

'This doesn't prove anything you know,' said Argand. 'Of course it won't match the prints in the file. All this proves is the lengths to which these people are prepared to go to deceive you.'

'Nevertheless, I do wish you would take this card and make the comparison. I think you should. I think your conscience will tell you you should. And your conscience will tell you what to do about the result.'

22

Delusions

Conscience or no, Argand refused to go back to
Wilhelmstras that night. Later in the evening he wished
that he had done. He found that his mind would not let
the case rest, that the Pastor had stirred up sediments
that had begun to settle, memories that had lain dor-
mant. Of course there was nothing at all in what the
Pastor had said – that was clear. The man was a dupe.
No doubt he was sincere, and intelligent, also clearly pos-
sessed of a very strong moral will, and very strong convictions about right and wrong. All this Argand admired
intensely. Kant was the sort of man his father had been,
the sort of man, though without the faith, that he hoped
he was. And the Pastor stood for values that had dominated Argand's childhood, which, in the way a child does,
he had assumed to be unassailable – values that he now
saw degraded, neglected and worst of all abused all
round him. He had forbidden Mrs Esslin to buy a brand
of brown bread he had always assumed to be especially
wholesome when it launched an advertising campaign
with the slogan: 'This is your Daily Bread'.

But Kant was a fanatic. You could see the man was
consumed by some internal fire, you could see it in his
burning eyes, in his ascetic but hectic cheeks, in his tall
thin frame. Well, you can't budge a fanatic, Argand

thought, a fanatic will cling to beliefs against all sense, all proofs that he is wrong, and Argand knew Kant was wrong about this false Herm he thought he had seen. He was probably wrong too in his attitude to the Spartshaven Project; in his support, no, it was more than support, it was fervent fostering of a campaign of civil disobedience against it. Yes, thought Argand (who believed in hierarchy, who believed that the great and the rich and the powerful are also good, who believed this in the face of a thousand instances a day to the contrary), the fanatic Kant is wrong there – no matter how good a man he is, he is wrong to ally himself with druggists, dropouts, demonstrators and the like, and moreover, he has brought his church into disrepute by doing so.

What worried Argand most that night was the death of Emil Schneider. He relived his interview with the artist, his shock at the sight of that foul painting, his dislike of the man's drinking and taking pills – even if they were only Librium. He had said, what was it? that the day had been a nightmare. Why had he been so upset? Kratt had been there of course, but to offer the artist a commission, a very good commission it had sounded, that would bring him reputation, and no doubt a very fat fee. But when Schneider had opened the door he had said, 'This must be to do with poor Wolfgang's disappearance. I have already one guest in this connection.' And then after talking about the commission, (which Schneider so horribly parodied in his obscene cartoon), Kratt had gone on at some length about how the Project could not be stopped, about how Herm would know that, and what was it? that the whole board of EUREAC could be machine-gunned and still the Project would go ahead. Why had he said all that? Well, why not? It was no doubt true.

Then the day the artist died. The two chairs facing the bed, the indentation in the bed. Doctor Dael's assertion that LSD and sodium amytal make an efficient truth drug, and then the way he back-pedalled in his report. And where was the forensic report? Why had Argand never seen it? Of course it was odd, a mistake that he had seen any of the files after he had been taken off the case and reprimanded, (and that rankled, that still hurt quite bitterly), but why not the forensic – if any reports at all, then why not all of them? Schneider had vomited. Dael had been sure of that. The cadaver on the white slab, the stomach and upper intestine neatly dissected, proved it – yet there was no mention of this in Dael's final report. He had vomited, and cleared up afterwards, leaving the bathroom spotless, and then he had gone into a near-coma in which he had thrown himself over the fire-escape rail and broken his neck. Of course if there had been a forensic report, now suppressed, that said there had been two other men there *at the time* . . . which, thought Argand, is how I interpreted what I saw, then the whole thing becomes more real. Also more the way Kant saw it. Or rather, the man Kant is duped into thinking is Wolfgang Herm.

Herm was a "friend" of Schneider. A "friend". How Argand hated, abhorred all that sort of thing. And everything connecting Wolfgang with Schneider had been moved from the flat. Everything except the record with the message on the sleeve: 'This might remind you of me. Play it if you feel lonely.' Something by Mendelssohn. Someone had taken everything else. The police, Argand assumed. His colleagues. Here again was a contradiction, for that must mean that after all they – that is Gapp or Stent – connected the murder, no, *death*, with Herm; and the official reports so far, and therefore the inquest which would be based on them, avoided anything at all that might lead to that connection.

Of course Mrs Herm would not want it brought out. Perhaps the stuff had been taken at her request, and the relationship between her husband and the artist hushed up. Yes, that seemed likely. And highly understandable on her part, Argand thought. In her position he would have wanted to do the same. But he could not condone the fact that his colleagues had abetted her. Not at all. If ever that came out there would be a few more reprimands flying around, that was for sure.

And having drunk nearly a tumbler of dry plum-flavoured gin, instead of his usual thimbleful, Argand went to bed and mercifully slept, though in his dreams Victoria reiterated again and again: 'Did Kratt kill him? Did Kratt kill Emil so he wouldn't say where my Father is?'; though Roman Punt bled swiftly to death out of the hole in the top of his head more than once and Schneider spat at him: 'You should realise that acts of love offend you.'

In the morning he sat for an hour in his office doing nothing very much, trying to make up his mind to ask Commissioner Gapp for the Herm kidnap file. His relief was like a child's in its intensity when at about half-past ten Gapp rang him and invited him to have it, that is if he wanted it. 'The point is this,' the cool military voice explained, 'I expect to have the whole business cleared up tomorrow or on Sunday. Herm home and free, and everything back to normal. But then comes the paper work, making out our reports and so on, and it occurred to me that you'll have to do one on the early part of the business, and I shall be trying to get mine done, so we'll be in each other's way. So I thought you might like to get down to your side of things now. That is if you want to.'

Scarcely believing his luck Argand agreed, and ten minutes later two clerks arrived carrying bundles of dossiers and box files. However, everything was neatly labelled and dated, and it did not take him long to find the fingerprints of Wolfgang Herm and of the severed finger. They matched. Unmistakably they matched. And Herm's prints, taken from his house, were sworn to by Lena Herm as having come from objects in his private suite of rooms where only he and Mustafa could have touched them. Mustafa's prints were there and sworn to, so there was no possible doubt. Everything had been done properly, signed by the officers responsible, done on the correct forms, and dated 26th March.

Which, thought Argand, is a day later than it should be. He looked back through his desk diary. Monday the 24th it had all started, the day he had gone first to EUREAC and then the Herm house. Tuesday the 25th he had gone to Spartshaven because the Green Force note had arrived, leaving his subordinates to go back to the Herm house to do the fingerprinting, to start going through his financial papers and so on. Tuesday night was the night of the first Red Spectre letter, and on Wednesday, not Tuesday the Herm household had been fingerprinted and Wolfgang's prints attested to. Why a day late? No doubt there was a very simple explanation, oh, no doubt there was. Argand rubbed his face in the palms of his hands. This was absurd. He thought back to another conversation he had had the previous awful Sunday, a conversation which the shooting in Wilhelmspark had put right out of his head. 'In my job I have to know a bit about this sort of thing,' he had said to his son. 'I have to know what a paranoid schizophrenic is. The condition is primarily characterised by unrealistic, illogical thinking, delusions of being persecuted.' *If* there is a simple explanation, he thought, then I am on my way to being a paranoid schizophrenic, and no wonder with all this mess.

It took him some time and several telephone calls to establish what had happened. At first it seemed that the fingerprinting had been done twice, on both Tuesday and Wednesday. But then it appeared that the detectives had gone to the house on the Tuesday to do it, but Mrs Lena Herm had been either out or too busy, helping the other young detective to go through her husband's affairs, to do the witnessing that was required, so they had gone back on the Wednesday to finish off the formalities. Establishing this not only took time, it wasted time too, other people's time. As he pursued the enquiry, Argand found he was becoming more and more apologetic, that the people he was questioning on the phone were becoming more and more irritated, and finally he was left feeling foolish and uncomfortably aware that he had behaved in a way which was not unlike his wife's behaviour six years before when the first symptoms of madness had appeared.

It is not surprising then that he was not at all inclined to pursue the one or two other things that continued to bother him – most notably the fact that the forensic report on Schneider's flat was still missing; nor was there any forensic report on Kant's church – which there should have been, even if it had proved to be completely negative, as it no doubt had. If I try to track that down, Argand thought, they really will come for me with a strait-jacket.

Kant phoned him ten minutes after he had returned home. Argand told him that the fingerprint he had given him the night before was spurious, quite certainly spurious. No doubt at all. There was a pause, then Kant said: 'There has been a third wave of searches in Spartshaven and of other people in my address book. Did you know?'

'No.' But it occurred to him that he had not seen the book in the file.

'This has been worse than all the others. We reckon it must have involved about two hundred policemen of whom at least half were EUREAC Health Guards. It started about an hour after I left you last night, and is still going on. Property has been damaged, children disturbed and upset, and I believe that there have been at least three beatings. I myself have been under constant surveillance. You should ask yourself why, Commissioner. You should ask yourself why these things are happening.'

'I don't know why they are happening. Why should I *believe* that they are happening?'

He heard Kant draw a deep breath. 'Why don't you come and see for yourself, Commissioner?'

'I'm sorry, Pastor. I have no intention of doing that. If there is any police activity out there, it's nothing to do with me and it would be quite improper of me to interfere. And I'm sure if there is any you are exaggerating its extent wildly, and totally misunderstanding its purpose.'

'I see,' and the phone went dead.

Now Argand had another thing to worry about. How had Kant known his number? It was not listed. Only his son, the Hearts Haven Nursing home, and the office in Wilhelmstras knew it. He prowled miserably about his room for nearly an hour obsessively trying to remember where Kant had stood. The Pastor was tall – was his eyesight good, could he have read the number off the phone itself, which stood on the sideboard? The obsession would not shift, and at last he picked up the phone book and found the number of the Church of Inner Salvation, Spartshaven.

A recorded voice answered him.

'The number caller requires is now unobtainable through reasons beyond our control. The number caller requires is now unobtainable. . . .'

Two hours later he rang his doctor and said he was under strain, would like a sleeping draught. His doctor agreed to make one up, would bring it round.

'No, no,' Argand replied. 'I'll come for it. The five minute walk may do me good.'

On his way to and from his doctor's house he began to feel that he was being followed. He could not decide which frightened him more – the possibility that he *was* being followed or the possibility that he was now subject to paranoid delusions, even auditory hallucinations.

The next day, Saturday, the weather cleared, the sun shone, the daffodils, now fully out, nodded in window-boxes and municipal flowerbeds, the chestnuts looked splendid, the fresh lime green of new leaves glowing against the greys and blacks of the anonymous buildings in Wilhelmstras. As he mounted the steps into the build-ing, Argand said to himself that he would not after all come out again a moment after and follow the man in a pale blue mackintosh who had followed him from the Louis Bonaparte: it was too absurd to think that the man behind him had been any different at all from the hundred or so other pedestrians that must have come along the route, on the same pavement, just as they did every day at that time. Still, there was no doubt, this Herm business had had a very nasty effect on him, and he would be glad indeed if today or tomorrow it was all finished, as Gapp had promised.

He worked hard for an hour or so, made one of two ad-justments to the arrangements for the Euro-Cup tie, and collaborated with his colleagues in the Rural Guard over another matter that had turned up. A procession of daf-fodil growers threatened to drive their tractors into the centre of the town and dump part of their crop in protest against Community regulations that had laid down that all daffodils with stems of less than twenty-eight centi-metres were to be class two. The Brabt growers specialise in a small daffodil which, they say, combines the delicacy and lasting qualities of the wild mountain jonquil with the richness of colour associated with cultivated varieties. The Rural Guard put him in mind of what Kant had said – that the shanties in Spartshaven had been searched by State Security Police. It should have been a job for the Rural Guard, or at any rate shared with them. No doubt the pastor was mistaken, had perhaps mistaken the Rural Guards for the EUREAC Health Guards he had said were there.

At half-past ten he was through – with a couple of hours left he reluctantly decided that he had better get on with his report on his part in the Herm case, as Gapp had suggested he should. It was best at any rate to get it done while it was still fresh in his mind. Never put off to tomorrow what you can do today, had been one of his mother's constantly reiterated sayings, and the hundred proverbs that she had of a similar nature, expressing virtues like thrift, hard work, care, thoroughness and so on that she had learnt in a farmhouse not four kilometres from the North Sea, were as deeply embedded in his mind as the teachings of the Church of Inner Salvation.

His secretary told him that the file had gone back to Commissioner Gapp's office. There a duty-clerk told him that Commissioner Gapp was not in, and that he could not release the file without Gapp's permission. With the particular blend of frustration and anger that had characterised so many moments in the early part of the case, Argand used his phone like a weapon to track down his colleague, who turned out to be at Secretary Prinz's house which was on the hill behind the castle, not far from the Herms'.

'Gapp? Look, would you mind very much giving your office a ring and asking them to send down the Herm file. I have come in this morning especially to finish my report, as you requested, and find that your people have taken it back.'

'Oh I am sorry, Argand. I had quite decided that you would be far too busy today with your football match, so I took it without asking. . . .'

'I understand. But in fact I do have the time, so if you could ring your clerk and ask him to release it . . .'

'No. I'm afraid you don't understand. Our final preparations for the exchange of Herm for Punt and the Jansens are going ahead. For reasons I won't go into on the phone, Secretary Prinz's house is being used as the Headquarters for this operation and the file is here. I'm sorry old chap, but you'll just have to wait until Monday.'

For half an hour Argand managed to invent work for himself, then realised that he was becoming more and more conscious of the silences around him, and the muffled rumble of the traffic outside. He felt low and dispirited. Although his doctor had assured him that the sleeping draught he had prescribed was very mild, non-addictive and had no unpleasant after-effects, he felt heavy, slightly too hot and a headache hovered behind his eyes. He might, he thought, be a little constipated. Certainly that is what his mother would have said — exercise might do the trick.

In fact he did not want to go back to his flat, and he could not or would not explain to himself why this was. Instead he decided to go for a brisk walk, and then perhaps treat himself to a better lunch than he usually had, perhaps at the Louis Bonaparte.

The streets were busy with week-end shoppers, and in Rinusplatz he came upon about twenty Scots. They wore tartan floppy berets, long scarves that went down almost to their feet, and they were drunk, with bottles of duty-free whisky sticking out of their overcoat pockets. 'Keep right on to the end of the road, keep right on to the end,' they were singing over and over again, as if they had forgotten the rest of the words. One of them was trying to ask a young policeman where their hotel was, but it was clear that the policeman could not understand him, nor he the policeman. Argand intervened and sorted out the difficulty – his English was quite good. 'Thank you, my verrry good Sor,' said the Scot, making a sort of half bow accompanied by a flourish of his scarf, 'for shedding light in darrrk corrrners, a light to lighten the gentiles you are, sor,' and Argand went on his way.

To avoid the crowds he headed down towards the river and so on to the bridge, heading for the park, but half way across he stopped, suddenly afflicted with a feeling of anxiety and revulsion that was almost sickening. In front of him was the pond with its river gods and water nymphs, above it the dry cascade climbed to the fairy castle. To the left, grassy slopes climbed to shrubberies and pines and the wooden bench where Roman Punt had crashed into the daffodils. Argand turned brusquely and strode back into the town. For the first hundred metres or so he found it was he who was following a man in a light blue raincoat, instead of the other way round, and he pulled a wry face at this continuing evidence of the uncertainty of the state of his mind.

He lunched off *Wiener schnitzel*, a half-bottle of Moselle, and an ice-cream, finished up with coffee, and took as long as he could over it. But in the end he had to pay the bill and go home – there was nothing else for it; then on the way home it occurred to him, for the first time in four years, that he might go to a cinema – he would have to buy a paper to find out the programmes. At the kiosk a newspaper board announced: 'SLIK STIEN – SPECIAL EDITION, NEW REVELATIONS ABOUT EUREAC.' He ignored it, bought the paper he needed and went to see a re-showing of *The French Connection* – everything else was pornographic or for children. He found the plot too simple but the unravelling of it unnecessarily obscure, and the scene where the girlfriend of the second detective walks about her flat with no clothes on gratuitously offensive. The chase at the end did not excite him, and the morality of the detective played by Gene Hackman depressed him.

He spent the evening watching television quiz games with infantile questions and moronic competitors, and a 'show' centred around two 'personalities', a French male singer and an English woman, both in their fifties and simpering coyly at eachother as if they were seventeen. They held hands when they sang a love song together and Argand sipped his dry gin. After the show came the news.

23

Leaders and Reports – 2

SLIK STIEN

'Two days ago it seemed we would never publish
again. Two days ago, quite frankly, many of us did not
want ever to publish again. It is a very frightening
moment when the glass window of your first-floor office
is shattered without warning by a heavy metal canister
about half a metre long, with a diameter of about twenty
centimetres. It is even more frightening when you realise
that the thing is fizzing and pumping out a thin stream
of white smoke. Then the moment after it has exploded,
while one's heart is still pounding and one's bowels still
feel insecure, one feels an odd mixture of emotions: relief
that one is alive, anger that one is hurt, perhaps seriously, and above all a strong desire never, never to have
to live through the experience again.

'But one recovers. And perhaps it is the anger that
lasts longest. That and a sort of bitter pride that this is
the ultimate proof that one is doing the right thing. If
what we publish can provoke this sort of response then
we are on the right lines, we are attacking precisely the
sort of people who ought to be attacked – people who are
not above employing thugs and bullies when they find
that official ways of stopping us are closed, and that
there is still protection under the laws of the Province for

those of us who are concerned to print the truth and the whole truth as early and as accurately as we can.

'We had not expected to go to press before next Monday but yesterday evening another tape cassette was delivered here purporting to be from the kidnapped millionaire industrialist, Wolfgang Herm. This time we saw the man who brought it. He was tall, dressed in a long tweed coat and with a trilby hat to match. Round his neck was a woollen muffler. He was thin, had high, pinkish cheek-bones, and deep-set eyes, looked respectable.

'After he had gone (the police have asked us why we did not follow him – the answer is that the youngest and most fit of us for such a job is still on crutches and likely to lose three toes as a result of the bomb), we played the tape. Again it is not our business to speculate on whether or not it is spurious, beyond repeating what we said last time – that a member of our staff who knows Herm is convinced that it is him. To which we would add that the laboratories beneath Wilhelmstras have yet to publish their report on the first tape, and until they do, and show that it is not Herm in these tapes, and produce the evidence for saying it is not, we will continue to believe it might be.

'If these tapes are genuine then we are faced with an extremely serious situation, just how serious will be seen when this second transcript is read. It is not mere journalistic rhetoric to talk now about Brabt's Watergate, it is a matter of sober fact. Meanwhile, genuine or not, we feel it is our duty to print, and to take the consequences. Our legal advisers have warned us that we may be liable for prosecution under the libel laws – certainly we would be in, say, Great Britain, but here we believe we can plead justifiably that we are printing in good faith and in the public interest and thus remain within our Province's more liberal laws. What other consequences there may be we will also face with what courage we can muster. At least the shock will not be quite so terrible if we are bombed a second time.'

THE SECOND TAPE

"This is Wolfgang Herm again, the real Wolfgang Herm. Following the reports that Red Spectre have killed Hector Macher, and severed my finger, my actual captors have asked me to do another tape, which they hope will convince police and public that I am the real Wolfgang Herm. They discussed severing a finger in imitation of the so-called Red Spectre, but decided that this would achieve nothing. They believe that records of my fingerprints in the possession of the police must have already been altered.

"In place of savagery they have asked that I should put on this tape information of a sort that cannot possibly be denied, and which no one, apart from the other principals in EUREAC, could possibly know. I have done my best — partly out of fear of what will happen to me if the Spartshaven Project goes forward on Monday, partly because I am beginning to feel unsure myself about that Project, and am not unwilling to go on making revelations like those I am about to make, until the Project is cancelled.

"Right then; for the second time, here goes.

"EUREAC is effectively ruled by an inner board, a cabinet. Its members are Baron de Merle, my cousin by marriage, who is also the President of the Company, Joseph Dax who was once finance minister of the Province and later our chief minister at Brussels, Paul Brandt who is in charge of the River Flot Plant, Christian Kratt, who is now Company Secretary, and my wife Lena Herm, née de Merle. Henry Macher sits in on most meetings as secretary, though all meetings are taped. Paul Brandt only attends those meetings when technical decisions have to be made, my wife only when her cousin feels he needs her vote to be sure of getting his way.

"Almost exactly four years ago Paul Brandt brought to a meeting a detailed analysis of the extent and nature of the effluent that the new processes we were then planning to implement would produce. It was clear that no government would permit the discharge of these effluents into the environment by conventional means, and it was thus out of that meeting that the Spartshaven Project was born, for that project is nothing more nor less than an excuse to build the vast concrete tanks or reservoirs of slowly decaying effluent that Brandt believed we needed if the planned expansion of our operations was to go ahead.

"Two years and two months ago it was clear that we would not be able to avoid a public enquiry into the Project, since opposition had turned out to be far better informed and far better supported than we had anticipated. The inner board met to discuss this crisis. Present were myself, my wife, Kratt, de Merle and Dax. After some discussion Dax declared that he would be able to use his influence in government circles to ensure that Judge Sterling would be appointed Official Enquirer. He intimated that some money would have to be put out to secure this appointment but that once secured we need no longer fear the result of the enquiry. The reason for his optimism was that he could produce proof that in 1943 Judge Sterling, then a Provincial Investigating Magistrate in the Wilhelmspark Banlieu, not only collaborated with the Nazis, but collaborated enthusiastically in the naming and rounding up of people of Jewish descent in his area, and later in other areas of the City. The inner board then authorised Dax to secure, by whatever means he thought suitable and at whatever expense might prove to be necessary, the appointment of Judge Sterling to the enquiry. The fact that the enquiry passed the Spartshaven Project with only minor recommendations for adjustments to the original plan was the largest and most irrevocable blow to informed opposition of the Project, and without it the other legislation needed, as for instance the compulsory purchase of dwelling places in Spartshaven that I mentioned in my first tape, could never have gone through. In a meeting that took place eighteen months ago the inner board recognised the importance of Dax's contribution to the success of the enquiry by voting to double his holding of company stock and making his purchase of a villa in Jamaica a charge upon the company.

"I can substantiate these allegations, and will do so on my release, if not before, by producing the original tapes of these meetings, which have just recently come into the possession of the Green Force who now hold me. If the police and EUREAC make no move at all towards acknowledging that this tape you are now listening to is genuine, I shall be forced to record a third. This, using inner board tapes, will show how Christian Kratt and a certain Brabanter official now a senior policeman but then seconded to NATO gained NATO contracts which will absorb some expected expansion of EUREAC's productivity capability following the implementation of the Spartshaven Project."

RTVE NEWS SATURDAY 5TH APRIL 2100 HOURS

'Commissioner Gapp, of the State Security Police, has just issued the following statement from Wilhelmstras.

'At 1900 hours today, Saturday 5th April, the planned exchange of members of the Red Spectre terrorist gang, who were serving life sentences for acts of terrorism, for Wolfgang Herm, Vice-president of EUREAC, was put into train. During the course of the exchange, which had been planned with the greatest care to avoid any incident, a member of the Red Spectre gang

214

attempted to shoot Mr Herm, just at the critical point of the exchange. In the ensuing gun-fight Hans Punt, Susan Jansen and Pier Jansen suffered gunshot wounds. Hans Punt's body has been found, but the Jansens are so far still at large though believed to be seriously hurt. Mr Herm also received a minor wound, but is not in any danger. He has however suffered extreme privations while a prisoner of the Red Spectre gang, including the mutilation earlier reported, and is now being taken care of in a private ward of Brabt State Hospital. His wife, Mrs Lena Herm, and his cousin, Baron de Merle are at his bedside.

'The Commissioner congratulates all the members of his force who put their lives at risk tonight and who acted with great coolness, skill and courage at a very critical moment.

'Full details of these incidents will be put before the public just as soon as they have been fully analysed. It is hoped that Mr Herm will be well enough to give a short press conference some time tomorrow.'

24

Conversion

Sports Union Brabt Stad is a modern concrete stadium elegantly designed with generous cantilevers which give it a light, open appearance. It holds thirty thousand in numbered seats and a further ten thousand standing at each end on terraces behind the goals. When Sports Union plays a British team the visiting supporters remain in one of the terrace blocks: seats cost anything from five to twenty English pounds and British football supporters still come predominantly from the lower paid section of the working class.

The amenities for players, directors and their guests are sumptuous and include a large reception room where the directors entertain officials of the visiting team before the kick-off of every home match. Also among those invited are the police officers responsible for public order on the day, any 'personalities' from the entertainment world who happen to be in the area and any senior members of EUREAC who may care to come. These last are invited because a substantial part of the capital put up for the stadium came from EUREAC. EUREAC workers are given priority for season tickets and so on, and the company runs coaches for them from the housing estate near the River Flot Plant.

On Sunday 7th April the kick-off was timed for seven

o'clock, and the reception started at half-past five. Shortly after that time Argand stood in the long broad window with a glass of orange juice in his hand (he did not like champagne or whisky which were the alternatives) and looked out over the still empty seats towards the terrace behind the goal to his left. That is where the trouble will start, he thought, for there spectators were already flooding in — all Scots, all dressed absurdly in tartan gear with red and yellow scarves, all three parts intoxicated but whether on whisky or football was difficult to say. It could hardly be whisky, Argand thought, since most of them had arrived the day before and would long since have finished their one litre of duty-free, and in Brabt one couldn't get a bottle under seven pounds.

Already they were chanting, already those who had gone right down to the level of the pitch were testing the iron cage which hemmed them in from the rest of the stadium. Argand's men stood stolidly in a line between the fence and the pitch, armed only with truncheons. If the fence goes they will be swept aside, Argand thought, and it will then be a case for the six bus-loads of riot police with helmets, shields and nerve gas who wait silently in the car park but can reach the pitch through the tunnel in a matter of seconds. It is after the match that the trouble will come — especially if Kirkshield Wanderers lose on a disputable decision.

Behind Argand the brightly-lit rom was filling with the directors' guests. There were exotic girls in furs, provocative dresses and absurd hair styles. At least two of them had appeared in the centre pages of *Slik Prik*, and one was in the satirical nude show Argand's men had had to close the night before when it was invaded by Scots. There were middle-aged men who wore their hair long though their heads were already bald on top, and who wore bright suits with huge flares — on one of these

Stent had unsuccessfully tried to pin a dope-pushing charge. There was a pop singer in dark glasses and a white suit with a huge wide-brimmed hat that he would not take off, and there was the chanteuse who was to sing the Province's entry in the Eurovision Song Contest in a week's time. Near her was the Brabanter novelist most likely to win the *Prix de Flot* next autumn – an untidy bearded man whose teeth needed attention, who wore an old leather coat and patched jeans and who affected to be a modern Thersites. There were lithe but muscly young men also in bright suits, who kept silent, drank orange juice, and eyed the girls who eyed them back – these were the members of the Sports Union squad who would not be playing today. They and all the officials of the club were wearing black armbands out of respect for Hector Macher who had been a club director and a very keen supporter – or so it was said. However, mourning had dampened no one's spirits and Argand could not remember that he had ever seen Macher there.

Secretary Prinz, however, was a familiar figure – he boasted a passionate enthusiasm for the game – and at the moment was the centre of a sycophantic group of burghers and their wives who offered suggestions of refined brutality about what should be done to any surviving members of Red Spectre, who attempted to cap each other's wit on the subject of the League for Life and the Spartshaven shanty dwellers, and who congratulated Secretary Prinz in tones of warm, rich sincerity on his handling of the business. A Trade Union leader who was drinking Scotch and iced water at the rate of a tumbler every ten minutes was particularly insistent that the full weight of his men was right behind the government in this; they might have their differences in other areas, ha, ha, but in the matter of terrorism Secretary Prinz could rely on the support of the working classes, at least that section of them which he, the Trade Union Leader, was privileged to represent. And through them all passed large silent men, dressed as waiters, carrying trays of champagne and scotch, of lumpen fish eggs disguised as caviare and spread on leathery toast, and small spicy sausages, the speciality of the Province. These were EUREAC Health Guards, loaned to the club for the day.

At five to six Secretary Prinz disengaged himself from this crowd and, to Argand's surprise, came across the big room and joined him in the window. At just that moment the floodlighting above the darkening ground began to glow, and the Scots on the distant terrace raised a sarcastic cheer.

'Well, Commissioner, everything under control? Of course it is, silly of me to ask.'

'So far I'm satisfied.'

'I'm sure you are. That little difference between the ambulance people and the riot police smoothed over all right? Yes, I thought you'd sort them out. What time do you have? Nearly six? Good gracious. I'm told Wolfgang Herm is going to be on the news. Let's ask the Chairman if we can go to his office. I happen to know he has a set there. You'd like to see it, I'm sure.'

Argand followed Prinz down a short passage and into a small but expensively furnished room. On a cocktail cabinet there was a small colour television set which was already on though there was no one else there. A fluffy dog was gambolling with a rag doll and a snail, and then they all got on a toy roundabout. A painted speakerine, less human than the rag puppet, took its place followed by the signature tune of RTVB News.

Lena Herm sat next to a man whom Argand identified almost immediately as Hector Macher in spite of the fact that his hair had been whitened, his face lined, and he wore dark glasses. Argand did not ask himself why he was so sure it was Macher – indeed it was less the outcome of keen observation than a sudden conversion – in a flash of insight he realised that here was what explained all the anomalies, all the mysteries. If that is Macher, he thought, then everything falls into place.

In a tired voice the man was answering questions put by invisible press men. It had been a terrible ordeal. The doctors did not think he was in any danger now, but he needed rest, rest and peace. It had been decided that he and his wife (here he put his bandaged hand over Lena Herm's on the table in front of them) would go abroad for a time, for as much as a month or more. A fellow director of EUREAC had put a villa at their disposal for as long as they needed it, in Jamaica. That's where they were going. He was wearing dark glasses because his eyes hurt – his captors had kept him in a brightly-lit room for over a fortnight without ever turning the lights off. This was one reason why he was so exhausted. He had nothing but praise for the way the police had handled the affair and was glad that his release had been achieved with little or no cost, that the terrorists who were to be set at liberty were all dead. (Here Argand made a movement and Prinz who was watching him closely whispered: 'Didn't you know? The bodies of the Jansens were found in a car park an hour ago.') He was dreadfully grieved at the death of Hector Macher, it was a terrible blow to him, the worst of the whole awful business.

Did Mr Herm know that he had been impersonated by an opponent of the Spartshaven Project? Yes, he had been told. Had he any comment on the allegations of corruption of government officials by EUREAC? There was not a grain of truth in any of them. They were the fabrications of a sick, perverted mind. He felt bitter about them, because he might have escaped mutilation but for this ridiculous impersonation. And here he held up his bandaged hand. It was clear, in spite of the dressing, that he had indeed lost half a finger. Had Mr Herm also heard of the death of Emil Schneider, the artist? Yes, he had. That too was very painful news, though not unanticipated. Emil, though a wonderful painter, had been a very disturbed person, with serious personality problems. Without wishing to anticipate the inquest he had known for some time that Schneider had been taking drugs, indeed he had been trying to help him break the habit. Perhaps but for the kidnap he would have been able to do more. . .

A white-coated doctor intervened. Mr Herm was by no means off the danger list. He was deeply exhausted, it would be some days before the effects of his terrible ordeal were fully understood, he must now insist that no further strain be placed on his patient, he must close the interview.

'No wonder Macher's body never turned up,' Argand murmured to himself; the shock, scarcely less great than that suffered by St Paul on the way to Damascus, was still exacting tribute from the Commissioner.

'Eh? What did you say?' asked Prinz.

Argand felt the cold sweat on the back of his neck. I must, I must get a grip on myself, he thought.

'I wonder when Macher's body will turn up,' he said more loudly. Then: 'Well, Secretary, that's a relief. It must be a great relief to you now it's all over.'

Aware of something hard, enquiring in Prinz's eyes, Argand almost flinched away, back to the TV which was now showing the scene at the stadium itself, and the crowds gathering outside.

'Yes,' said the Secretary. 'It's been a tiring business. I'm quite worn out with it. You don't realise how tired you are at times like this until it's over and you can relax. That's so, isn't it?'

'Yes, yes indeed.' Argand wondered what he was meant to do now, what Prinz expected from him. Did he want to be convinced that Argand believed that the man on the news really had been Wolfgang Herm? The reporter droned on about the Scottish supporters, and the buzz of live excitement outside the windows of the office seemed to swell in the silence that lay between the two men.

Prinz slapped him on the back. 'We're not all lucky enough to have a villa in Jamaica waiting for us, eh? Never mind. I must see if I can organise a spot of leave for you. And for Gapp too. What a strain that man has been under! We don't want any more of this, do we?' He leant forward and switched off. The Manager of Sports Union Brabt collapsed in mid-sentence, folded in on himself, and disappeared into a rapidly diminishing spot in the middle of the screen. 'Coming back to the party?'

'No,' said Argand. 'No, I really should be up in my little cubicle from now on.'

'Your communication centre up by the press box? Right you are, old chap. I'll know where to find you if anything else crops up.'

No title, however grandiose or official sounding, could alter the fact that the room Argand had referred to was little more than a cupboard boarded off from the rest of the press box, but from there he could see the whole of the inside of the stadium and was in touch with events outside through three telephones and a radio. Argand, or one of his staff, spent every home match there. He found the small room oppressive and usually did not go there until the last moment, content to leave a subordinate to watch over things and report to him if necessary — now he was grateful to have somewhere where he would be alone: with the door shut there was not room for a second person.

Perched high above the steeply terraced seating which was beginning to fill with a military band wheeling and counter-marching, the bright lights gleaming off its silver instruments and imparting a bright unnatural glow to the striped green turf far below him, Argand felt a little godlike. The elation that comes with sudden illumination, the fulfilment of revelation, enhanced the feeling. But a voice still murmured in his mind: Jan, is not this the very stuff of paranoia? Are not feelings of keen insight and revelation precisely the symptoms a doctor would now expect you to display? Are you sure it was Macher, are you sure you are not hallucinating again, as you did when you fancied you were being followed?

His radio bleeped, he flicked a switch. A scuffle round a coach-load of Brabt supporters just offloading in the carpark had broken out. Apparently the Scottish queue came between them and the turnstiles they were heading for. Coolly Argand ordered the deployment of a section of civic police, and put a bus-load of riot police on stand-by.

I am not paranoid, he told himself. That *was* Macher. He reminded himself that in his view no one was mad without wanting or needing to be mad. For him to hallucinate Macher for Herm, he would have to *need* Macher to be Herm, and that was nonsense, clear nonsense. He knew what he needed. He needed Herm to have been held by Red Spectre. He needed the official version to be the right one. He needed this so much that he had wilfully blinded himself to the facts, to the obvious, had refused to listen to his better judgement in evaluating, for instance, Pastor Kant's statements, or even Victoria Herm's. It was then he had been, if not mad, then so willing and ready to be deceived as to be just about mad. Now he was sane.

As he thought this, the other Argand reasserted itself in response to reports from outside — the cold, desensitised Argand, Commissioner Argand, who again busied himself with his radio and telephones and moved police about in the unseen streets outside. Five minutes later ten Scots had been arrested, and three more, with two police were in ambulances on their way to Brabt State Hospital where there was a new psychiatric ward, with all the latest treatment available, or so his son said. . .

He thought of his wife and swung away again, again doubting himself, his newly-won sense of self-awareness. For she, had not she, when she could no longer bear living with him yet had no rational reason for this consuming antipathy, had not she then hallucinated things about him, that he was trying to poison her, was planning to gas her, and all so she could get out of his life and into Hearts Haven? So now, might not he, with a deep, irrational hate for his work, for the Commissioner who so punctiliously did this work, and for the system that needed that work and trained and employed him to do it, might it not be that now, faced inescapably with the intolerable contradictions of his life, might he not have hallucinated Macher for Herm? And done this so they would come with their straight-jackets and their chlorpromazine and lock him away in the new ward in Brabt State and dope and shock him there until the responsibility of being human dropped from his tired shoulders like a sack of coals.

The teams came on to the pitch, Kirkshield Wanderers red and gold, Sports Union in green and white. They lined up, stood to a sort of attention. The band played *Land of the purple heather, land of the high endeavour,* and the Scottish supporters now safely locked into their huge steel mesh cage, whose walls were topped with ferocious in-turned spikes, set up cheers which turned to a wild hysterical scream as the Brabt Anthem followed the Scottish. Then the band played *Freude, Freude, schöne Götterfunken. . . . Alle Menschen werden Brüder* for Europe, for after all it was a Euro-Cup tie, but no one paid much attention, both teams having already wheeled away towards opposite ends to warm up in front of their most fanatical supporters.

Argand in his eyrie leant back and relaxed – barring anything unusual, nothing would happen down there to worry him now until the match was over; and, as he relaxed, the thought occurred to him – *if* that was Macher, and *if* I insist it was, then sane or not they will come for me with strait-jackets. The irony of this reflection produced a wry smile, more a grimace than a smile and a return too of the euphoria that had come with revelation.

25

Penalty

The referee blew his whistle and with an underarm wave
set the game in motion. Argand, isolated in his glass box,
said, aloud: 'Well then, let's be rational. Let's work out
the implications. If that was Macher, then what else
fits?' and he felt in his pockets for paper and ballpoint.
The paper he found was the list of the members of Kant's
congregation, a week before, that he had decided Gapp
would not need, since Gapp and everyone else then was
so sure Red Spectre had kidnapped Wolfgang Herm.
Argand smiled again at this, as he began to write down,
in haphazard order, as they came to him, all the things
that had bothered him over the last fortnight, all the
anomalies, all the moments when he had had to make an
effort to maintain his faith in the rightness of things.
When he was done the blank side of the paper was filled,
although he had used a sort of improvised shorthand,
and the game below was a quarter gone. In spite of his
euphoria he felt a touch ashamed at the length of the
list, but reflected that even the most cool and rational of
people will go on believing sheer nonsense in the face of
all the evidence, if the stability of their personalities
depend on it. His father's insistence on literal accept-
ance of every word of the New Testament had been the
first time he had come consciously in contact with such

226

stubbornness; it was not beyond his wit to see it now in himself, not, at any rate, at this moment of euphoric liberation.

At the top of the list: 'Wrong date for fingerprints'. Tuesday's fingerprints were, no doubt, Herm's. Wednesday's had replaced Tuesday's and Macher's had replaced his employer's. Well, that meant that right from the start Kratt had accepted the authenticity of Green Force – Kratt and who else? The rest of the inner board of EUREAC including Lena Herm who, it seemed, was a monster; Secretary Prinz; Commissioner Gapp, or at any rate Gapp as soon as he was brought in, which must have been earlier than appeared: all had believed all the time that Herm was with the co-freaks, had suspected it perhaps before the letter, were certain of it after. And . . . and (here Argand became very excited in his glass box, almost jumped up and down with excitement, so much that an outside observer might have thought the game below had captured his attention) they had supposed what Argand himself had first nearly worked out for himself – that Herm's disappearance was voluntary, that the truth was that he had not been kidnapped when he went out into the street off Schneider's fire-escape, but had simply walked to his place of hiding and remained there ever since, playing this game of being kidnapped to put public pressure on EUREAC to cancel the Spartshaven Project, which he, Wolfgang Herm, had lost faith in and finally hated.

That's what was happening, that's it, said Jan Argand aloud to himself again. They all knew it, guessed it, no, *knew* it because Herm had tried everything else he could think of to stop the Project, had argued and threatened in meetings of the inner board so the tapes could not be handed over, not to Argand anyway, nor print-outs prepared, and he ticked off another item on his list.

Half-time. No score.

Jan put down his paper and his pen, checked round his men by phone and radio that all was as it should be, watched the moving geometry of the marching band. The door opened behind him, he smelt Prinz's pipe, felt the Secretary's hand on his shoulder.

'Enjoying the game then, Jan? I think we should be doing better than we are, if we're to win on aggregate in Glasgow, don't you?'

Argand shook his head, for a second quite lost, the words had had no meaning for him at all.

'Everything all right with you, is it?' Prinz went on, 'no trouble down below, I take it.'

'No, everything is very quiet. Well, as quiet as it should be at this stage.'

'Of course, of course. But it may turn out to be a different story if our lads get a couple in the net, eh?'

Argand said nothing. He could not yet think of the man behind him as a criminal, an utterly corrupt man, probably an accessory to murder, and who knew what else, but he felt irritated at his puerile enthusiasm for the game.

'I've heard no more on the Herm business. Though I gather Gapp has said they can go as soon as they want to, to Jamaica I mean. Wolfgang and Lena.'

Argand ran his tongue over dry lips, but still refused to stand up in the little room and face the man behind him. However, he managed to say: 'I don't suppose there will be much more to hear about it, will there? I mean, only details, only details to be filled in.'

He heard the suck of the pipe behind him, and felt the hand on his shoulder again.

'No, Jan. Nothing more. Just odd details. Ah. Here they come again. Well I must say I hope we get a bit more action this half.'

Argand left the door open, let the draught in the passage beyond sweep out the fumes and stink.

Again the referee's whistle, and then suddenly, unbe-
lievably, a goal, one of the simplest in the game. The
Sports Union striker had kicked off sideways, the forward next to him had played deeply back to the captain
who then played a long swinging pass forward to the
striker who had run on like an Olympic sprinter to find
the ball at his feet again, and only one defender and the
goalkeeper to beat. He was a Dutchman, an international, who had cost the club six million gelds, and he
made no mistake. The Scots pursued the referee down
the field as he raced back to the centre spot; they waved,
gesticulated, protested off-side, even that they had not
been ready for the restart, and one of them pulled at the
official's arm, who, accompanied by a second howl of fury
from the Scottish terraces, pulled out the yellow card.

Argand bent over his telephones and his radio, moved
his forces, put others on alert, waited tensely until all reported back that all was well, that the steel cage had
held, that no Scots had got into any other part of the
ground. Then he leaned back and got out his sheet of
paper and ballpoint again.

Of course if Gapp and EUREAC had believed from the
start that Herm was with League for Life supporters
somewhere, that explained their continuing harassment
of the remaining residents of Spartshaven and the other
people in Pastor Kant's address book. Wryly he turned
over his paper, looked at the typed names on the other
side. Were any of these *not* in the address book, then it
was possible that they had not after all been investigated,
that the State Security forces, the EUREAC Health
Guards had missed just that place where Herm had been,
indeed, he reminded himself, probably still was. And perhaps had missed them because he, Argand, had taken the
list of the Sunday congregation out of the file. Though
there was probably a copy — nevertheless, it was a
thought.

And no wonder the searches intensified, with increasing aggravation and even brutality as it seemed Herm would continue to make revelations not only about EUREAC, but the Province's most respected and senior public servants. Here, such was Argand's newly discovered euphoria, he reflected with amusement that it would be interesting, very interesting, to see what was to be on the next tape that Herm would produce. It would have to be something very good in the face of EUREAC's latest move. But perhaps there wouldn't be another tape. Macher, disguised as Herm, had probably blocked off that tactic – there was really only one thing left for Wolfgang and the League for Life to do now, and that was to produce the real Herm. It would be a dangerous moment. Argand wondered how they would bring it off.

Dangerous, to say the least. For the search for Herm had been conducted ruthlessly in more than one way. Argand himself, and his own men, had uncovered the fact that the artist Emil Schneider was the one person most likely to know where Wolfgang was to be found. And then what had happened? Secretary Prinz, no less, had said to him that he need not bother to investigate the people who had possibly paid their rents with a banknote that had been issued to Herm – not, that is, until his men had finished going through the address book; not, that is, until Schneider had been interrogated less openly, less officially, and, as it turned out, fatally.

Doctor Dael. His autopsy report. Well, that was sad, Argand reflected, as he ticked off another item – had it been simply that Dael respected his superiors, did not wish to offend them? Or had he been blackmailed? Argand suspected the latter. For he knew that the doctor too, as a medical student, had been a collaborator; he had seen the file on him. It was not something Argand held against him. Collaboration was often little more than acquiescence to what had, after all, been the legitimate government, and Argand himself had been a legitimist all his life; until Macher appeared on TV as Herm.

So, who had killed Schneider? EUREAC Health Guards? Perhaps Kratt and Macher themselves. Why not? Kratt had called on Schneider earlier. Kratt, under the strain of Herm's disappearance, still smoked, and one of the visitors to Schneider's flat had been a smoker. No wonder the forensic report had been suppressed. With modern techniques it was almost unthinkable that Kratt, if it were him, had not left behind some identifiable trace, a hair, fibres from his clothes, something. And no wonder the obscene cartoon of the Company Secretary, together with everything that connected Schneider with Herm, had later disappeared from the flat.

Tick again.

Except that Mendelssohn record. They had missed that. Argand looked down at his list. What else? How was it that Gapp had had the file on the case ready for him on Saturday, just when he wanted it to check the fingerprint Kant had given him the night before? No, it was surely no coincidence . . .

But before the Commissioner could apply his mind to that problem, the Euro-Cup tie reasserted itself. With three minutes to go and the score still one – nil, the Dutch striker jinxed his way between two converging defenders, and had no one but the goalkeeper to beat, when one of the defenders recovered quickly and went into a scything, skidding tackle from behind and brought him down on the very edge of the penalty area. The referee, an Italian, did not hesitate, but pointed to the spot. Immediately he was engulfed by the entire Kirkshield team, and two yellow cards and finally a red one were waved above their heads before they finally left him alone.

There was more provocation to the Scots to follow. The Dutchman took the penalty, the Scottish goalkeeper saved brilliantly, the linesman flagged furiously and the Italian pointed to the spot again – the goalkeeper had moved before the kick was taken. This time there was no mistake, two – nil and Argand watched grimly as a section of side fencing gave way and a tartan flood began to fight its way through the Brabanters towards the pitch. Already his radio told him that those at the back of the terraces were pouring out of the ground and into the carparks where a bus had been set alight, and several windscreens smashed. The referee blew time and Argand's first line of defence, the Civic Police, moved between the retreating players and the advancing Scots. Argand called for two squads of riot police, deployed the rest in the carparks, and made his way down to the pitch as quickly as he could.

Ten minutes later the worst was over. His men, using carefully conceived and practised techniques, drove wedges between the rival groups and most of the home supporters had got out of the ground unscathed. The remaining thousand or so Scots, however, were turning even nastier, and the reason was plain: if they retreated up the terraces and out into the car park they would get into the battle that was still raging there, and most of them had had enough; but in front there was now a solid wall of riot shields and visors, of weighted truncheons and tear gas canisters.

Argand was down on the pitch now, standing on the back of a converted and armoured Renault van, placed just behind the second line of riot police. To his left the stands were almost deserted and the exits unblocked. He gave an order and two tear gas shells popped at the back of the rioters' terraces and simultaneously he pulled in the line of police. The Scots surged forward away from the gas, across a corner of the pitch and up into the empty stands. The fight had gone out of them now and most were happy to spill out of the ground on the opposite side from where the battle continued outside, and so disperse back to their hotels.

It was at this point that Argand saw Victoria Herm. There were few Brabanters on the side the Scots were leaving by; she stood out as the only one who appeared to be resisting them, trying to push her way across the flow, though buffeted and occasionally carried along with it. But she was a big girl, and determined. Only the line of riot police between her and the Commissioner was to much for her, would not give way in front of her. She was shouting, he could see that, waving . . . waving at him? Then a truncheon was flourished above her fair hair, a policeman's grey arm momentarily obscured her face, and she was gone. No, there again, ten metres further up the terrace, there she was again, but this time with two Scots who helped, half-carried her towards the nearest exit above them while blood streamed between the fingers she held in front of her face.

26

Blunder

It was nearly eleven o'clock before Argand got home, dropped by a police car at the entrance to his apartment block. As usual he opened his mail-box, but found nothing this time other than two advertisement circulars. He stuffed them in his coat pocket without looking at them and dragged himself up the three flights of stairs round the lift cage, and so to his own front door, where he fumbled for a key and let himself in. Upstairs, above him, a door clicked shut a fraction of a second before his; he paused in his hall, shrugged and went through to his kitchen. There, so they would not develop bulges, he emptied his coat pockets on the table – keys, gloves, the circulars – then went back to the tiny hall to hang the coat on a hanger with his hat. The routine of all this was soothing, a comfort.

He was now very tired, drained of energy, all euphoria gone. At Wilhelmstras, while sorting out the aftermath of the football riot, he had seen on the news a film of Wolfgang Herm and Lena Herm boarding a EUREAC plane at the airport. They had been seen off by Christian Kratt. The film showed them getting out of a company car, walking down long marble-floored corridors with glass walls black to the night beyond. There had been a brief interview outside, at the foot of the steps leading up

into the plane, then Kratt had shaken hands with Wolfgang, kissed Lena Herm. She and her husband had
waved briefly at the top of the steps and then gone.

Watching this, with three of his subordinates and the
rather jolly but efficient secretary who looked after him,
and listening to their commonplace but sincere and feeling comments on the business, Argand had imagined
himself facing them and saying out boldly: 'That is not
Herm, that's Macher, Hector Macher, who you think is
dead', and had concluded that he *was* ill. And as for
seeing Victoria Herm after the football match, what he
had seen was surely a wild Scots girl, and as for the click
of the door on the landing above him, well – all the text-
books agreed that auditory hallucinations precede visual
ones.

He sniffed. Mrs Esslin had left a casserole. That was
nice. By the stove he found a note from her: 'I do hope
this is all right, and I'm sorry if it's not. I know you'll be
late what with the match, so I've put plenty of water in,
it should be all right, nice and tender, I hope, since it will
have cooked a long time.' He lifted the lid. The gravy
had certainly shrunk away down the sides, looked thick
and brown with a skin on top, but not burnt yet, though
it must have been on for near enough twelve hours. It
was a long time since she had left him a casserole, not
since the Friday before last, he thought, the night
Schneider drugged himself to death. He shivered, decided
to have a thimbleful of gin before he had his supper.

He sat back in his father's leather chair and sipped.
He would go to his doctor tomorrow. It would be a relief
to do so, but clearly a duty as well – he could not go on
like this, holding a responsible position as he did. How
much would he tell him? Anxiety welled up in him as he
considered this, and his hand went to his inside pocket
where he had put the list of Kant's congregation and his
table of all the so-called anomalies his diseased mind had

discovered in his superiors' handling of the case. He couldn't show that to a doctor, not to anyone. Jan Argand looked at the paper and suffered agony at the thought of the state he had allowed himself to get into. What was this? *File on Saturday*. Gapp, his diseased mind had told him, had had the file ready for him because he already knew that Argand wanted to check the fingerprints. Knew, in other words, exactly what had passed between him and Kant the night before, in this very room as if the flat were bugged. . . .

He flinched away from the idea, and, prompted by the rich smell from the kitchen, his mind went back to Mrs Esslin. She had surprised him ten days earlier coming out of his flat as he went in; she had been carrying a bucket of rubbish which she would not let him see, she had spent the day, from the early morning, at her sister's and had only just got in to clean his rooms and make his supper, *yet the casserole had been as well-cooked as the one now in his oven.*

It took him less than ten seconds to reach Mrs Esslin's door, yet when she opened it he managed to control his agitation and she was not alarmed. He managed to get her into her hall with the door shut behind them, before seizing her by the arm and hustling her into her kitchen. A large fat black cat hissed at him, and slid away into the rest of the flat as he forced her down into a chair and swung a back-handed slap across her face.

She remained still long enough for her cheek to redden where he had hit her, looking up at him from small eyes set in a wide, soft-skinned face, the skin just losing its elasticity, just beginning to collapse into plump turkey-like wattles. Then she put one hand on the table beside her as if to gain purchase, the other fastened over the lapels of the mauve quilted dressing-gown she was wearing, and she put back her head and screamed, a long, forced, deliberate scream which she kept up until he had hit her three more times, the last blow knocking her sideways off the kitchen chair and on to the floor. Something clattered away from her as she fell, and in spite of pain and terror her plump hand went groping after it – her top denture.

Argand seized large handfuls of mauve nylon and heaved at the totally unresponsive weight, trying to hoist it back to the chair. The body inside shifted lumpily but remained inert, like separate joints of meat rolling at the bottom of a sack, and through the gap that appeared Argand became aware of more nylon, frothily pink and mounds of greyish ochre skin. 'Has she got you into her bed, yet?' his mad wife had asked, and the memory was not exactly unbidden, for the last time he had beaten a woman it had been his wife, a long time ago, ten years or more, at the breaking point of six months' sexual frustration.

Eventually he did get her into the chair, but nothing it seemed would now stop the sobbing that followed the scream, and it was twenty minutes before he was satisfied that he understood what had happened the day State Security had come to his flat and bugged it. She had been there when they came, at about half-past eleven, when he was safely tied down at Wilhemstras trying to sort out the initial quarrel between the ambulance people and the chief of the riot police. She had just put the casserole in the oven, was about to leave. There had been four men. They had explained what they were doing, showed their authority, enlisted her support, and promised her two thousand gelds a week if she would keep a record of when Argand came and went, of who called on him. Then they had done a lot of work, lifting the floor boards (the block was an old one) running new wires into the sockets that were already there so they would not show. They had made a mess, but had joked with her saying how fortunate it was she was there, she would be sure to put back everything exactly as it had been, and they paid her another thousand gelds for that.

When at last it was all out, Argand gazed down at the widow gloomily, then fetched her a damp cloth and told her to wipe off the streak of clotting blood that had trickled down her chins from her split mouth.

As she wiped at it, he asked: 'Why? Why, Mrs Esslin, did you do this to me?'

She looked back up at him, her eyes baleful.

'Every Friday for five years,' she said, 'I have had to go down to your flat to settle my accounts with you. Never, never once did you come here to do it. You made a servant of me, Commissioner, a servant. We had our own shop, my Fred and I, our own shop. We were as good as you are, as good as you.'

The Commissioner heaved a deep sigh of hollow wretchedness at this, then shook his head very slowly from side to side.

'Well, well,' he said at last, 'never mind, never mind. I shall have to tie you up now Mrs Esslin, and gag you too . . .'

But as he said this she made a lumbering dash, head down towards the hall and the outside world and the scream came again too. He caught her from behind round her wide waist and together they went to the floor, sending two chairs tumbling away from them. She fought this time, fought hard and bitterly, biting till her dentures came adrift again, scratching for his eyes. He had to beat her insensible before she stopped, before he could tie her hands and ankles with flex so the twisted, plastic-coated wires bit into her plump flesh, and he gagged her with a dish-cloth and a drying up cloth.

'She might die,' he thought, as he let himself quietly out, and 'she might die,' he reiterated on the stairs.

His own flat seemed intolerably quiet. The heavy brown velvet drapes kept out most of the traffic noise, and the presence of four electronic ears made an event out of every breath he drew, every rustle of paper or footstep. He wondered if they had picked up Mrs Esslin's screams, thought probably not — he had never himself heard the slightest sound from above: the building was old, the walls and floors both thick and hollow. Nor did he fear that neighbours upstairs would be concerned — few families go through a year these days without at least one bout of screaming, hysteria, and even beating — one of the privileges of having one's own front door is that one can be sure that when these occasions come round, the neighbours will ignore them.

What was to be done then? He felt exhausted now, sick, and wretched, yet dreadfully aware that something had to be done, but what? He was too tired to think, too tired even to stand. He remembered, with terrible longing, his bed, suffered a vision of himself beneath the down quilt, knees pulled up, thumb. . . . This would not do. Perhaps if he had something to eat — could he face that woman's casserole? Why not? He pulled the brown glazed dish from the oven and carried it to the kitchen table, lifted the lid, spooned a helping out on to a plate, then went to the bread-bin and cut himself a thick slice.

He ate automatically for nearly five minutes, then, scarcely thinking of what he was doing, reached out and pulled towards him the circulars that had been in his mail-box and were still on the other end of the table where he had left them. The first was glossy, a pamphlet advertising in colour Eurama's new range of furniture, a Spring collection it said, with daffodils round three piece suites, and love-birds over the 'Pompadour' bed.

The second was a cheaper affair — a single sheet announcing the opening of a new dry-cleaner in a neighbouring street. The paper was thin enough, shoddy enough for Argand to realise that someone had written in thin fibre-tip on the other side. He turned it over and read: 'I have seen my father. He wants to see you. He believes he needs you to help him show that EUREAC's charade is a lie. He will be in the café-bar opposite Liesbet Dock from eight o'clock tomorrow morning. He will wait there for you for one hour. Please go to see him. Victoria Herm.'

He chewed on the last piece of beef and forced it down. So. They had bugged his flat and left him to investigate the League for Life after Gapp had ostensibly taken over the case and was supposedly negotiating with Red Spectre; but all the time he had been Gapp's stalking horse, the factor that Gapp and EUREAC had hoped would lead them to the real Herm, while they set up the 'charade' of Red Spectre and Macher's 'death'. And in doing it they had incidentally been able to illegally execute — well, murder — three, no four leading terrorists. That had pleased Gapp no doubt, but also Baron de Merle who no doubt felt that life imprisonment for shooting him in the knees was an inadequate punishment for Hans Punt.

And still he was the bait. Kant and Victoria and now the real Herm came to him, trusting his reputation as an honest public servant, and he was bugged, contaminated. He looked round the room, wondered where the microphone was, and shuddered. He was infected, as dangerously infected as Gapp, Prinz and the rest, but Herm did not know it.

He turned the dry-cleaner's handout over and over. Of course they had opened his mail-box. That is how they had known Victoria Herm was going to meet him in Wilhelmspark, they had even guessed correctly that she was going to bring Roman Punt to meet him. How long had this bill been in the box? It was rare for them to be delivered later than six o'clock, though common enough for them to come on a Sunday since most of the deliverers were students or people doing a second job. He supposed Victoria had intercepted whoever was stuffing them in the boxes some way away, paid to have this one put in his box. She had been at the football match, perhaps fearing that the note would not reach him. It must have lain in the mail-box for five hours at least. It must have been seen.

Herm must be warned, Argand thought, but how? The telephone is tapped. If I go out I will be followed. Well, perhaps that can be dealt with. I know the techniques. Nearly midnight – eight hours. He went to his bureau, unlocked a drawer and took from it the 7.65 standard police issue Mauser that he had not carried since he first became Deputy Commissioner for Public Order back in 1969, then back to the hall where he put on coat, gloves and hat. The gun weighed heavily in his pocket, but he preferred to leave it there – the only holster he had was a shoulder one and would be little use under jacket as well as coat. He checked he had money and keys, and turned out the lights. Only then did the thought occur to him: they know I have seen that note; they know I have not reported it; they know I was reprimanded for not reporting a similar note a week ago. He put the light back on, went to his telephone and dialled.

'I want to speak to Secretary Prinz,' he said. 'I am Commissioner Argand. I know it's late, but this is very urgent.'

'Jan. Whatever is it at this hour?'

'I'm sorry, Secretary, but something has cropped up which I think I should tell you about immediately.'

'Go on, Jan.'

'When I came in tonight there were two handouts in my mail-box. You know the sort of thing. I did not look at them properly at first, but now I have done.'

'Go on.'

You know very well what I am going to say, thought Argand.

'There is a handwritten message on the back of one of them. Shall I read it to you?'

'If you think it's important.'

Argand read out the message.

There was a long silence at the other end. The suspicion that after all Prinz had not seen the handout, that Victoria had delivered it after the match, after failing to see him there, dawned monstrously in Argand's mind.

The Secretary answered at last: 'Jan, I don't think that can after all be very important, can it? I mean the girl must be off her head, mustn't she? We'll look into it in the morning, but I shouldn't lose any sleep over it, if I were you.'

'All right, but . . .'

'Now don't worry, Jan. I understand. After that reprimand you don't want to make any more mistakes, I can see that. Well, don't worry. You're on record now as having reported this message, you're in the clear. Now you get off to bed. You must be exhausted. By the way, I think you handled the business after the football quite magnificently.' He rang off.

Jan Argand replaced the phone, closed the sitting-room door, then took the precaution of operating the toilet-flush so the noise would cover the click of his front door as he pulled it to behind him. But already the thought that he had blundered horribly by phoning Prinz spread like a poison, like hemlock, through his limbs and left him cold and heavy with despair, and mistrustful of his judgement.

27

Ebb-Tide

It was not a well-conceived plan, but it's difficult to see what else Argand could have done. The first part went well enough. It is easy to shake off followers once one knows they are there. Argand used conventional tricks, not caring now how blatant they were – descending into the small metro system, getting off a train just as it was about to leave the platform where he had boarded it leaving his tail helplessly carried away in the carriage behind; then losing the back-up by going into a cinema, and leaving almost immediately. The cinema had an all-night show of relatively hard porn – it stank of whisky, and the snoring of Scots drowned the panting and grunts on the screen. Twenty minutes later Argand was satisfied that there had been only two tails, furthermore they had been so clumsy that he was almost certain that they were not State Security Police but EUREAC Health Guards in plain clothes.

The problem remained: how to get in touch with Herm when he still had no idea at all of the man's hiding-place.

He started by trying to phone Kant from a public phone box, but again the recorded voice monotonously informed him that the number caller wanted was not available. He now turned to the list of the Pastor's

Sunday congregation, and using the phone book rang three Spartshaven numbers with names corresponding to those on the list. Each time the same recorded voice answered him and he at last remembered what the Rural Guard lieutenant had told him a fortnight before — that as a part of their campaign of civil disobedience, and to impede EUREAC's operations, the remaining residents had pulled down the telephone wires.

There still remained two courses of action open to him and he chose the wrong one. Instead of taking a taxi out to Spartshaven he moved back into the middle of Brabt, into the old part near the university, and prowled the streets for two hours or more before coming across Victoria Herm's name by the street-level bell-push of an attic flat. The block, though old, had been partly modernised and a street door put in with a night lock that could only be released from inside, or from each flat. There was an intercom.

Argand pressed the bell-push and waited. After a pause there was an audible electronic click in the tiny speaker above the console of bell-pushes and Argand, without pausing to consider, announced himself. There was no answer, though he felt sure someone was there, perhaps he detected the sound of breathing. Then the click again and a moment later, the sound of a lift. It was enough for him to realise that Victoria Herm would have spoken to him, that whoever was on his way down was probably an enemy. He took to his heels and escaped into the narrow alleys of that part of the City.

It was now gone four o'clock and he was on the very edge of exhaustion. This, and no doubt everything he had been through in the previous weeks, deepened his despair. He gave up hope of finding Herm before the time appointed and decided that the best he could do was to be at Liesbet Dock at eight o'clock and hope that he would be able to warn Herm personally before either or both of them were taken. He passed the next three hours in an all-night café near the docks, drinking coffee and dozing. At about half-past seven he approached the Liesbet Dock gate, mingling with workers coming on the early morning shift, and finally taking up a position in a bus-shelter from where he could see the café-bar opposite without being himself conspicuous. Thus, with his back to the gate he could see several hundred metres up the road in both directions and hoped to see Herm approach in time to warn him.

Liesbet Dock is the furthest upstream and marks the limit between the docks and the riverside lunapark that separates the industrial area from Wilhelmspark. Since containerisation it is no longer much used. Lower down, the river is wider and deeper and with fewer and larger ships calling the upstream docks do little business, handling little more than barges carrying local produce from the interior and providing facilities for refits and repairs for smaller boats. There was only one boat that morning, a British trawler, and when Argand arrived it was already flying the Blue Peter on its forepeak, preparing to take advantage of the tide that had just begun to ebb. He gave it a brief glance across the hundred metres of rails, small derricks and sheds that separate the wharf from the road and then forgot about it. It seems it did not occur to him to ask himself just why Herm had chosen this particular spot to meet.

The half hour went past and the stream of workers in car and on foot diminished to a trickle. It was a pleasant morning, breezy, a touch chilly, but with sunshine and high white clouds once the early morning haze had dispersed; seagulls swooped and cackled between the cranes, and the pale sun picked out the fresh blue-green growth on the pines which Argand could see through the iron lace-work of the big wheel in the lunapark. A gilded weathercock on the topmost spire of Archduke

Wilhelm's fantasy castle gleamed brightly but briefly.

At eight o'clock exactly the trawler behind Argand gave three short blasts followed by the rattle of gangplanks being taken in. Still he did not look behind him, for his eyes were now fixed on the café though occasionally he still glanced up and down the now almost deserted dockside road. There were people inside, he could see that; he thought that at least two had been there since he had arrived. Was Herm already there? Or were they Health Guards waiting for Herm? Then just as he was about to step off the curb and cross the road to see for himself, shouts behind him and the sound of running feet arrested him.

He turned. The trawler was now standing out in the middle of the river and he could see letters painted boldly along the hull: FRIENDS OF LIFE and on the stern FINGAL'S CAVE, SOUTHAMPTON, beneath the Red Ensign of the British Mercantile Marine. Between him and the trawler, walking towards him from the wharf, was a tall figure in a short tweed driving coat – hatless as he was, the characteristic hair style was immediately recognisable. As Argand saw him, he broke into a trot, then a run. Two more men, at least, had appeared in the litter of rails, wire hausers and empty sheds, and were also moving quickly towards the chain-link fence and open gate, but were obviously ready to cut off the first if he broke away from the gate back towards the wharf. Seeing them, the first man checked, still fifty metres from Argand, remained motionless for a second, but poised as if to move off with even greater energy – then the tension dropped out of his body as swiftly as sand from a broken egg-timer. He walked towards the gate. Argand turned and saw four men in dark suits ranged on the pavement outside the café, and a large chauffeur-driven black Peugeot pulling out of a side street. As it came across the carriageway and slid along the curb

towards him he identified the passenger as Christian
Kratt. I should shoot him, Argand thought, his hand in
his coat pocket hefting the Mauser so it no longer pulled
on the fabric, but I can't.

Three dockers, hurrying down the road, aware that
something was happening, paused beside him, and he
made his last gesture to prevent what now seemed inevitable.

'That's Wolfgang Herm,' he said. 'The real Wolfgang
Herm.'

The men looked at him blankly, totally uncompre-
hending, then fear blanched the face of one of them.

'Come on,' he said to his mates, 'let's get out of this.
This is nothing to do with us,' and their heavy boots clattered away over the paving.

Herm came through the gate. He was taller than Argand
expected, had more presence, distinction even. He
ignored the dark suits closing in from all sides, and the
car now parked behind Argand, and held out his hand.
'You must be the honest Commissioner,' he said.

Argand mumbled: 'I didn't want this . . . this is
not . . .'

'No. But I'm sure you did your best.' The voice was
dry and steady. He turned to the car. 'I don't suppose
you have the gall to kill us here, do you Kratt? Are we to
get in with you?'

The Company Secretary spoke through the open
window: 'Please, Herm. But first the Commissioner can
give his gun to the man behind him.'

Within moments they were cruising away through the
high rises and the warehouses, with two other black cars
behind them. The whole episode had taken no more than
two minutes, no one had remarked it except the three
dockers, and perhaps the café owner. What they had
seen was unusual, sinister even, something to mention

over a lager in the evening, but no more.

The car, the estate version, had two seats behind the driver, both facing forward. Herm was in the further forward of these. Kratt and Argand were in the very back. A glass screen shut them off from the chauffeur.

'I don't think you'll pull this off,' Herm said, twisting so he could see Kratt.

'Oh yes. If there was any *other* hope for you, you would not have come out the way you did.'

Herm shrugged. 'Nevertheless, you still don't know where the inner board tapes are.'

'They're not important now. Macher and the rest of us are already re-recording them. He mimics your voice quite well enough and of course he speaks most enthusiastically about the Project. And if the real tapes turn up anywhere, well then we have dear Hector with us to say that he is *you* and the real tapes are forgeries.'

'He might get by on television and so on but he won't fool people I've worked with for years at the Plant.'

'He won't have to. He'll take a long time to recover in Jamaica. A year or more. During that time your team will be split up. After all their work is more or less done now. Actually it's not beyond the bounds of *possibility* that once the tapes have been re-recorded and one or two other loop-holes have been filled, the *real* Wolfgang Herm may have a relapse, or a water-skiing accident, something of that sort. It will depend on Lena.'

Herm's mouth set at this, perhaps he paled a little. For a minute or so he looked out of his window. Dockland was giving way to suburbia.

'We're on the way to the Plant,' he said presently.

'Yes.'

'And the Project is under way.'

'Yes. It started at seven o'clock though as *you* know we can't start damming the tide-gap until one o'clock

248

when the tide is almost right out.'

'Exactly what are you going to do with us?'

'Shoot you, and put your bodies in the cement at the bottom of the dam.'

A kilometre ticked away in silence.

'You are very blunt. Almost I was sick then. Why don't the Commissioner and I overpower you now and escape?'

'The result will be the same. More *messy*, that's all.'

Herm looked at the impassive chauffeur on the far side of what was presumably a sound-proof screen. There was a large automatic under the dashboard. Then he glanced back at the cars behind them.

'Your Praetorian Guard. You are very sure of them.'

'Yes.'

'And Pastor Kant, and . . . my daughter?'

'No harm will come to *them*. They can say what they like, no one will *believe* them. If your daughter is a nuisance she will be institutionalised.'

'Given psychiatric treatment until she shuts up?'

'Yes.'

'Kratt. Do me one favour. Tell her not to be a nuisance, from me, and spare her that.'

Kratt's lips moved again, but whether or not in assent neither Herm nor Argand could say.

'It's all very untidy. Loose-ended,' Herm said after another silence. 'Very improvised. Doesn't that bother you Kratt?'

Kratt was perhaps stung by this, or tension was telling on him. At all events he became more talkative.

'But of course it is. It has to be. Reality is never ideal. We patch up as we go on. We do not create things, they happen, and we *cope* with them. That's where you were wrong Herm, in thinking you had created the Project and that you could stop it. The one is not true, the other is impossible. The corporation created it and the cor-

249

poration created it in inevitable *reflex* to a complex of outside factors beyond its control.'

'But yet you could stop it. If you wanted to. You could get out of this car when we get to the Plant, and tell them to halt everything, and they would.'

'You know that is not so. If I did *that*, what would happen? In a week, in a month, the corporation would react, it would identify me as a threat to its existence, and it would expel me as it has you. It is not I who has put you in this position. It is the corporation working through me. If I did not allow myself to be its instrument it would find another. There is no place for individualism under corporatism, or only in so far as individualism promotes the corporate. There is no room for individual morality. The *only* morality is the survival of the whole.'

Another pause. Then: 'I'm still surprised that with all your resources you couldn't find me.'

The thin lips lengthened into their version of a smile. 'Well of course we hoped our friend the Commissioner would look after that side for us.'

'Nevertheless it was good of Emil not to give me away.'

'Oh, he gave you away all right. He babbled on about Scotland, and a symphony, and the Hebrides, *and* Fingal's Cave. I failed to make the connection with that absurd English trawler.'

He was silent for a moment, then his cold grimace returned. 'Sometimes the improvisatory element was *overdone*. In the kidnap of Macher, in the presence of the Commissioner here, it was a clumsy extra to try to kill him as well. Gapp's idea. You see he knew Argand had, that morning, questioned Dael's autopsy report on Schneider.'

Argand recalled the EUREAC Health Guard, how he had levelled the pistol and fired and the glass door intervened and shattered. He shuddered. There would be no glass door this time.

There was one moment on the way when Argand thought they had a chance of escape. Just as they were leaving the City they came upon an extraordinary sight, a bank of thousands of cut daffodils heaped up in a huge mound on one side of the carriageway. The breeze whipped the top layer off and drove them across the road, a blizzard of yellow and green. Argand remembered that they had been dumped the day before by growers protesting against Community grading regulations. In the middle of it two Rural Guards, with their bikes parked beside them, were directing the traffic in single file round the end of the mound. Perhaps a decisive movement then, under the Rural Guards' eyes, might have been successful, but there were only two of them, and not much traffic, just a small mechanical shovel scooping the flowers into the back of a lorry.

Argand supposed that the flowers, two or three of which settled momentarily on the bonnet of the car, must be beautiful, but he couldn't see it. They were all of a length, of a size, exactly the same shade of yellow. It occurred to him that he was not sorry to be leaving a world where daffodils had become dull.

The small fleet of black cars paused at the River Flot Plant for about ten minutes and Kratt got out, leaving them alone apart from the screened-off chauffeur. Argand had never been inside the fences round the Plant before. He was impressed in spite of everything by the scale, the complexity, the size. There were not only the huge concrete structures like giant silos, the enormous stacks, and the cooling towers one can see from outside, but also a vast campus of smaller buildings as well, offices, laboratories, store-houses and buildings fed by pipes that hissed, and leaked steam or worse. Above everything except the highest structures an intricate mesh of cables and lights fed power in and kept the thing going regardless of weather or the turn of the earth's surface away from the sun.

He felt awkward now, in Wolfgang Herm's presence, but had to say something. Almost blushing at the banality he muttered: 'It's a big place.'

'It's a botched-up disaster.'

The Plant's principal creator went on: 'You know why developing countries find it difficult or impossible to run places like this? It's because they have them built in one stage, and like that things go wrong, often, several things at once. There's nothing planned about a place this size. When it started expanding fifteen years ago no one had any idea that this would be the end . . . not that it is the end. It will go on sprawling and spewing, and going wrong until it really does get too large to handle. Not too complex. Complex is not the word. It's a muddle, a mess. Kratt was right. No one person can understand it, because so many people have put it together, but not, as *he* says, corporately, but each improvising, at each stage, just for the moment, each just concerned to keep his job . . . or get out of it unscathed before it gets beyond him. There are things going on in there simply because someone started them a few years ago and now no one remembers why. But they daren't stop them in case they are important. A lot of things are like that nowadays. Most big things. Industries, bureaucracies, governments.'

He turned now and faced the Commissioner, eyes cool and serious. 'You know, Argand, Kratt doesn't want to kill you. If you've got a price, you name it. He'll pay. Any price but the one I'm asking.'

Argand's stoicism inhibited any reply. The truth is that all he had to live for was a blind self-respect. But even if it had been possible for him to get out of the car at that moment, with this self-respect intact, and walk away, it is doubtful that he would have done. At that moment there was nowhere to go and nothing to do. Presently he thought of his wife in Hearts Haven; thought of her with an odd sense of relief. She would get well now, take her place in society again. After all he had not done badly by her, and she would have his pension.

Kratt returned, bringing with him the sour odour Argand had noticed at their first meeting. As he settled himself beside Argand again, and the three cars slid into motion, he pulled out his cigarette case and tapped a cigarette against his thumb. Even unlit the tobacco smelt acrid. Argand clenched his fist and looked out of the window as the Plant began to slip away to his right, then forced himself to say: 'I should like to go with fresh air in my lungs.'

There was an awkward silence, then the click of the gold case as Kratt replaced the cigarette.

Herm murmured: 'Well done.'

Presently the huge structures petered out into smaller ones, then waste ground, and finally a high fence with a barrier. They went through the barrier and everything seemed lighter and cleaner, though the shingle spit in front of them and slightly below them was covered with a litter of heavy mobile plant, huge slowly revolving drums of pre-mixed concrete, men in yellow safety helmets that made them look like bugs, and, protruding out of the sea, in the gap between this spit and the Spartshaven one beyond, giant coffers made out of timber form work, ready to receive the concrete as soon as the tide had drained out of them. But above all this the sky was blue and clear, to the left the mudflats of the marsh were coming fresh and glistening into view as the waters receded, and to the right shingle was giving way to wave-rippled sand glinting in the sunlight. Only directly in front, on the other side of the gap, thick clouds of black smoke billowed inland and orange flames blossomed beneath them.

Kratt looked at his watch. 'It's half-past eleven,' he said. 'We have to wait until one. Only then will the tide have ebbed *enough* for us to begin pouring the concrete.' He got out of the car, pulled his coat round him, and lit a cigarette.

'They're bull-dozing Spartshaven and burning the débris,' Herm said. 'But Kant will survive. And my British friends on the boat. It's possible they're working out some way of getting to us even now.'

Argand said nothing. There was nothing to say. An hour and a half was a long time to wait. Herm leaned forward to where a radio was set in the partition behind the driver, and fiddled with the dials. 'There's a British station I used to listen to when I was working at the Plant,' he said. 'You get good reception here, by the sea.'

A woman's voice: '. . . Scottish Symphony Orchestra is conducted today by Karl Anton Rickenbacher. The main work will be Brahms's second Piano Concerto in which the soloist will be Alfred Brendel, but we begin with Mendelssohn's concert overture *The Hebrides*, also known as *Fingal's Cave* . . .'

'Well!' said Herm.

'That's the name of the boat you were on.'

'Yes.'

With the music Jan began to feel better. He recognised it from a long time ago, but it was no longer familiar, and the repeated rhythmic rise and fall of the opening phrases set something stirring in him that he thought had died years ago. Presently a small white bird, with black head and black wing-tips caught his eye. It was hovering above the edge of the water, not a hundred metres away, and it had a small forked tail like a swallow or a martin. It wasn't much bigger than a martin. Well, he thought, an hour and a half is a long time, anything may happen. It doesn't do to give up hope.

He sat back in the car seat and listened to the music.